"YOU'LL FIND ME A BIG DISAPPOINTMENT."

Puzzled by Joelle's words, Zach tried to reassure her. "I've never found anything about you disappointing."

"You've never made love to me."

Zach felt anger leaping fiercely inside of him. Not at Joelle, but at the man or men who had made her devalue herself. Now he understood why she didn't like being touched, why her acceptance of his love was such a miracle. "No," he said evenly. "I haven't been that lucky yet. And when we do make love, I won't be disappointed."

"How can you know that?"

"Because making love isn't a performance. It's something that happens between two people, hopefully who care about each other. It's both giving and taking. It's not a concert, and the audience isn't going to be angry if they don't get their money's worth...."

ABOUT THE AUTHOR

Emilie Richards lives in romantic New Orleans with her minister husband and her four children. This prolific author has written many romance novels, including this, her second Superromance.

Books by Emilie Richards

HARLEQUIN SUPERROMANCE
172—THE UNMASKING
204—SOMETHING SO RIGHT

These books may be available at your local bookseller.

Don't miss any of our special offers. Write to us at the following address for information on our newest releases.

Harlequin Reader Service
901 Fuhrmann Blvd., P.O. Box 1397, Buffalo, NY 14240
Canadian address: P.O. Box 2800, Postal Station A,
5170 Yonge St., Willowdale, Ont. M2N 6J3

Emilie Richards
SOMETHING SO RIGHT

Harlequin Books

TORONTO • NEW YORK • LONDON
AMSTERDAM • PARIS • SYDNEY • HAMBURG
STOCKHOLM • ATHENS • TOKYO • MILAN

Published March 1986

First printing January 1986

ISBN 0-373-70204-3

Printed in Canada

To Kathy,
a coal miner's daughter.
And to Michael,
who was always absolutely confident.

CHAPTER ONE

THE MAN LEANED against the ancient trunk of a sugar maple and watched the woman on the hillside chopping weeds. Shards of occasional sunlight reflected off the curving scythe that she gripped with capable hands. Her movements were fluid as she swung from side to side, bending at the waist as if she participated in a primitive, partnerless dance. In the eerie haze of a western-Pennsylvania morning, she alone seemed alive. She alone seemed real.

As he watched, the woman stopped, her back still turned to him. With one hand she pushed damp strands of wheat-colored hair behind her ears. The hand not holding the scythe stretched above her head, and she stood on tiptoe, soothing muscles that were taut from the punishing exercise. The movement pulled her thin white camisole tightly over the prominent bones of her back, accentuating the spare, clean lines of her body.

Again she bent, gripped the scythe and began to swing. The first few strokes were clumsy. As if to combat the lapse in rhythm, she began to sing in a voice just loud enough for him to hear, "'Tis a gift to be simple, 'tis a gift to be free..."

The voice was familiar, and the man listened intently as the husky sound tugged at the edges of his consciousness. "'Tis a gift to come down where we ought to be..."

The waist-high weeds fell in bundles at her feet like biblical sheaves of grain, but these bundles would be left to rot where they fell, not gleaned to provide sustenance. The same motion, the same effect. Different reasons. One to harvest, one to destroy. Both important.

The woman stepped forward as she swung the scythe, turning to present the man with her profile. He saw that she was made up of intriguing angles, and that she had smooth, heavily freckled skin. Under the golden hair, streaked silver in places by the sun, straight black brows and heavy dark lashes lent an element of surprise to the austere beauty of her face. He could not see her eyes, but as the man pushed away from the tree and stood staring in bemused recognition at her features, he knew that when he could see them, they would be green and tilted slightly. "Cat's eyes," publicity about her always emphasized. The soul-searching cat's eyes of Jo Lynd.

Maybe the woman was a trick of his imagination, a wraith formed from the morning mist to torment him, to remind him of his past and of his humanity. Maybe her existence was as ephemeral as his thoughts of her had been during the fourteen years since she had made her first appearance in his life, changing it forever.

She hadn't seen him yet. If he turned and retraced his path, he could disappear and perhaps, eventually, even forget that he had seen her. But as he straightened, a half-planned retreat in his head, he knew that he could not take the first step. His days of running had ended.

SWINGING RHYTHMICALLY back and forth, Joelle Lindsey completed her turn, lifting her face to the sky to stretch her aching neck. She finished the song, lowering the scythe to the ground beside her. Every muscle in her body protested the punishment she was inflicting. She shut her eyes and stretched her hands over her head again, swaying to silent music. How long had it been since she had used her body so completely? She was testing herself to the limits, and yet, surprisingly, she was discovering that she still possessed much of the strength and stamina of her childhood and teenage years.

It had been here, on this farm now overgrown and neglected, that she had risen every morning of her youth to sing a silent litany to the mysterious world that offered endless possibilities. As she had helped her father and older brother, Hoyt Jr., with the myriad farm chores, she had absorbed the sights and sounds of a new day, relishing the colors and the textures and the music. Especially the music. There had been birds singing melodies she could never hope to improve on, the distant lowing of their milk cow, the occasional rumble of a car on the dirt road that ran by their house. There had been the sound of a pitchfork whooshing cleanly through hay, the sound of an ax chopping wood. They had all been the sounds of home and love and security.

Here she had needed strength and endurance. It hadn't been an easy life; every member of the Lindsey family from Grandma Jo Ellen down to the baby, Rae, had worked hard raising the food that they needed to supplement Joelle's father's coal miner's wages.

Years had passed, and Joelle had worked hard since that time, too. But her job had taken her away from early-morning mysteries and strained muscles. Now the heaviest thing she ever lifted was a guitar, the earliest she arose was noon. Her life was lived at night, under artificial light.

At least that had all been true until she had found herself on an airplane, flying back home to the little town of Russell Creek, back home to the farm that was now an abandoned tangle of weeds and dilapidated buildings and possibilities. In the week since she had been back, she had tested herself again and again to see how much of the old Joelle Lindsey still existed. She hadn't expected to find that so much did. The revelation that she was somehow unchanged filled her aching body with hope and a spark of pride. It had been a long time since she had felt either.

Stretching once more, she relaxed and opened her eyes. As she did, her vision registered the figure of a man almost hidden beside the massive trunk of a tree at the bottom of the hill. Calmly, she observed him. She had no idea how long he had been watching her, but it seemed only fair to return his attention. If he had recognized her, she would need to know what kind of person she was confronting.

The man stepped forward into the dim sunlight, out from under the partially leafed branches of the tree. Sensing that he was giving her time to examine him as penance for his own secretive observations, she obliged him.

He was tall, she decided, and the color of the earth. Brown hair, tanned skin. Only the neatly trimmed beard was different, a lighter, redder shade that offered an interesting contrast. His hair was neatly trimmed, too, but longer than style dictated, waving back from a broad forehead.

He was smiling at her. It was a quiet smile, and somehow she was sure immediately that this man rarely grinned. Under most circumstances he would probably smile that pleasant smile of genuine good humor, and when he was serious again, the smile would still linger in the faint crinkles around his eyes.

The woman allowed her gaze to flicker over his clothing. He wore work boots, worn jeans and a faded T-shirt with a barely identifiable slogan: "Split wood, not atoms." He'll know who I am, she thought with resignation. No one who'd wear that shirt would fail to recognize Jo Lynd. She waited, muscles tensed, for the questions that would surely follow.

"I'm Zach Smith. The farm over there is mine." The man pointed over a sharp rise, beyond a broad field that had once held corn and now held only weeds and pesky varmints.

She nodded without smiling. Zach Smith. The name meant nothing to her. "I'm Joelle Lindsey. I didn't hear you drive up."

"I walked." He climbed up the gentle slope with the swinging grace of a man in complete control of his body.

"Why are you here?" she asked.

"I noticed your car pulling into the driveway last night. I came to investigate.

"And?"

"I wanted to know who was here and why."

Joelle pulled the scythe in front of her to lean on the long wooden handle, arms stiff. "I own this place. I've been here a week now."

"I've been remiss then; I should have come sooner."

"Why the interest?" Let's get it over with, she thought. Ask me. What is Jo Lynd, the folksinger, doing on an overgrown Pennsylvania farm?

"A Mr. Fedders asked me to keep an eye on the place for you. I wrote last year about buying this property to display some of my equipment. Fedders said you wouldn't sell, but that I could use some of the land in exchange for watching out for intruders and keeping your driveway clear.''

Vaguely Joelle remembered Sid Fedders, her accountant, coming to her with the proposition to sell the land. ''It's a good offer; I've checked into it,'' he had told her. ''Land in that part of Pennsylvania is worthless. Dump it while you can.''

Joelle lifted her head and straightened her lanky body. ''As I told Sid, the land has always belonged to my family. I'd never sell it. I didn't know he had worked anything out with you.''

''He should have told you.''

Perhaps this Zach Smith didn't know who she was after all. If her accountant or her manager came to her with every little detail of the empire that was Jo Lynd, she would never have time to sing. And singing was what the empire was all about. The rest they handled without her.

''Don't worry, Mr. Smith. It sounds like a good idea.'' Joelle gestured toward a distant field where tall steel structures surveyed the surrounding land like whooping cranes looking for a place to nest. ''To be honest, I didn't even know that the land those machines are on was mine. When I was growing up here, that land wasn't used for anything by anybody.''

''It's rock strewn and not good for much. Those are wind machines. I own an alternative energy supply house.''

''I've seen your sign.'' Joelle remembered a wooden sign, skillfully designed and hand lettered, on the highway leading into the little town of Russell Creek. Don Quixote on a donkey with a lance. Windmill Chargers, Inc. She watched him move closer.

"As long as I've lived here, no one has ever shown any interest in this property. It's good to see that change," he said.

Joelle was beginning to believe that her identity was a secret from him, although the man's penetrating eyes failed to ease her doubts completely. But Zach Smith was regarding her with the steady gaze of an old acquaintance, not the adoring look of a fan who is about to ask for an autograph.

Before coming to the farm, she had cut her hair shorter than it had ever been—halfway to her shoulders—and added a thick fringe on her forehead. She had not packed any of the dramatic designer originals that looked so severely simple on stage yet cost enough to feed half the poor folks in America. She had come here with nothing except her guitar, one suitcase and a fading grip on reality. Perhaps her attempt at disguise was successful.

"I've never had any time to fix this place up. I'm on a leave of absence from my job, and I decided to spend it here."

"You're going to wear yourself out if you take on the whole farm with that." Zach gestured to the scythe.

"I'm just clearing the land around the spring. It's so clogged with weeds that the water barely flows into the springhouse."

"I watched you. You've had practice."

"Is that why you were staring?"

"I was staring because you're beautiful."

Joelle looked down at her body as if to figure out what he was talking about. The tight camisole was damp with perspiration and clung tenaciously to her slender frame revealing every line of her body. She had become so thin in the past year that to her own eyes she resembled a concentration-camp survivor. But on Jo Lynd, the prominent bones, the hollows, the denial of all that was soft and feminine, were high fashion, to be much admired and copied.

Nothing about her today seemed like it was worth a second look. A hunter's plaid flannel shirt was knotted around her waist, and she wore expensive, well-cut khaki jeans, rolled up at the knee. Her long legs were streaked with mud. In the right clothes, with the right lighting, she knew she could be stunning. But beautiful?

"What a strange thing to say," she marveled.

"Not so strange," he said. "I'm sure you've heard it before."

Her eyes searched Zach's face, but there was only male approval and something almost like concern written across his strong, even features. His words were a compliment from a man to a woman. They appeared to be nothing more. Stifling the spark of interest that was igniting inside her, Joelle asked, "Is there anything else that you need to know?"

"Where you sleep."

She wasn't really surprised at the question. She had thwarted more passes in her lifetime than there were weeds on this hundred-acre farm. "My business."

Zach blinked, and then the sound of his words came back to him. The smile he flashed was a genuine appreciation of her response. "You should know we don't move quite that fast around here, Miss Lindsey. I'm just concerned about your safety. That house hasn't been lived in for years. Without some shoring up, it could tumble down around you."

She didn't smile, but she could feel her face relax. "Call me Joelle," she said. "Actually, I'm sleeping in the springhouse. It seemed the safer of the two buildings.''

Zach looked in the direction of the springhouse. It was two-story and tiny, sitting on the small hill. ''I've been in it once. I came over to investigate when there were tales of fugitives in the area. It's safer, but not safe. And hardly habitable.''

''Safe enough.''

Zach faced Joelle again and watched the retightening of her facial muscles. It had been years since he had found it necessary to interpret emotional reactions by reading expressions. Talking to Joelle Lindsey was like watching a foreign film without subtitles. She gave almost nothing away.

''I gather you don't want me to pry or to talk down to you because you're a woman. I appreciate that. But as one neighbor to another, may I take a look at the springhouse so I won't have nightmares about you living in it?''

''Why should you worry about me?'' she asked at the same time that she pivoted and motioned for him to follow her.

The question shot quicksilver shivers through Zach's body, and he tensed. ''Why indeed?'' he answered after a pause. ''We're neighbors.''

The springhouse was stone. Originally a one-story building, it had been enlarged sometime in the past fifty years by adding a wood-frame second story. The one-room addition had been used to store animal feed and tools for the chores that needed to be done close to the farmhouse. Over the years the area had become a dumping ground for farm refuse.

Remnants of the refuse lay in neat piles fifty yards from the rickety steps leading up to the addition. There were signs that anything that could be burned, had been. Other trash had been bundled or compacted to be carried away. Zach examined the steps, noting they had been inexpertly patched with wood that was sturdy but not cut evenly to size.

"The stairs are safe to climb," Joelle informed him.

"Yes, I can see they are." Taking the steps two at a time, Zach pushed the door open and peered inside. The room had been thoroughly cleared and scrubbed so that the old wood was now free of cobwebs and filth. Where there once had been several broken windows, now there were holes covered by mesh nailed to the window frames. Insulation was packed between the long wooden studs, waiting only for walls to cover it.

In the corner, away from the screen windows, was a foam-rubber pad covered by a sleeping bag. A large suitcase sat next to it acting as a makeshift table. A guitar case lay at the foot of the bed. The only other objects in the room were an ice chest and a kerosene lantern.

The stark simplicity was reminiscent of a nun's quarters or a prison cell. Had Joelle Lindsey been anyone else, Zach would have immediately offered her a loan. Under the circumstances, that action would only be incongruous.

"You certainly have cleaned it up," he said as he climbed down the steps to where she stood.

"You can sleep unencumbered tonight."

They were standing close together and Zach found that the intense green of Joelle's eyes was a surprise. One expected less of a famous face in person, not more; her album covers paled in comparison.

She was waiting for him to leave, and there was no doubt in his mind that he should. He should leave and never come back. But standing there, close enough to stroke the smooth freckled skin, to run his finger over the harsh cheekbones and trace the winged eyebrows, Zach knew that he was not going to be smart about this. Not smart at all. "This is no place for a woman alone."

Joelle raised her green eyes to his brown ones. Men rarely had eyes that color, she noted. Brown flecked with gold. Sparkling eyes that were warm and liquid. Eyes to be trusted. "Do you always move right in and take over other people's lives?"

"Is that what I'm doing?"

"It certainly feels like it. Why?"

Why indeed, Zach wondered. Because Jo Lynd had haunted him since he was old enough to drink hard liquor? Because her voice was still intertwined with the most important decision he had ever made? Because having been part of the machine that almost destroyed her, he wanted to make amends?

"If I said that I was just being neighborly, would you believe me?" he asked finally.

Joelle liked his slow smile. It started at his eyes and worked down to his lips, and for a moment watching the process absorbed her completely. "I think I prefer that answer to others you might give," she said.

"And?"

"And, I think that good fences made good neighbors."

"In that case, you and I have a lot of work to do. The fences between your place and mine are in terrible shape."

"I think you know what I mean."

There was a shining strand of hair caressing her cheek. Zach lifted his hand slowly and tucked it behind her ear, brushing his finger across the smooth hollow of her cheekbone as he did so. "I truly wish I could oblige you, but I think this situation is out of our hands."

"Fate?" she asked, an unexpected quiver tracing the muscles of her stomach in the wake of his touch. "I don't believe in it."

"I'd like to think you were right," Zach said softly. "It would be nice to feel that you and I were in complete control of our lives. But suddenly I have my doubts."

"Well, I am in control," Joelle answered, turning sharply to begin the trip back to the spring where she retrieved the scythe. Zach Smith would not charm his way into her existence. What she needed right now was solitude and hard work. Not an attractive man. There was no point in beating around the bush. "Leave me alone, Zach Smith," she said calmly. "I do not want you in my life."

"For better or for worse, I'm there already," he replied.

Zach watched the heavy colorless mist drift in the air to change his visual impression of the woman before him. She was fluid grace, ramrod caution, secret vulnerability. She was a mixture of everything he had ever found intriguing. Although he didn't trust his acute response to her, Zach felt his head turn from side to side. "I'll do what I can, Joelle, but until I'm satisfied that you're at least safe and comfortable here, I'm going to find it hard to stay away."

Joelle gave him a disgusted look that was the most mobile her features had appeared at any time during their meeting. "What kind of convincing do you need?"

"From what I can tell, you have no electricity, no running water, no windows to keep out the rain and no place to keep food cold or to cook. Why don't you start there?''

''None of this is your business,'' she said, her temper flaring.

''I know.''

''Listen, if you're so determined to play do-gooder, just drive around the outskirts of Russell Creek. There are probably some old miners living in shacks that make my springhouse look like the Ritz. They need you, I don't.'' She began to swing the scythe.

''Have you thought that your spring might be polluted?''

''I'm not drinking the water, only using it to wash in. I'm hauling drinking water from Taylerton.'' The scythe moved back and forth in meditative monotony.

''Good.'' Zach was sure that if Joelle realized how captivating, how earth mother incarnate she appeared, she would abandon the pretense of weed chopping immediately.

''Anything else?'' she snapped when she saw he was not going to leave.

''Food, electricity, windows . . .''

Flinging the scythe to the ground, Joelle faced him again, hands on slender hips. ''I'm only eating food I don't need refrigeration for. I have a kerosene lantern, and I've ordered windows. I pick them up next Friday. Furthermore, I've hired a crew to come out and begin renovations on the house in a couple of weeks. Now, please go!''

Zach turned to walk down the slight slope to the long, graded driveway that would take him back out to the road.

Joelle watched as his tall form began to disappear. He moved with such masculine grace, such certainty. He had come to offer her advice and concern, and she had offered him nothing except arrogance.

Apologies. She hated them. Still, there was no excuse for her rudeness. Had she lived so long among careless, self-absorbed people that she had become like them? "Mr. Smith?"

He stopped and looked over his shoulder. "Zach."

"Zach, I'm sorry." Stuffing her hands in her pockets, Joelle followed his path, coming to stand in front of him. "I was overreacting to your questions. You see, I've..." How much could she tell him without stirring his curiosity? "I'm just sensitive to being pushed around. I came here to get away from that."

"I never push people around. It's a solemn oath I once swore on a copy of *The Grapes of Wrath*.

The smile that lit up Joelle's face in response to his joke was breathtaking. Zach knew that she was thirty or so, but the smile took years off her age. She was transformed into the eighteen-year-old Jo Lynd, fragile, vulnerable, thrown suddenly into the spotlight with no defenses to shield her. He could see why she seldom smiled; it was dangerous to appear so unprotected.

"Perhaps I'm just not used to people who are genuinely concerned about strangers," she said.

"Perhaps you'd better be careful, then. It might grow on you."

Joelle straightened a little and shook her head, the sun-streaked hair whirling around her face. "Zach, I do appreciate your kindness, but I want to be left alone. I'm here to work out some things, and I have to be by myself to do it."

She was giving him the perfect excuse to turn and walk away, to put distance between them before she discovered who he was. Zach knew he should take her words and use them to escape, like a magical incantation issued to a flying carpet. It made all the sense in the world to leave. Why then, wasn't he able to?

The answer was complicated. But at least one thing was clear. She needed him, even if she didn't know it. She needed the warmth of human contact. Walking away would be unconscionable. Especially walking away from Jo Lynd.

"How many hours are there in a day, Joelle?"

"Your point?"

"Only that I intend to leave you alone...most of the time." He lifted his hand in a casual wave and continued down the driveway.

Joelle stood, eyes focused on the proud retreating back. Zach walked like a man who knew where he was going. That quality alone made her choke down the angry words rising in her throat; it had been so long since she had known where she was headed herself. Reluctantly she let herself wonder what it would be like to trust the man, Zach Smith.

Shrugging her shoulders, Joelle turned and strode up the path to the spring. She had worked for days to clear debris from the source of the bubbling water. What had once been a sparkling, free-flowing stream was now barely producing, saturating the ground around it instead of running unimpeded into the underground pipes that led to the springhouse.

Bending, she began to pull weeds, hand over hand, until her tired muscles screamed for a respite. Instead she pushed on. There wasn't much that she could do about her life, but when the spring was clear again, at least she would know that she had accomplished something.

ZACH CROSSED THE LAST FIELD that connected his land
to Joelle's and swung himself onto the gray porch of the
tall white farmhouse—neglecting the front steps and
just missing a bed of nodding scarlet tulips. The wife of
his foreman had dug up the fertile rocky ground several years before, designing borders that waved around
the stark lines of the house like an undulating river.
Early in the spring yellow daffodils graced the curving
beds. Then came the tulips and when they were gone,
summer annuals of whatever hue and height struck her
fancy. The tulips were everyone's favorite. What else
could be as appropriate for a business that sold windmills?

Inside the house he flicked on the radio, then thought
better of it, turning it off with a sharp snap. The last
thing he needed right now was to hear Jo Lynd's husky,
sensuous voice drift across the airwaves.

Zach could not believe that she was living next door
to him, although it should hardly have come as a surprise. The few people in town who knew that the Lindsey family still owned the land next to his had made sure
that he was informed who his absent neighbor was.
Over and over again he had been reminded.

The town of Russell Creek had not died completely
after the Pennington Alloy coal mine had closed down.
Those who had chosen to stay had gotten a perverse
pleasure from flaunting Jo Lynd's name in front of
him. He had never tried to hide his identity, and they
had never hidden their animosity.

He hoped that with great effort on his part, local at-
titudes would change one day. Even now, there were
people who had accepted him and what he was trying to
do. Slowly he was proving himself. With Jo Lynd living here, however, Zach knew that his presence would

be questioned again. He pictured some benevolent being in the clouds expounding to a group of adoring angels. "Let's play a trick on Zacharias Smith," the voice boomed. "Let's turn his life inside out."

The comfortable sofa beckoned, and although Zach normally never paused to rest during a workday, he flopped down without a second thought. Dropping his head on the sofa's back, arms folded in front of him, he shut his eyes.

The radio was off, but it didn't seem to matter. As clearly as though he was being given a personal concert, he could hear Jo Lynd's voice. The vibrant, smoky alto was singing a recent hit, "When I Come Home to You." It was blatantly commercial, a far cry from her first songs.

To call her a folksinger now was incorrect. She sang soft rock and occasionally country, but she never quite stepped over the line into hard-driving rock and roll. Some of her songs retained their haunting folk quality, most did not. More and more she had followed the path of her famed mentor-lover, Tim Daniels. Blowing with the winds of change, singing what people wanted to hear.

Her album covers mirrored the changes, and Zach had all her records. Restlessly he slid to the end of the sofa, and opened the walnut cabinet under his expensive, outdated stereo. Jo Lynd's records were kept together in an inviolate corner. He rarely played them, but he kept the albums in one place so that he could find them easily if the need arose. And late at night on those rare occasions when the past began to torture him, he would pull them out and play them one by one.

The albums were arranged from the most recent to the first. Zach pulled them onto his lap and ran his

hands over their smooth surfaces. When he realized
what his fingers were caressing, he stopped, moving his
hands to the edge to hold the album as a child is taught
to hold a photograph. Jo Lynd stared out at him, looking the same and yet not the same as the Joelle Lindsey
he had met today.

In the photograph she was dressed in black. A stark
silk blouse cut almost to her waist exposed the inner
curves of her softly mounded breasts. Flowing sleeves
dived down into cuffs that threatened to swallow her
painfully thin wrists. The blouse was tucked into sleek
black jeans and fastened at the waist with a chain of
heavy gold links. Her long blond hair billowed out behind her in a relentlessly contrived manner, still, con-
veying exactly what it was supposed to. The woman on
the album cover was pure flame, lighting dark desire in
the heart of every man who chanced to see the photograph.

The woman he had met today was not flame. She was
earth and cool gray mist. And she had smiled. Never, on
album covers, in performance, during interviews, did Jo
Lynd smile.

The next cover was similar, and the one after it was
similar too, with candid black-and-white photographs
on the back taken during recording sessions. One of the
photographs showed her with Tim Daniels. Zach noted
the expression of rapt attention on her face as she talked
to the magnetic folk performer who had discovered her
and boosted her meteoric rise to fame.

The fourth album portrayed another side of her. She
looked pensive, not sexy, and her waist-length hair hung
over her shoulders like a summer rain, falling to caress
the guitar she held on her lap. This was Jo Lynd, the

folk musician, not Jo Lynd, the object of nameless men's lust. She was younger. Pure, almost holy.

Zach came to her first recording. On the album cover she was standing, looking sadly at the camera as though it were trying to take her soul. The print on the cover almost eclipsed her photograph, in the way that record albums had been typically designed in the early seventies. Her freckles stood out in sharp relief against the gray background, and a lone braid curved over her shoulder. She held a guitar beside her as if it might offer her the comfort that nothing else could. "The Voice of Corruption," the album title read. "Jo Lynd Tells Her Story."

The record was still wrapped carefully in its original cellophane; the seal was unbroken. Although Zach could repeat the words to the title song verbatim, he had never played this album. He had never needed to feel that much emotion. Flipping it over, he read the familiar cover notes. Everything anyone would ever need to know about Jo Lynd was there. The world had not been spared any detail. It was a story that he knew by heart, a story he had played a part in. It was a story that never should have happened.

Zach gathered the albums against his chest and stood to open an old sailor's trunk that he used as an end table. He set the albums underneath an afghan that was stored there. He did not want to see them again. Jo Lynd was no longer a story, no longer a symbol. She was the young woman who was living next door to him. She was Joelle Lindsey, and he was Zach Smith, a man she had never met. A man whose life she had changed forever.

He had an unsettling premonition that she was about to change his life again.

CHAPTER TWO

LIKE SO MANY SPRING MORNINGS in western Pennsylvania, this one had ended in rain. Joelle ignored the insistent drops of water until she realized that she was shivering. After hesitating, she picked up her scythe and small shovel, retreating to the dubious shelter of the springhouse. Storing the tools under the steps, she climbed wearily to the second floor, stopping at the top to remove her clothes and allow herself the luxury of the divinely inspired shower. It did not rival warm water and fragrant French soap, but it was better than the sponge baths that she had been taking in buckets of rusty spring water.

Too cold to stand the rain any longer, she opened the door and stepped inside. The room was not warm, due to the absence of windowpanes, but it was protected, and mostly, it was dry. There were several small leaks and occasional raindrops coming in through the screens, but with some attention those problems would soon be fixed.

Still shivering, she opened her suitcase and dug out her last clean towel. She dried off quickly, stepping into corduroy jeans and an olive sweater. Her sleeping bag was made of goose down, and she crawled in gratefully, allowing the feathers to provide her with the warmth that she needed. A peaceful contentment stole over her, blocking for a time the problems that she had wrestled with for so long.

Joelle drifted off to sleep, aware in her sinking lethargy that it was the first nap she had taken in years. Of course that didn't count the days she had slept through because she was on tour and needed to switch her schedule. But this nap was different, and the luxury of it contrasted sharply with the austerity of her surroundings.

It was well into the afternoon when she awoke. Hunger assailed her, surprising her with its intensity. She sat up and rummaged through the ice chest, pulling out a package of crackers and some peanut butter. She ate them with an apple and found that she was surprised again. Apples, usually just another way of staving off starvation, could actually taste good. Her appetite, long dormant, was beginning to come back.

The day had been full of surprises. Zach Smith had been a surprise. The rain had been a surprise, her nap, her impromptu lunch, all had been interesting developments in what should have been a boring day. With a fleeting smile she wondered what the people she knew in Los Angeles would think of her enjoyment of such basic pleasures. And what would Tim, who often sang of the simple life but never lived it, think of a day and a place such as this? She shut her eyes and imagined the look of horror on his face. Forcing Tim to live this ascetic life would be similar to catching a fox in a trap by one leg. Tim was always on the move, always restless. He never took time to listen, not to himself, not to others. His restlessness had been the most primary of problems in their stormy relationship.

Rising, Joelle went to the window and noted the gray rain with disappointment. Her options for the rest of the afternoon did not appear interesting even with her renewed enthusiasm for the simple life.

Since coming to the farm, she had begun writing songs again, something that she never seemed to have time for in California. When she had put pen to paper before her flight to Pennsylvania, it had been to sign contracts and business documents. Her songs had always served to record her progress or lack of it, and not writing at all had been another sign of the impasse in her life. Now that she had the time, she found herself exploring thoughts and images, setting them to music as landmarks on her life's journey. Rainy afternoons were perfect for songwriting, but now Joelle was restless, and the thought gave her no pleasure.

She had been alone for a week. It was exactly what she had needed, what she wanted, but Zach's entrance into her life that morning had awakened another need. She needed human contact. Although she had been putting off the moment when she would have to confront more of her past, that moment had arrived.

The apprehension that welled up inside her was unfamiliar. Jo Lynd sang in front of roaring waves of admirers, unafraid and completely self-confident. Joelle Lindsey was afraid to start her car and drive the two-mile blacktop to Russell Creek. Since coming to the farm, she had managed to avoid driving into the little mining town, traveling the extra miles to the small city of Taylerton instead when she needed supplies. Was it what she would find or what wouldn't be in Russell Creek that was most frightening?

Throwing on a brown raincoat and rubbing her hands together for badly needed warmth, Joelle picked her way down the path, opened the door of the Pontiac that she had leased in Pittsburgh, and slid into the driver's seat. The only truth she had to find comfort in was that nothing she would ever do would be harder than this trip into her past.

AFTER SEVERAL MILES of green, lush country, Russell Creek appeared over the last rise of a group of heavily forested hills. It was a small town, smaller now than it had been when it thrived as a place for the Pennington Alloy miners and their families to live. There was no operating mine now. No coal was loaded on barges and shipped down the Monongahela River to Pittsburgh.

Joelle parked and slowly noted the changes in the town. It had been fifteen years since she had last stood on this same hill looking over the neighborhoods of two-story duplex houses, each like the other except for the small touches their occupants had added to establish separate identities. The company had owned the houses, selling them to the miners if they were able to come up with the money to buy them. Occasionally someone had, sometimes evicting the family living on the other side to spread out in glorious freedom.

Instinctively Joelle searched for the "yaller house." It had been at the end of a block of plain white houses, a testament to creativity in a town that had little use for the unusual. She remembered how as a child she had looked out the school-bus window one day and seen the "yaller house." It had been white the day before, plain, as ordinary as everyone else's. By the next day, with a whole family of painters slapping the gaudy gold paint on the weathered boards, the house had been transformed.

Today there was no sign of that particular house. Either its color had faded with time and with neglect, or it was one of many of the duplexes that had been

abandoned and finally torn down. There were numerous gaps now where once there had been houses. Those
that were left ranged from shacks to well-kept little res-
idences. Joelle had expected the shacks. The many
neatly cared for houses interspersed among them were
a surprise.

Starting the car, she followed the road into the center of town and parked again, this time getting out to
walk the two-block street that was the heart of Russell
Creek. It was with amazement that she realized her legs
were shaking.

There were few people walking in the drizzle along
the side of the pothole-covered blacktop, and she ignored those who were, hoping to blend into the stark
colorless buildings beside her. She passed what had once
been a thriving club patronized by the miners for the
sole purpose of trading stories and getting drunk. In a
society that had stifled expression of feelings, the club
had served as a therapeutic outlet for men who faced the
end of their lives each time they plummeted down the
mine shaft. Now it was closed.

What had been the company store was closed, too.
Joelle faced the door, tentatively lifting her hand to
touch the scratched metal knob. As she had known they
would, memories flashed in front of her, formless and
fleeting. Her mother holding a younger sibling on one
hip, collaring another sibling to push him through the
door. Her father emerging with a brown bag in each
arm and a sober expression on his face. Her brother
Hoyt, Jr.... Quickly Joelle turned and continued down
the street.

Not all the stores were closed. Russell Creek was still
occupied and where there were people there was com-
merce. Joelle stopped at a small white building at the

end of the street and looked through the mud-splattered window. Her memory could not dredge up what the building had been originally. Now it was obviously the town grocery store. No larger than a quick-stop market in any other town, the store evidently met the needs of Russell Creek's citizens until they could drive into Taylerton.

As she watched, the old man behind the counter lifted his head from the newspaper spread out before him and saw her face at the window. Reaching behind him to pull wire-rimmed spectacles from a pocket, he plopped them on his nose and squinted. Through the grimy window Joelle watched as he finally mouthed the words, "Let me take a look at you, girl."

"Mr. Kincaid." It seemed impossible, but perhaps sixteen years was only a long time to her. Her apprehension growing, Joelle pulled the door open and stepped inside. "Mr. Kincaid?"

"The same." The old man examined her, taking off the spectacles as she came closer. "Hoyt's girl?"

"The same." Joelle felt a smile burst through the apprehension. "The very same."

"Nah. I'd say different." Mr. Kincaid smiled. "It's about time you came home. There wouldn't have been much left if you'd waited."

"There wasn't. The house is about to tumble down. I'm staying in the springhouse until I can get it repaired."

Mr. Kincaid nodded, examining her. "You turned out prettier than I'd have thought possible. You were always a skinny little girl, with eyes as big as hubcaps."

"I'm still skinny."

"From what I hear, you work hard enough to keep anyone skinny. Even me." Mr. Kincaid patted his huge stomach and Joelle watched it bounce against the counter. She smiled again.

"So you've heard about me?"

"News even gets to Russell Creek. C'mere, let me look at you up close." She leaned against the counter, submitting to the indignity of a full examination without comment. "You don't look famous, girl. Just hungry."

It was good to be in the store, to be with someone who hadn't always known her as a symbol, as a success. Joelle nodded at the old man, glad that he was standing there and that she had found the courage to come back. "Mr. Kincaid, who's left?" She swept her hand behind her toward the street.

"You'd be surprised at the ones who stayed." Toddling down to the end of the counter, he lifted the top off a plastic cake dish that covered a small wheel of cheese and cut a hearty slice. He put it on a napkin and toddled back over to thrust it at Joelle. "Eat."

She took a bite. "Your Cheddar tastes just like it always did. I'll buy a pound." She noted the price and took money from the wallet in her pocket. Finishing her sample, she listened.

"When there was no more work, there was a parade out of here the likes of which I never want to see again. Seems to me you were in it." He cut more cheese and squinted at her again.

Joelle nodded. "We went to West Virginia. My mother had a brother living there. He took us all in."

"People do what they can with what they have." Mr. Kincaid busied himself wrapping Joelle's purchase and cleaning up cheese crumbs off the counter. "There was some who had no place to go. The miners who could went other places, to other mines. Some found work, most didn't, or so I hear.''

Joelle knew her face was grim. "If there'd been work in other places, no one would have ever stayed in Russell Creek."

"You're too young to remember. Even with all its problems this was a good place to live. Still is in some ways." The old man was lost in thought for a moment. "Some folks stayed and lived off their pensions if they was old enough to qualify. More'n a few of the younger ones stayed and found work in Taylerton or Awnsley. Livin' here's cheap. Nuthin' to spend your money on."

"Why did you stay?"

Mr. Kincaid shrugged. "Too old to start over, too young to die quiet. The company closed down the store, so I was left without a job." He grinned at Joelle's nod. "I'd saved some money, and I bought this building dirt cheap. People were used to buyin' from me. They didn't care if it was me or the company bringin' the food in."

"I can't remember what this building used to be."

"Fire hall."

"That's right. Dances on Saturday night, Halloween parties. We lived so far up the road that we didn't get to go out as much as the kids in town did."

"I still saw plenty of all the Lindsey kids, though. Where are the rest of you now?"

"Both my sisters married miners in southern West Virginia. My brother's an engineer in Maryland. Ma died years ago."

"And you ended up with the farm and no time to use it."

"No one else wanted it. They'd never come back here. All three of them were a lot younger than I was. What memories they have, they've walled off."

Mr. Kincaid stopped wiping the counter. "And you, girl? What about your memories?"

Joelle finished the last crumb of cheese and balled up her napkin. "I guess they're about as bad as memories get."

"Your songs kept it all alive. I can't listen to 'em. I don't know how you can sing 'em." Joelle met his eyes and was surprised at the compassion she saw there. She was standing in a tiny grocery store, talking to a casual observer of her past, and she was more touched than she remembered being in a long time.

"I don't sing coal-mining songs anymore," she said. "Now I just sing for money."

"Do you sing for old friends? There's plenty of folks hereabouts that would love to hear you."

The door behind her opened and Joelle turned slowly to look at the newcomer. A young woman with crisply curling brown hair came in and began to put some canned goods in a basket. "How many people who live here will even remember me?" Joelle asked casually, although the question wasn't really casual at all. She didn't want to be a local celebrity.

"More'n a few. Folks are real proud of you. And there's some new blood in town, too." He nodded his head at the woman who was in the back of the store examining a meager supply of vegetables in a lone cooler.

"I'd like to keep a low profile for a while," Joelle said softly, her voice an unconscious plea.

Mr. Kincaid nodded. "I won't give you away, but folks'll catch on soon enough if you keep comin' around. They notice new faces. Ain't nuthin' much else to gossip about."

"I met a man today who wasn't familiar. Zach Smith. Do you know who I'm talking about?"

She was surprised to see the old man stiffen. "He's not exactly a new face. Did he tell you who he is?"

Joelle's skin prickled. "He said he runs an energy-supply house, although why he picked Russell Creek for it is a mystery."

"Not so much." The old man clamped his jaw and shook his head. The young woman came up to the counter, her basket heaped with vegetables, and stepped behind Joelle.

"Go ahead," Joelle said. "We were just chatting."

The young woman smiled and then her brow furrowed briefly. "Do I know you?"

"It's possible," Joelle said smoothly, "but I'm afraid you don't look familiar." Unwilling to stay and face exposure, she turned to leave. "Mr. Kincaid, I'll see you soon. It's been good to chat." She waved when she reached the door, stepping out into the street to let it bang shut behind her.

Outside, Joelle hugged herself against the chill in the air and started back to the car. She had planned to visit the mine, too, but the encounter with Mr. Kincaid had stirred up more than enough memories for one day. Facing one person from her past and standing at the door of the abandoned mine were hardly the same things. She was not yet strong enough for the latter. Starting the car engine, Joelle whispered a prayer asking for forgiveness for her cowardice and turned the steering wheel to head back to the farm.

THE GRADUAL CHANGE from dark afternoon to darker evening crept over the wide expanse of sky, leaving Joelle restless with the pent-up energy that her reminiscences had not tapped. The constant drizzle had slowed enough for her to stuff her hair under a Greek fisherman's cap and put on a windbreaker to venture out to brave the elements. The rain had washed the earth and the spring-budding trees, leaving the air fresh and redolent with the smells of ozone and decaying leaves.

She had been so busy clearing and cleaning that there were still portions of her farm that she had not explored. Choosing a direction, she trampled through the weeds, following fence posts that had long since lost their barbwire. The land had been long abandoned, but with the patience of Mother Nature, it had calmly waited, growing more beautiful with the passing of time.

The woods she came to were full of trees that she couldn't identify, along with sycamore, buckeye and maple. A thick carpet of slippery leaves protected her from the mud below, and she walked for an hour, crisscrossing her original path, getting to know each inch of forest again. There were spring wildflowers and interesting fungi. Joelle saw chipmunks and a fat opossum as she crouched quietly, letting the woods work its calming magic.

It was almost dark when she reluctantly headed back to the springhouse. She wasn't tired, but there was little that she could do by the light of one kerosene lantern, and a boring night spread out before her. As she walked through the door, Joelle saw that she had a visitor. A tiny gray field mouse was sitting cheerfully on her ice chest, eating the crackers that she had left out after lunch.

"Hey, that's my dinner!"

The mouse scampered off to the corner carrying one cracker, but the hole that it evidently resided in was too small to pull the cracker through. "It's a mouse's ethical dilemma," Joelle said sternly, shaking her finger at the tiny creature. "Leave it and your family starves; stay with it and I could trample you."

The mouse had no trouble with its decision and disappeared into the hole. With a sigh and a muttered oath against do-gooders, Joelle crumbled the cracker and stuffed it in the hole behind the house. "My treat."

Still squatting, ear to the wall, she listened for the sounds of mousy ecstasy. "Aren't you even going to say thank-you?" she prompted.

"Thank you." The man's voice resounded through the room, and as Joelle rocked back on her heels, she lost her balance, sitting with a thump on the floor behind her.

"I'm sorry, Joelle. Are you all right?"

She swiveled to see Zach Smith watching her. He was trying very hard not to smile. He extended a hand, but Joelle ignored it, pushing herself to stand upright in front of him. "I'm glad to see you're not a hundred-eighty-pound mouse," she said, brushing off the seat of her pants. "I was worried there for a moment."

"If you keep feeding those varmints, you actually may have a hundred-eighty-pound mouse keeping you company." He dropped his hand to his side.

"A temporary lapse in sanity."

"Is the solitude getting to you?"

Joelle removed her hat and shook her hair free. "I have to admit it is. When I start talking to mice...watch out!"

"I thought it might be. I've come to invite you to my house for dinner and a shower."

Her eyelids closed for a moment as the thought of warm water and a hot meal swept over her. "Zach, I told you, I want to be left alone."

"I know."

Eyes open, she focused wearily on his face again. "Do you thrive on rejection?"

"I thrive on beautiful, grubby women who look like they haven't eaten in weeks."

The room was getting darker as they talked, but Zach's brown eyes seemed to absorb the fading light. Again Joelle found herself admiring their warmth. "Your towel or mine?" she finally asked in defeat.

"Mine. Bring your laundry, too. I've got a washing machine and dryer. You can do it while we eat."

Joelle picked up her suitcase and followed Zach to the door, but she stopped to warn him as he climbed down the steps. "I'm not going to make a habit of this, you know."

He turned and smiled. "Good, I'm not sure how long my solar hot-water heater will hold out."

"That's not what I mean, Zach."

"I know it's not. Let's just see what happens, shall we?"

Considering that she had lived most of her life just waiting to see what happened, it was hard to say no.

Zach reached up for the suitcase and lifted it from her as she followed him down the steps. The day had darkened to that mysterious time when the stark canopy above them showed no stars, no moon, no sun. Joelle stopped and tilted her head to watch. There had been times like this when she was a little girl, times when she and her two younger sisters would sit quietly on their front porch, as they waited for day to end. She realized that once again she was holding her breath for that second when day would be night, when light would finally, irrevocably, become darkness.

Zach lifted his arm and pointed a long finger to the north. "Right over the horizon. The first star." He watched Joelle's lips move silently. Star light, star bright...what did Joelle Lindsey wish for, he wondered. Would her wishes be different or exactly the same as those of Jo Lynd, who already seemed to have everything?

"I'll take that now." Joelle, amazed at having fallen into such a comfortable trance with Zach standing beside her, reached for the suitcase.

"Let me," he said. "I haven't worked as hard as you have today."

Joelle liked his answer. There was no condescension, no "stronger than thou" insult in his words. She nodded in gratitude. "Thanks."

They walked down the path to the driveway. A blue Ford pick-up truck was parked at the end next to the rental car. Old and battered, the truck looked perfectly natural parked in front of the tumbling house that had been Joelle's childhood home. Zach hoisted the suitcase over the truck tailgate and continued around to open the door for her. Joelle, who was used to the complete absence of manners in rock stars and their bands, was surprised by the old-fashioned courtesy.

"Thanks," she murmured again. She could remember no occasion in the past ten years when it had been necessary to say thank-you twice to the same person in a five-minute period. It was a sad commentary on her life.

The truck inside was worn but obviously well taken care of. The seats had been carefully patched, and there was a scrap of carpeting at her feet. When Zach got in and turned the key, the truck purred like a kitten. He put it in reverse, head turned to look behind him as he rested one arm on the seat behind Joelle. The gesture was casual, but she could feel the wool sweater that he wore tickling the back of her neck. Her feelings, though natural, were not welcome. She inched forward slightly.

Casually Zach removed his arm and gripped the wheel with both hands. "How do you like Pennsylvania?" he asked, trying to lighten the tension.

"I always have," she answered.

"But you live in California."

Joelle felt a rush of anger at his words. He had known all along who she was. "How did you know that?"

"I wrote you there, remember? I got your address at the county courthouse."

"Oh, that's right." She relaxed slightly.

"Do you like California?"

"I get tired of all that sunshine."

He had a rich, deep laugh that filled the cab of the old truck. "I understand perfectly."

"Why?"

"I lived there for a while, among other places. One morning I was lying in bed in San Diego and there was sunshine flooding the room. Bouncing, golden sunshine. I was so sick of it that I got up and pulled every curtain in the apartment closed, and I still couldn't shut it all out. I was hanging blankets in front of the curtains when I came to my senses."

"What did you do then?"

"I bought a one-way ticket back to Pennsylvania."

"Most of the world would think you were crazy."

Zach turned and smiled, and his teeth, surrounded by the soft auburn beard, gleamed white in the darkness. "I've never cared very much what the world would think."

Perhaps, Joelle decided, that was why he was such an attractive man.

Zach's farmhouse sat on a low rise like a white dove nesting in the moonlight. Joelle glimpsed tulips and carefully tended shrubbery in the darkness. "Our place looked like this once," she said. "I can still shut my eyes and remember exactly how it was."

"Your place is unique, really. There aren't too many one-story houses in this part of the country. They aren't energy efficient." Zach opened his door and climbed down out of the cab, coming around to help her out. "And the long porch surrounding it is the only one like it around here. I like your house. It's too bad it's in such rough shape."

"Actually I'm ashamed I've let it deteriorate so badly. But it's been abandoned for such a long time."

Zach held out his hand and watched Joelle hesitate as she decided whether to accept it. He stood perfectly still as she struggled, fighting the impulse to move closer and make the decision for her. Finally she put her hand in his and stepped down. Her hand felt fragile; surprising really, he thought, for someone who could swing a scythe with such expertise. He felt a slight swelling on the palm and turned it over with curiosity to examine it. "You've got an interesting collection of blisters there."

Joelle grimaced. "I'd feel better if you called them calluses."

"You ought to put something on them."

"I didn't come prepared for medical emergencies." Her shoulder lifted in a careless shrug.

"I'll rig up a first-aid kit for you tonight before you leave." Zach dropped her hand and started toward the house.

"Were you a Boy Scout?"

"For years. My father was a great believer in the basic American virtues."

The irony in his voice seemed to come out of nowhere. Pausing for a moment, Joelle watched him climb the steps. *I wonder who he is,* she thought. *What would Mr. Kincaid have told me if we hadn't been interrupted?* Certainly, however, she was in no position to begin asking questions that could be turned back on her.

Joelle picked her way around concrete planters that promised to be filled eventually with cascading flowers. Now the planters stood empty. They looked like stone lions guarding Zach's door. "I can't tell in the dark, but I'd guess that someone here is a gardener," she said.

"Carol is. Every time I turn around she's digging up some perfectly good plot of my grass and planting something new. In the summertime we look like an advertisement for a seed catalog." He opened the door and motioned Joelle inside.

"Am I about to meet Carol?" she asked, surprised at the disappointment that she felt. She had never considered the fact that this man might be married.

"I doubt it. She's rarely here in the evenings." Zach flicked on a light, surprised by the bleak expression on Joelle's face. "Is something wrong?"

"I feel a little strange being in another woman's house without her being present."

A warm chuckle welled up deep inside him, and Zach restrained it as best he could. "I didn't think how my remark sounded, Joelle. For some reason, I forgot that you don't know me. I'm not married. Carol is. To my foreman."

"I see." Joelle's noncommittal expression hid the satisfaction that his words gave her.

"Why don't you take a shower first, and I'll see about dinner? When you're done I'll show you where the washer and dryer are." Zach pointed to the dark oak staircase. "First door on the left."

Flashing him one of her rare smiles, Joelle followed his instructions. The bathroom was finished in tiny, old-fashioned hexagonal tile. There was an elaborate claw-footed bathtub with a hand-held shower head. To Joelle, whose house in Los Angeles had a Jacuzzi and a hot tub, but whose springhouse in Pennsylvania had only a rusty bucket of water, the bathroom was luxury itself.

She showered quickly, taking his remark about the solar hot-water heater seriously. She washed her hair, forgoing the deep-treatment conditioner that her stylist insisted she couldn't live without. When she emerged she felt renewed.

She changed back into the olive sweater and brown corduroy jeans that were the cleanest things she owned. She hadn't thought to bring a comb up with her, and she used Zach's, conscientiously washing it when she was finished. In the mirror Joelle's face was rosy with the well-scrubbed appearance of a child going to church. But her face was not a child's. The thirty years she had lived had left their mark.

After cleaning the bathroom, Joelle ventured down-stairs, stopping this time to admire the photographs lining the walls of the stairwell. They were beautifully done, portraying everyday scenes of a miner's life. Although the subject matter was unusual, the photographs were appealing in their black-and-white simplicity.

"I like the photographs," she told Zach when she found him in the kitchen. "They're like the house, simple yet rich in detail."

Zach looked around, trying to see the familiar room through her eyes. The kitchen was modern enough to be functional. There were few items to distract one's attention, but those that did were worth looking twice at. A set of cobalt-blue enameled cannisters graced the top of a butcher-block counter. One wall was papered in the same vivid blue. The color was picked up once again in an island in the middle of the room that was covered in Delft tiles of windmills.

"I'm glad you liked the photographs. I enjoyed doing them."

"I didn't realize that you were the photographer. I'm surprised."

"Why?"

Joelle thought of all the photography sessions that she had endured in the last thirteen years . . . and all the photographers. Little by little she had felt her spirit was being whittled away, given to an admiring public to keep on a shelf for posterity. No matter how much she learned about keeping a part of herself untouched, the endless photographs seemed to get closer and closer until she was sure she would no longer have anything left inside her.

"Most of the photographers I've known have been insensitive. They're so busy looking for the perfect image that they forget the people they photograph are real."

"I think that's why I never wanted to be more than an amateur camera bug. When your livelihood depends on that perfect picture, you lose sight of all the not-so-perfect pictures that also need to be recorded." Zach bent to check something in the oven, and the scent of rich tomato sauce and herbs filled the kitchen.

"That smells wonderful. What is it?" Joelle came around the counter to stand beside him.

"Eggplant Parmigiana." Zach straightened and shut the oven door. "I had a feeling that you might be a vegetarian."

"Why?" she snapped suspiciously. Her publicist always made a point of her meatless diet. It was part of her image.

"Well, you told me this morning that you're only eating things that don't need refrigeration."

"Actually," she said, relief spreading through her body at his answer, "I am a lapsing vegetarian. I've become obsessed with the idea of a hot meal since I started living on the farm. Sometimes I dream about a huge, rare chunk of meat. I always wake up just as I'm about to bite into a steak."

"I could fix you one."

"Nothing could beat Eggplant Parmigiana. My body's just craving something hot and full of calories."

They were standing side by side, leaning on the oven door, which was sending welcome heat into the coolness of the kitchen. Zach allowed his eyes to travel over Joelle's slender frame. She was tall, but so tiny. All bones and skin. "When was the last time you had a real dinner?" he asked gently.

It had been the evening before the party that had catapulted her life into upheaval. A lifetime ago. "Last week sometime," she said, trying to sound nonchalant. "Before I decided to come here."

"There are restaurants in Taylerton, you know."

"I don't like restaurants," Joelle said. And she didn't like being recognized even more. Sunglasses and scarves might work as a disguise at airports and grocery stores, but they were useless in a restaurant.

"Well, you will like my cooking. I'll make the salad now, and then we can eat."

"Let me help." Joelle followed Zach to the refrigerator and took the vegetables that he handed her to the sink to begin to wash them. "Salad is my specialty. In fact it's about the only thing I ever fix." The comment was too revealing, she realized.

"Well, if that's all you eat, it's no wonder there's not an ounce of fat on you anywhere."

They finished the preparations in silence. Conversation was difficult when both were hiding themselves and beginning to regret the necessity. Joelle watched Zach through lowered lids. He worked quickly and moved around the comfortable kitchen with fluid motions. He was perfectly at home, doing what needed to be done with no fuss, no boredom. Still, Joelle knew that he would be more in his element outside in the wind and the sun. He was a man who was obviously good at a lot of things, including inspiring trust in a woman who had hardly trusted anyone since she was fourteen years old.

When the salad was finished, Zach pointed Joelle to the basement laundry room, and she started the washing machine. She took a long time familiarizing herself with the dials and buttons on the relatively elementary equipment. As a child she had often helped her mother wash clothes using the old wringer washer in their dirt-floor cellar. Since that time she had sent her laundry out to be cleaned professionally. Zack's simple automatic washing machine had the fascination of a high-powered computer. She realized that there was an entire decade of basic home technology that she was unfamiliar with.

Returning to find that dinner was completed, Joelle carried the salad into the small dining room and set it on the antique pine table. Zach's house was furnished with American primitives, a subject Joelle knew little about except that she had grown up with much of the same furniture. When she was a child, however, the primitives were there because they had been carefully passed down through the generations to save buying new items that were never affordable.

"My youngest sister has a pie safe that you'd love," Joelle told Zach when he entered with the casserole and a loaf of crusty French bread. "She was the only one in our family with enough sense to value our heritage."

"Not the only one. You refused to sell the farm."

Joelle lifted her eyes to Zach's face, pleased to be reminded that she hadn't failed the Lindsey family, either. "Yes, I did," she said softly. "I did do that."

Something very much like pleasure passed across her face, and Zach, who had conscientiously tried not to stare at her, forgot to be careful. She was so lovely, her wet hair parted on the side and sculpted to her well-formed head. He remembered that the sun-streaked hair used to be much longer, almost a trademark, and he smiled inadvertently as he realized that cutting it had been an attempt at disguise. Nothing could have been a worse idea. With her hair shorter, her distinctive bone structure and slanting jade eyes were even more prominent and easily recognizable. Half-smiling, lost in thought, Joelle was too exquisite to believe.

Zack shook himself, ignoring the shudder of desire that was passing through his long frame. She was the last person on earth who he could ever take to his bed. "Let's eat," he said, pulling them both out of their reverie. "It's best when it's very hot."

Joelle savored every bite of the dinner, lingering over each mouthful as if it might be her last. Zach watched with satisfaction as she accepted a second helping. "There's dessert, too, if you can manage," he told her.

Something like a groan emerged from behind her napkin. "Not another bite. I couldn't, not for hours."

"We'll have to wait then." He offered her another glass of the Burgundy that he had served with the meal. "Would you like to take this out on the front porch, or have you had enough fresh air today?"

"I'll help you with the dishes," she said, "and then I'd better be going."

"Your laundry's not done yet," he reminded her. "Stay at least that long."

Zach was right; she was trapped by her dirty clothes into spending a lovely evening with a very attractive man. Worse things had happened to her. "I'll see if it's ready for the dryer yet," Joelle replied, acquiescing "and I'll meet you on the front porch."

She stood, reaching for her dishes, but Zach's large hand on her shoulder stopped her. "Is your hair still wet? he asked. His fingers threaded through the silky strands tugging gently. "I'll get you a hat if it is."

Joelle was frozen to the spot, vulnerable and suddenly frightened of the man standing next to her. No one had really touched her in such a long time until Zach Smith had stepped into her life. She remembered his finger brushing across her cheekbone, his hand as he helped her out of the truck. The contacts had been casual. Much more casual really than the bone-crushing hugs that she had to endure from other show-business people who always treated her body as if it was another obstacle to get around. But when Zach touched her, she felt as though something intimate had occurred.

He felt her tension, and he withdrew immediately. "I think you'll be fine," he murmured. "Just let me know if you get cold."

Joelle watched him disappear into the kitchen. "I'm not sure I want to remember what it's like to be warm, Zach Smith," she whispered. "But I don't think you're going to let me forget."

CHAPTER THREE

THE FIRST STAR of the night had been joined by a universe of twinkling kin. Zach was comfortably ensconced in a tall wooden rocking chair when Joelle joined him on the front porch. He stood, pulling another chair beside him, and waited for her to be seated. When she was, he joined her, trying not to notice her discomfort at their close proximity.

He felt some of the same discomfort himself. All afternoon he had tried to convince himself that his reactions to Joelle Lindsey were solely because of the mutual past that they shared, a past that she wasn't even aware of. He had hovered between swearing never to be alone with her again and wanting to see her immediately.

He hadn't even made a conscious decision about asking her to dinner. He had prepared a meal, straightened the house and gotten into his truck without admitting to himself that he was going to invite her to spend the evening with him. As he had driven to her house, he had cursed his lack of objectivity. Nothing good could come of a relationship between them.

She was obviously at a crossroads in her life; he had no right to interfere. But most of all, he didn't trust his strong response to her. Jo Lynd had been a symbol to him when he needed a symbol to force a change in his priorities. But Joelle Lindsey was a human being with deep needs of her own. He wasn't certain which person, Jo or Joelle, he was so powerfully attracted to. Now, hours later, he still wasn't sure.

They sat quietly, each striving to develop a topic of neutral conversation. Finally Zach began.

"Do you know anything about the history of your land?"

Joelle turned slightly to watch his face as she talked. "Not a whole lot. My grandmother's family was Polish and they settled here generations ago. They did subsistence farming, shipped whatever they could up to Pittsburgh to sell. When the coal mine opened, my grandfather came up from West Virginia to work in it, married my grandmother and settled down here. With the mine, there was no need for serious farming."

"It's a nice piece of land. Rich soil, good water source. There's quite a bit of hardwood in the forest, too."

"You know more about it than I do."

"Originally my land belonged with yours. This house is the older of the two. Your relatives probably lived here, then sold this chunk and built the house that's on your land now."

"Your house is in much better shape, though."

"That's because it's been lived in continuously. The old man I bought it from only sold it to me because his kids had moved away, and they didn't want it."

"I remember him. Mr. Barrows. A crotchety old guy who used to shoot at us with his slingshot if we stole walnuts. My brother, Hoyt..." Joelle's voice trailed off. "Anyway," she began again, "I imagine selling this property was about the hardest thing in the world for Mr. Barrows. Moving is hard even when you don't have any roots."

Her tone was so wistful that Zach felt a rush of sympathy. Try as he might, it was difficult not to react emotionally to the woman sitting beside him. He wanted to school his feelings, maintain his own defenses, but Joelle melted them, leaving him a receptive vessel, touched deeply by everything about her. He tried to sound casual. "You've obviously spent a lot of time moving around."

"Yes, I have. You mentioned that you had, too."

It was a neat change of subject and Zach respected it. "I lived in thirteen different states before I settled here. I don't intend to move again."

Inclining her head in his direction Joelle asked, "So what took you through thirteen different states?"

Zach realized that there was a possibility that if he told Joelle who he was right now, without apologies or self-recrimination, she might be able to accept him. Accept him perhaps, but nothing more. And he realized with dread that more was what he wanted. Much more. He forced his eyes open and turned slightly. She was staring at him, puzzled by his long silence.

Instead of an explanation, he answered her question. "Wanderlust. I was looking for something. I worked for a big corporation when I first graduated from college, and I discovered that I didn't like it. So I started traveling, doing odd jobs, moving on when I chose to. It gave me a chance to live in some unusual situations."

"Like what?" Joelle asked with genuine curiosity. Her life had been so prescribed, so regimented. What Zach was describing had enormous appeal to her.

"Well, I lived in a desert commune for one year. The people who started it were dropouts from a variety of professions. They wanted to develop a self-sufficient life-style devoted to researching ways of rehumanizing society.''

''Why did you leave?''

''We kept fighting about who was going to wash the dishes.''

Joelle snorted.

''I'm serious. We couldn't get past those little human interactions that can be so irritating. No one wanted to participate in any drudgery. Everyone in the commune, including me, felt they had better ways to spend their time. After a year, I just packed and left. I still hate to wash dishes, but at least when I do, I only have mine.''

''And mine tonight.''

''For the pleasure of your company, I can handle the extra.''

Joelle shifted uneasily in her seat at the personal remark. ''Tell me more.''

''Well, I helped organize migrant workers in Texas one year. Another time I worked on a back-to-the-land magazine as an energy consultant. And once, a very long time ago—'' he stopped as if to consider his words ''—I worked in a coal mine.''

''Why?'' Joelle was wide-eyed in the darkness. ''Why would you want to?''

''Not for the thrill of it,'' he said softly. ''It was an investigation of sorts.'' He stopped, knowing that if he went on Joelle would know who he was. ''I imagine it was just the kind of mine that your grandfather worked in down in West Virginia,'' he said, changing the thrust of his explanation.

''Strangely enough,'' Joelle mused, ''my grandfather liked being a miner and so did my father. It was all they knew, and they were very proud men.''

"The men that I worked with were proud men, too. They had a right to be."

"Pride doesn't keep them alive." Joelle stood and walked to the porch railing, reclining against the edge. Zach's face was clear in the moonlight, and she drew in a sharp breath at the pain etched on his features. "I'm sorry. I shouldn't have gotten so serious," she apologized.

Zach shook his head as if to clear it. "Don't apologize," he said. "There are a lot of people in this town with bad memories." He stood. "Can I get you some wine?"

Joelle nodded, and he bent to fill her glass. He brought it to her and leaned against the railing, sipping his own. "You've never told me what brought you here," he said with studied casualness.

"I'm running away."

"From someone or something?"

"From everyone and everything." Slowly Joelle rotated her head, easing the strained muscles in her neck that were the aftermath of weed chopping.

"Let me," Zach said, setting his glass on the railing. His hands gripped her shoulders at the base of her neck and his thumbs began a slow assault on the tension he found. He could feel Joelle's body go even more rigid at his touch. "I'm not going to hurt you," he soothed, hoping it was the truth. "Relax. Let me."

Slowly his thumbs traveled beneath the silky hair that caressed the backs of his hands as he worked. Inch by inch, muscle by muscle, he felt her let go of her tension. "That's better," he encouraged. When he was finished with her neck he began to work the knots out of her shoulders. "You worked too hard today," he chastised her.

It wasn't the work she had done that was making Joelle tense. The unfamiliar hands were spilling shivers down her spinal column. When had a man touched her with such genuine concern? When had a man touched her for any reason except his own pleasure? Zach's hands were traveling down her back, kneading and stroking, encouraging her response. "Better?" he asked finally.

"What do you want from me?" she asked, turning to face him. They were so close that a slight motion would bring their mouths in contact. She moved back a step.

Zach's face was shuttered. Instantly Joelle wished that she could take back her words. Instead she waited for his answer.

"Someone's hurt you very badly, hasn't he?"

"What do you mean?"

"You interpreted a simple massage as a means to some devious end. Have you considered the possibility that I might have done it just to give you pleasure?"

Joelle lowered her head, ashamed of her reaction, but Zach put his fingers under her chin and lifted it. "This may be hard to accept, but I just want to take this one step at a time. Will you believe that? Because it's going to be difficult for us if you don't."

"Zach," she said softly. "There isn't going to be an 'us.' I'm here to straighten out my life, not to complicate it."

"I'm not a complicated person."

His smile was intriguing, and against her better judgment, Joelle returned it, enjoying the warmth of his eyes as she did. "You really are much too nice a person to keep pretending that you don't understand what I'm saying, Zach."

"Oh, I understand." He dropped his hand to her shoulder. "Tell me. Is there a man in California that I'm competing with? If there is, I'll keep my distance." Zach waited for her answer, not sure what he hoped she'd say. He was beginning to realize that his own good sense was not going to prevail. He needed a stronger reason to force him to leave Joelle Lindsey alone.

Joelle knew that Zach was giving her an easy out, and she almost took it. But something behind the warmth in his eyes stopped her. She read a deep yearning and a flicker of fear. Zach was vulnerable, too. She couldn't lie. "No, there's no one waiting there for me."

Her answer was a surprise. Zach had steeled himself to accept the reality of her relationship with Tim Daniels. Even though his own taste did not run to celebrity magazines, Zach knew that Jo Lynd and Tim Daniels had been an acknowledged couple for years. Now she was admitting to no involvement with anyone, even though she knew that it would keep him away if she pretended otherwise. "Well..." He exhaled slowly. "I'm glad." Unaccountably, he really was, but he could feel the web of complications ensnare them both a little tighter.

Joelle closed her eyes. What was she doing? This was exactly what she didn't need right now. But when she opened her eyes to repeat those words to Zach, he had moved a step closer. She tensed as he leaned toward her, but she could not make herself break away.

"I'm only going to kiss you," Zach comforted her. Then, slowly and with great restraint, he bent down and took her mouth with his. His fingers tangled lightly in her hair, and his thumbs traced the sharp lines of her cheekbones. The caress, more than the kiss, sent waves of feeling through her body. His hands were so gentle, so obviously intent on soothing her fears.

The kiss deepened. Joelle allowed Zach to pull her closer. She could feel the heat of his body surrounding her, drawing her further into intimacy. His hands moved down her neck, down her back to encircle her waist and pull her unresisting body against his. At the same time his tongue began to caress her soft lips, encouraging them to part for him.

Joelle often experienced dreams where she was trying to escape from danger, but her body would not, could not move. Zach's kiss had exactly the same effect. Try as she might, she could not make herself break away.

Once when she and Tim had taken a highly publicized pilgrimage to visit a reclusive spiritual teacher, Joelle had told the wizened old man about her dreams. His response had been that she should stop running away. In her dreams she was to turn and face what was threatening her and to give herself to it. Asleep, she had never been courageous enough to follow his advice, but now she forced herself to relax, to stop trying to escape. Instinctively she knew that Zach would not take advantage of her acquiescence, that she was safe with him.

The inky blackness closed in around them, and Joelle felt as if only Zach's presence kept her from becoming part of the night. She could sense his reluctance as he ended the kiss. Tentatively she put her arms around him. He felt so good. His wiry strength was more substantial than mere muscles and sinew; it seemed to come from inside him, and she held on to it, molding her body to his.

"Am I competing with anyone?" she asked finally. She knew so little about him, and truly, she was afraid to know more. But she did want that one answer.

"No."

"I don't know why I asked," she said, finally forcing herself to pull away from him. "I want to be left alone."

"I've always been alone, and I just realized it," Zach answered quietly.

There was loneliness written on his features, and before she knew what she was doing, Joelle had reached up to stroke it away. She ran her fingers beneath the golden-brown eyes, along the fine, straight nose. Her fingertips tangled in the soft auburn beard, around his ears and into his thick wavy hair. For a moment she locked her fingers behind his neck, memorizing his features.

"I needed you a long time ago," she whispered. "But now it's too late for me, Zach. I don't have anything to give you."

"I haven't asked for anything, and I won't."

Joelle shook her head as she untangled her fingers, stepping away in the process. "You're asking for everything. And you don't even know me."

Zach knew that she was partly right. He was asking for everything. But she was wrong about the other conclusion she'd drawn. He did know her. And he knew that he had impetuously created an avalanche. The irony of his audacity hit him forcefully. There was no one in the world who had less right to ask anything of her.

There was nothing left to say. Joelle moved past him toward the door, and he watched her disappear into the kitchen. When she returned a short time later with her

suitcase, he took it and walked with her to his truck.
The trip back to the springhouse was silent.

JOELLE CONTINUED TO STAND on the top step of the
springhouse as Zach's truck pulled out her driveway.
For a moment she panicked at the thought of going inside. Solitude was what she had come for, but it was not
what she wanted at that moment. She wanted Zach.

She wanted his strong arms to hold her. She wanted
to open herself to his kiss and to feel it change from
gentle affection to dark passion. She wanted to unbut-
ton his shirt and let her fingertips discover the solid
muscles, the contours of his body. She wanted to lie
with him, to make love until the sun came up.

Instead she had run. Not only because it was the
wrong time in her life, but because he was the most
frightening man that she had ever encountered. Zach
cared. Not in the way that many men of her acquaintance did. Joelle knew other men who thought of
themselves as caring people. They cared about the
planet, about the population explosion, about the nu-
clear-arms race. They cared who won the presidential
primaries and whether the supreme court upheld the
constitution. When it came to a woman's feelings,
though, they were not as concerned. And after all, in
the global scheme of things, what were the feelings of
one female folksinger worth anyway?

Tim Daniels was such a man. Zach Smith was not.
She suspected that Zach also cared deeply about social
issues, but instinctively she knew that an abiding concern for the individual made him the man he was.

Joelle opened the door and stepped inside. She allowed her eyes to become accustomed to the greater
darkness of the room and then found her way to the

corner where she kept her lamp. With the strike of a match, the room was illuminated. She pulled the suitcase inside and closed the door, locking it behind her.

Her bedtime ritual took only a moment. Joelle blew out the lantern flame and crawled into the goose-down bag, trying to let her mind drift into sleep. But sleep would not come. Instead, images of the past came back to haunt her.

Giving up the pretense, she sat up and leaned over, pulling the guitar case up beside her. She unfastened the snaps, reaching inside to pull the expensive handmade instrument from it. Music had always been the source of her salvation, and tonight would be no different. Joelle sat cross-legged on the sleeping bag and strummed, feeling the pleasant bite of the steel strings against her calloused fingertips. She closed her eyes and began to sing and to remember. It seemed only right that she should begin with the song that had brought her down the long road that had finally led back home.

Joelle had been fourteen the day she became an adult. She had awakened early to the smell of bacon frying, the sound of shuffling feet and the low murmur of voices as her father and Hoyt, Jr., got ready to go into the mine. Joelle had turned over, smothering the noise with her pillow, but sleep had eluded her. Swinging her feet to the floor, careful not to disturb the two sisters who slept in the double bed with her, she had padded barefoot into the kitchen, leaning on the doorframe for support as she covered her mouth with her hand to smother a yawn.

Hoyt, Jr., was at the breakfast table, wolfing down the pancakes that their mother fixed every morning from self-rising flour and instant milk. Broad shouldered and good-looking, with a cocky smile that melted hearts, Hoyt had glanced at Joelle and gestured to an empty place at the table.

"Sit down and eat."

"I've got to help Ma."

Mrs. Lindsey, at the sink with her back turned, had echoed Hoyt's words.

Feeling slightly guilty at the unaccustomed luxury of a leisurely breakfast, Joelle had joined her brother at the table noticing, as she had more and more often in the past days, how much of a man he had become.

She nibbled at a piece of bacon, making it last as long as she could by letting the salty tang melt on her tongue. Bacon was a treat, made possible now by Hoyt, Jr.'s contribution to the family. "Do you miss school?" she asked him shyly.

"Never did like school." Hoyt, Jr., flashed her a smile. "But then, I don't like the mine, either. Might as well get paid if you're going to do something you don't like."

Mrs. Lindsey interrupted in a voice as old as the world. "Sixteen's too young to be in the mines."

Joelle finched at her mother's remark. "Hoyt's happy, aren't you Hoyt?"

"Let's just say I'm not unhappy." He pushed his chair back and wiped his mouth on his sleeve. "Got to go. Pa's waiting."

Hoyt, Jr., had stood next to Joelle's chair, the picture of maturing masculinity, and he had tugged at her long thick braid. "Behave yourself Jo-Jo. Don't forget, I'm watching what you do."

Not too mature to still need a mother's hug, Hoyt, Jr. had slammed the door behind him, and Joelle had run to the kitchen window to wave goodbye. She caught a glimpse of her father's profile behind the steering wheel of their old station wagon, and she watched as they started up the driveway.

It was later that morning when the tragedy that changed her life occurred. Joelle was shepherding her two younger sisters off the bus to the door of the elementary school, where she would catch another bus to the consolidated high school she attended in Taylerton. She had wrapped her long braid around her neck as protection against the cold October winds and snuggled into the first brand-new coat that she had ever owned.

The streets were filled with miners just returning from the cat's-eye shift. Her father joked that miner's called the shift "cat's eye," because "graveyard shift" was too close for comfort in an occupation so laden with hazards. Joelle saw some friends of her fathers and lifted her hand in greeting.

As she stepped up to the top step of the battered yellow school bus, a whistle screamed with a bone-chilling cadence. It was accompanied by an explosion that rocked the crowded street like an earthquake. The whistle was familiar. It signaled an accident in the mine. The explosion was unlike anything she had every heard.

The men milling in the street began to run toward the main shaft as pandemonium broke out. The skinny freckled girl found herself running, too. Everywhere there were people shouting and pushing. Rumors flew, but the truth was only too evident. Deadly underground methane gas, unleashed by the mining efforts, had collected and somehow been touched off, probably by a miner's carbon-tipped drill bit. It, in turn, had ignited coal dust, releasing enormous energy and spreading fire.

The fire blast had been so forceful that one of the electric rail cars that carried miners to and from their underground passages, had torpedoed from its housing and landed, a twisted molten mass, fifty yards from the shaft. It lay in plain sight of the crowd, a testimony to the impossibility of survival below.

Joelle fought her way through the masses, only to find herself herded along with everybody else to a spot a considerable distance from the mine entrance. She clung to people who were little more than strangers as they waited for news. When it came, it was what she had expected. The change of shift had been completed before the explosion. Hoyt Senior and Junior were both underground.

The town had few resources, but those it did possess were strained that day. The church where the Lindsey family worshipped opened its doors, and relatives of the men underground went there to wait. It was there that Joelle and her mother heard that twenty-nine miners, who had been able to grope their way, hand in hand, through the blinding fog of coal dust to an air shaft, had been rescued by bucket crane. The Lindseys and forty-three other men were not among them.

It was at the church that Joelle first heard her mother's bitter murmurings. Hoyt, Sr., had become increasingly aware of the lack of safety regulations being followed in the mine. After years of hard, backbreaking labor, he had recently been promoted to mine foreman, one of those overworked men whose pay increased only half as much as his responsibilities. What had always been calm resignation about mining's dangers had become a heavy load of responsibility. With his promotion had come a concern for the safety of the men he supervised, one of whom was his beloved oldest son.

Night after night Hoyt, Sr., had confessed his worries to his wife. Tests for the presence of deadly gases were not being administered often enough; the mine was not illuminated well; dusts were not being sampled or controlled correctly; and miners were receiving no training in safety procedures. In fact new miners were not even given the most elementary lessons in survival in case a mine accident occurred.

There should have been somewhere to turn, but the few federal inspectors who toured the mine were harassed or bought off by the company, resulting in little adherence to what were already loose federal regulations. The mine owner and the mine supervisors wanted no interference. As surely as if the company had set off the explosion itself, Pennington Alloy had trapped the men underground.

The vigil lasted a week. The underground inferno continued to rage out of control, melting the heat-measuring instruments that were lowered underground. The families of the forty-five miners alternately prayed and mourned. Photographers arrived to record their grief. They got the usual interviews of proud, strained women bearing up to the ordeal with acceptance and strong religious faith. They also got one interview that was different.

On the day the mine was sealed to extinguish the fire, entombing the men inside, Joelle's mother lost all control, screaming in her rage at the injustice of the mine owner walking away unscathed. Always available to pick up a particularly riveting human-interest item, the reporters interviewed her the next day, after she had regained some control. Mrs. Lindsey spilled the entire story. She talked about Hoyt's frustrations and fears, the poverty that the Pennington Alloy miners were subjected to, the lack of adherence to safety standards. Every detail was spread on the pages of newspapers nationwide.

There would have been a cursory investigation anyway, but the newspaper story hastened the process. Pennington Alloy was on trial in the hearts of America. The results were inevitable. What could one grief-stricken widow prove against an industry so large that it was said to own huge chunks of Pennsylvania outright? The investigation was carried out. Pennington Alloy was found to have violated certain minor safety regulations, but the disaster was blamed on human error.

Joelle was visiting a friend who had also lost her father, when together they saw the national television newscast explaining the investigation's findings. There was a segment about the Pennington Alloy president, Franklin Pennington-Smith, at a press conference after the report was released. Forever after, his smooth voice, his show of concern for the miner's families would haunt her. He stood, flanked by his wife and three sons, a good family man, an upstanding pillar of the community.

"The explosion was a great tragedy," he stated. "Although Pennington Alloy has been found blameless, we intend to help the families of the miners. Mining is a dangerous occupation, but it provides jobs for many of America's unskilled workers. We must all do our best to make their work as safe as possible."

The press conference should have ended there, but one interesting development was recorded for viewers. As Pennington-Smith was leaving, a reporter got between him and the door, firing questions that had not been sufficiently answered by the investigation. With a fluid movement and no change of expression, Pennington-Smith pushed the man out of the way, knocking him down as he did. The steel corporation president's sentimental show of concern was undermined by that one gesture that he had obviously thought was untelevised.

What weapons did a fourteen-year-old girl possess to fight a man like that? He had the resources of the universe at his fingertips. Joelle had only the beat-up guitar given to her by a long-dead grandmother and a grief inside her that could not be contained. But growing up in poverty, she had learned to take what she was given and squeeze every drop of life out of it. She went home that night and with her grief and her silently burning anger, she wrote the song that two years later would thrust her into the limelight. Simply but with extraordinary power, she told the story of her father's and brother's deaths, and of what it was like to hear the tragedy of the forty-five miners reduced to statistics by the steel-company president, Franklin Pennington-Smith.

Sixteen years later Joelle Lindsey was back home again. There were only ghosts to greet her, only memories to keep her company. She had told the story, and perhaps it had produced some changes. Certainly federal regulations were stricter, mines were safer. But what changes had the song and the journey to fame wrought in her? She was only sure of one. She no longer believed that she had any answers.

Joelle put the guitar back in its case and curled up once more in the down bag, pillowing her head on her hands. Her hair tickled her cheek and, as she pushed it back, she remembered the feel of Zach's thumbs tracing her cheekbones. She had been wrong once before about a man. Was that what was stopping her from letting Zach into her life? Was running from intimacy the only way that she could discover who she was again?

"Turn and face your pursuer," the spiritual teacher had told her. "Whenever you run, you give him your power."

By coming back to the farm, she was facing her ghosts, putting them in perspective. Already she could feel a faint lightening of the burden she had carried since that day so long ago when she was sure that her world had ended.

The danger Zach represented was another ghost. It was possible that the time had come to turn and face that fear, too. There were questions that needed to be answered; perhaps, she could discover the answers with him.

In return she might find that she still had something left to give. Hope eased the pain her memories had uncovered, and she drifted off to sleep, a faint smile on her lips.

ZACH HAD WATCHED JOELLE standing on the springhouse steps, silhouetted against the sky, when he turned his truck around in the narrow driveway. As he pulled up in front of his house, the image haunted him, and he leaned his head against the seat and sat quietly for a few minutes before he finally went inside.

He heard the telephone ringing as he opened the front door, and his mind was so filled with Joelle Lindsey that for a moment he even imagined that she might be calling.

"Hello."

"Hello, son." The man's voice was deep and powerful. It was unmistakable. Zach pictured the florid skin, the thinning hair, the smile of the man who had conceived him.

His father, Franklin Pennington-Smith.

"Hello, Father." Zach waited for the inevitable.

There was a silence. That alone was peculiar; his father was never at a loss for words. "I've missed you, son."

Zach sat down carefully, cradling the receiver between his neck and shoulder. Distractedly he searched the table beside him for the cigarettes he hadn't smoked in five years. "I'm sorry, Father. I've been very busy."

There was another silence. Finally his father said, "Zacharias, come home. I need to talk to you. There are things we have to straighten out."

"I haven't changed my mind, Father. I want no part of Pennington Alloy. Not now, not ever."

"There are other things to talk about."

"How is Mother?" Zach's voice was carefully polite.

"Well. She sends her love."

"Tell her I'll be in touch."

"Zacharias, come home."

"I can't," Zach said shortly. "I have a business to run, remember?" He sighed, trying to erase the emotion from his voice. "I promised Isaac and Jeremiah that I'd come to Pittsburgh for a long visit this summer. I'll see you then, if not before."

This time the silence stretched interminably. "All right, son." There was a click, and the line went dead.

Zach let the receiver dangle from its spiraling cord. Every one of his thirty-five years showed as he walked slowly to the window and looked out over the front porch. Staring at the rocking chair where Joelle Lindsey had so recently been sitting, Zach wondered if he'd been fooling himself all these years. Being with Joelle had dredged up every bit of guilt he hadn't been able to assuage for his family's responsibility in the Russell Creek mine disaster. He had thought that he had come to terms with it all, that Pennington Alloy's culpability had been put firmly in his past.

Zach knew that he was not responsible for what had happened. Actually no one person was responsible. Little decisions had been made by different people, people who didn't think of themselves as corrupt. The blame had been easy to spread out.

But when Joelle found out who he was, how would he explain his identity to her? *Don't hate me,* he could say. *I didn't do it; I wasn't there. Don't hate my father or my family, either. They knew some of the facts, but not all of them. There were so many people involved that no one was really to blame.*

Joelle would never understand. Zach wasn't sure that he did, either. At that moment the only thing he did understand was that he must tell Joelle Lindsey who he was and watch her become a part of his past, too.

CHAPTER FOUR

JOELLE FOUND THAT SHE WAS HUNGRY all the time. She woke up in the morning thinking about food, and she found herself snacking all day. The beginnings of contentment and the aftermath of grueling physical labor were doing what the fast life had never done. They were restoring her appetite and her optimism.

After chopping and clearing weeds from around the spring, she had gone to a hardware store on the edge of Taylerton and bought a spade and a hoe. Removing the rotting cover from the spring reservoir, she had pulled out as many of the rocks lining it as she could, using her new tools to loosen and remove the silt and mud that had accumulated in the fifteen years it had not been used. When the water began to settle and clarify, she hauled and scrubbed new rocks to line the larger hole, replacing what clay pipe she could with new pipe that she bought and installed herself.

The job had been backbreaking, but every minute of it had seemed important, every shovelful of silt and every rock rewarding. In comparison, cleaning the downstairs of the springhouse had been simple. With scrub brushes and bleach she had scrubbed away mold and algae, creating a clean destination for the spring water to flow into. When she was finished and drank her first glass of clear, cold water, she knew that no bottle of vintage French champagne would have tasted as good or been so treasured.

In honor of the occasion, Joelle decided to take a picnic to the highest hill on her land, a spot several hundred yards behind the house. Gathering crackers and the cheese that Mr. Kincaid had sold her, she took a blanket and bottle of spring water and carefully skirted the overgrown yard that had once been her mother's pride. Picking her way up the hill, over a fallen tree, and around boulders, she chose a spot where she had often come as a child. The view was still impressive, woods and fields and winding roads. In the distance she could see Zach's wind machines and beyond, a curling trail of smoke from his chimney.

It had been a week since Joelle had been to Zach's house, and she had not seen him again. Most of the time she had been too busy to think about his absence, but today, celebrating her success with the spring, she wished he was here to share it with her.

She had scared him away; that was certain. He had kissed her and she had reacted so strongly, that she was sure that he wouldn't be back. Throughout her thirty years Joelle had discovered that honesty and gut-level emotion scared most people away. She had learned to be careful, to be controlled, only allowing herself the luxury of sharing her feelings through her music. She had forgotten to behave that way with Zach, and she was glad. No matter what the consequence, she was glad that she had revealed some of herself to him.

Of course there were other things she hadn't revealed. She had not told him that she was Jo Lynd as well as Joelle Lindsey. She had not told him that she was running away from a career that was careening out of control and a life that no longer held much meaning.

But she had told him that she felt there was nothing inside her to give. Today, with the spring cleared and the sun shining warmly on her bare legs and arms, Joelle was not certain that she had told him the truth. The human spirit was indomitable. What had been a deep well of darkness inside her was beginning to run clear and free again.

Rising to stand on tiptoe, she squeezed her eyes shut and swung her arms over her head, swaying as the cool spring breeze whispered around her. Snatches of melodies ran through her head and she hummed, keeping time by continuing to sway. When she finally opened her eyes, it was to see a familiar blue pickup coming slowly down her long driveway.

Joelle scrambled to the top of a nearby pile of rocks, balancing precariously and waving with one hand to catch Zach's attention. The pickup was lost to view as he parked in front of the house, but a moment later she saw him cutting through the waist-high weeds in the yard and striding down the path toward her. She sat on a lower rock and waited.

Zach stopped about ten yards from her, casually raising one booted foot to rest it on a log. Neither said a word, quietly examining the other for long moments. Finally Joelle smiled and patted the rock next to her in an unspoken invitation to have him join her.

Zach shook his head. "I'll understand if you tell me to leave," he said without a smile.

Puzzled, Joelle wrinkled her forehead in contemplation. "Now why would I tell you to leave when I'd like you to stay?"

As if it were against his better judgment, Zach took the place beside her, turning to search her face. "I wasn't sure you'd want to see me again."

"I'm sure I've given you no cause to think otherwise," she assured him. "But a little while ago I was thinking that I'd like to see you today."

Zach's mouth tightened into a grim line, a startling contrast to the liquid warmth of his brandy eyes. "Joelle, before you say anything else, you should know something about me."

"Are we going to trade histories?" she asked, a catch in her voice, "because . . . I'd rather not."

"I'm not asking you any questions, Joelle."

"And I'm not asking you any." Joelle stood and turned her back to him, kicking a pebble with the toe of her expensive mud-encrusted jogging shoes. "I don't think the past is important."

"One day it may become important."

"On that day, you can tell me anything you want to." She turned and held out her hands. "For now, let's be friends. Let's be brand-new friends with nothing between us to make it impossible."

Zach stood and grasped Joelle's hands in his. Slanting jade eyes seemed to plead with him to give her time before she was forced to reveal who she was. It didn't matter that he already knew and that his own identity would rock her very foundation. Standing there, immersed in her vulnerability, he couldn't bring himself to let her know how exposed she really was.

Zach dropped her hands, stuffing his own quickly in his pockets as he turned away to compose himself. "How is the spring coming along?"

"It's finished." Joelle moved up to stand beside him. "Would you like a sample of the water? I happen to have one not more than two yards from your feet."

Shyly she motioned him to the blanket behind them. I'll feed you, too," she said, breaking off a chunk of cheese for him.''This is Russell Creek Cheddar. For some reason it always tastes better than cheese anywhere else. It must be Mr. Kincaid's special method of aging it.''

Zach accepted the cheese. "What's his method?"

"He keeps it under a plastic cake cover until somebody buys it all. Some folks get scared off by the layer of mold on the outside, so they won't buy it, and it stays around and ages for a long time until it's finally all bought up." Joelle flashed Zach a smile. "I'd say that piece you're eating now has been around since before the first space shuttle was launched."

Helpfully she pounded him on the back as he choked on the last bit of cheese. "Here, have some spring water," she offered.

Zach leaned back on the blanket, taking a long drink from the bottle. The change in Joelle's appearance was startling. He watched as he handed the water back to her and she took a long slow drink. The tautness about her mouth and eyes had disappeared to be replaced by an expression that could almost be described as contentment. She was still too thin, but under the layer of golden-hued freckles was a rosiness that hadn't been there before. She had pinned her hair away from her face with a child's plastic barrettes, and the sun had streaked it even lighter, in wide layers that emphasized her dark eyelashes and brows.

"Even with two coats of mud up to your knees, you're beautiful," he told her.

"One coat," she said. "As difficult as it is, I wash every night." Joelle ignored the compliment that was sending skittering pinpoints of warmth through her bloodstream.

"I could make life easier for you. Come take another shower at my place."

"I'd like that."

Prepared for the necessity of convincing her that he meant no harm, Zach was taken aback by her acquiescence. "Laundry, too?"

Joelle shook her head, dislodging a barrette. "No, I went to a Laundromat in Taylerton a few days ago." The trip had been enlightening. Since no one expected to find a superstar in a Laundromat, she had indulged in her anonymity, chatting with the young housewives about their children and their choices of detergent. No glitzy cocktail party had ever been more fun.

Zach watched as Joelle stared into space, a slight smile on her lips as if she was encountering a pleasant memory. Carefully he moved closer, untangling the barrette from her thick hair and pushing the heavy strands behind her ear to refasten the clasp. She didn't flinch or move away, but he could see her complexion pale and the pulse in her neck quicken. "You don't like to be touched, do you?" he asked, his mouth close to her ear.

Joelle focused on her hands, clasped carefully in her lap. "Most people don't notice that," she said.

"Then they haven't been paying attention," he said, moving away to a comfortable distance. "And if they haven't noticed, you haven't talked about it."

"I haven't needed to." Joelle stood, hands on her hips in a defensive posture. Only her smile assured Zach that he hadn't stepped too far over her boundaries. "Now, about that shower."

Zach stood, too. "Would you like a tour of my business while you're at it?"

"Very much. Just let me get a change of clothes."

Zach watched as she loped down the hill toward the springhouse, carefully skirting the immediate yard of her childhood home. He had come to tell her the truth, fully prepared to find that she had learned it already in town. Obviously she hadn't. She was pleading for anonymity, and he could give her no less. Yet the strain was immeasurable.

He followed her path, avoiding the house, too. He was a man who prided himself on his integrity. He had fought for it, sacrificed for it, and now he wondered if he was slowly watching it melt away.

JOELLE HAD TO RESTRAIN HERSELF from bursting into song in Zach's shower. With the warm water flowing sleekly over her shoulders and breasts, she experienced a sense of well-being bubbling up inside her. There was still so much she had to figure out, but at that moment she was just glad to be alive. And at age thirty, she wasn't naive enough to pretend that it had nothing to do with the man whose hot water she was fast using up.

At fifteen Joelle might not have recognized the bubbling feelings inside her for what they were, but at age thirty, she knew. She was immensely attracted to Zach Smith. She wanted him.

Not that she was going to tell him so. No, even if Zach initiated another kiss—or more—she wasn't sure what she would do. But at that moment, wanting him was enough. It had been a long time since she had felt this way, and she was just very glad to know that she still could.

''Thank you, Zach,'' she whispered as she towel dried her hair.

Wearing designer slacks and a hand-knit sweater, Joelle went downstairs to look for him. ''Zach?'' she called, peering into the kitchen. She wandered through the living room into the hallway. "Zach?"

A room that had probably originally been a small parlor stood off the side of the hall, and Joelle went in to look out the window. She saw Zach walking back toward the house talking to a white-haired man in a flannel shirt and jeans. Turning to meet him at the front door, she noticed an ornate silver tea service on a low table by another window. Filled with curiosity, she went to investigate.

The silver was very old and tarnished with disuse, but so exquisitely crafted that Joelle, who had not had time to learn about such things, could still tell that it was worth a fortune. Each piece was inscribed with a curlicued *P* that was so worn with time that it was almost illegible. Joelle looked around the room with new eyes. The furniture, which she had hardly noticed before, was antique and delicate, not at all like the furniture in the rest of the house, which was sturdy contemporary, or primitive pine.

This room could be a museum. Each item in it would have easily found a home at the Smithsonian. Although she had told Zach that she didn't want to know about his past, the room stirred Joelle's curiosity. Without asking him a single question, she knew at least one thing. Zach Smith was not a poor man. The furnishings in this one room would probably feed him for a lifetime if he chose to sell them. And the way that they were casually displayed was an indication that Zach had no intention of doing that.

Joelle was glad that Zach was at least comfortably well off. There were many people, the majority of them male, who were threatened by her status and wealth. If the time ever came when Zach was confronted with her identity, Joelle didn't want him to feel threatened. If he was wealthy in his own right, perhaps her own wealth wouldn't be a problem.

The door opened and she stood in the hall to greet him. "I was just looking for you."

Zach's eyes crinkled and she felt caressed by his glance. "Joelle Lindsey, meet Jake Byler, my foreman. Jake, Joelle Lindsey."

Joelle extended her hand and shook hands with the distinguished-looking man. In his late fifties, with a Santa Claus face and neatly trimmed white beard and mustache, Jake managed to look cuddly and imposing at the same time. "It's nice to meet you Jake," she said, meaning every word.

"It's nice to meet you, Joelle."

"Jake's got to use the phone. The one down at the barn is tied up with a long-distance order." Zach clapped Jake on the shoulder. "Go ahead, we'll see you outside later."

Joelle followed Zach out the door and onto the front porch. He pointed at a huge red barn in the distance. "The business is scattered through all my outbuildings, but we'll start at the barn. That's where I store most of my inventory."

"You store windmills in the barn?"

"Wind machines. Parts of them are stored there. But we aren't just a wind-power company. We market solar technology and four types of wood stoves, too."

Joelle whistled softly. "Big business."

"I wish." Zach put his arm around her back to guide her down the stairs, carefully removing it at the bottom. "No, alternative energy isn't a big business. At first there were months when I should have closed down and forgotten I ever thought this was a good idea."

"But you didn't."

"No. The business is comfortably thriving now. I'll probably hang on forever. It's in my blood."

The barn had been transformed into a warehouse with neatly stacked crates and space for loading and unloading. An office held several desks covered with invoices and assorted clutter. A young woman who looked vaguely familiar to Joelle sat at one of them.

"Dorothy Trotter, meet Joelle Lindsey. Joelle, Dorothy is my secretary." Exchanging pleasantries, Joelle realized that Dorothy was the same woman whom she had seen in the Russell Creek grocery store. Once again, Dorothy was examining Joelle as if she was trying to place her.

"Dorothy's not from here," Zach said casually, sensing Joelle's discomfort under Dorothy's scrutiny. "She's Pittsburgh born and bred."

"How did you end up in Russell Creek?" Joelle asked politely.

"My husband is from here originally. He came back to visit his grandfather and met Zach. Zach offered him a job and I sort of came with the deal." Dorothy wrinkled her brow. "You look so familiar."

"I have that kind of face," Joelle murmured.

"Are you from around here?"

There was no way of getting out of that one. "A long time ago," Joelle admitted.

"I bet Carl will remember you."

Carl Trotter. Joelle remembered that he had been a classmate of one of her younger sisters. It was very possible that he would remember her. But would he have been old enough to follow her career and connect the rising young star, Jo Lynd, with the Joelle Lindsey who had told him one day that she would tie his tongue behind his ear if he ever called her baby sister a name again?

"It's possible," Joelle said, hoping it wasn't.

"Carl's in Pittsburgh today, checking on some figures. He's an engineer," Zach interrupted. "He's working full-time on a design for a new wind machine that we're trying to get a grant for. Your land is one of our test sites."

"Will you show me?"

"When you leave here today, you'll know more about wind machines and solar energy than you ever wanted to learn." He steered her out of the office.

Zach was right. First they visited a small showroom that he had constructed behind the barn. It contained models of all the stoves that Windmill Chargers marketed: a Scandinavian enameled cast-iron model that could burn coal as well as wood, an airtight steel model that looked as if it belonged in granny's parlor, an elegantly designed cast-iron model in which the flames could be viewed and a wood-burning range that Zach swore was still in demand by a surprisingly large segment of the population.

"I notice you cook with electricity," Joelle chided him.

"Did you notice where my electricity comes from?" he asked.

Joelle hadn't, although how she had missed the towering wind machine sitting in an open field behind the house was a mystery. Zach laughed at her display of mock humility. "I'll show it to you after you see some of our solar equipment," he promised.

As they walked a hundred yards to another outbuilding, Zach explained that the woodstove showroom had been built using passive solar design—the building itself or some element of it served as the collector and storage of energy.

"This is where I work," he continued, opening the door to a simple wooden building that was arrayed with solar panels on the roof. It was more elaborate than the one they had just left, warm and comfortably designed inside. A drafting table stood in the corner and several practically upholstered sofas sat around a low table covered with catalogs. Two large desks sat against one wall. "When we have visitors, I bring them here to look through all our information and to see what's available to fit in with their plans." Zach shoved catalogs at Joelle. "Have a look while I check my mail."

There were solar collectors, solar greenhouses, solar hot-water heaters, fans and heat pumps, thermal shutters, special windows and an additional selection of solar gadgets, the likes of which Joelle had not known existed. Zach joined her on the sofa a moment later. "Obviously we don't sell all of that," he said, gesturing to the catalogs, "and we don't produce any of it here. There are several top-notch manufacturers that we work with on commission basis."

"You said something about visitors. Do people actually come to Russell Creek to do their solar shopping?"

"You'd be surprised. In the summer we have a steady stream of folks coming through. People who've bought equipment from us that just want to check in, people who are thinking about changing life-styles, people who are on vacation and want to check us out. Of course, we're not well-known enough yet or close enough to major population centers to get as much traffic as I'd like. Most of our business is conducted by phone or mail order."

Without knowing the volume of orders, and by casually judging the cost of the buildings that she had seen and the staff that she had met or heard about, Joelle was certain that her assessment of Zach's background must be correct. His inventory alone would be tremendously costly. Zach must be wealthy, or at least he must have been when he began Windmill Chargers. No operation as extensive as this started out on a shoestring. "This is quite an undertaking," she ventured.

"Isn't it?" he said with a glimmer of humor in his voice.

"So what's the five-year plan?"

Zach sat back contemplating her words. What were his goals? "To develop our own equipment and build a small factory to begin manufacturing wind machines on the premises," he said. There was no point in explaining that his dream was to use Pennington steel to produce a better life-style for the unemployed men in Russell Creek or that he wanted to produce an economical product that would lessen the demand on the nation's energy resources, one of which was King Coal. Those thoughts were too revealing. After all, why did a stranger care so much?

But Joelle was asking that question anyway. "Why here, Zach? Why here outside an abandoned coal-mining town in the middle of nowhere?"

"Land was cheap," he said with a shrug. "I can get my supplies from Pittsburgh, and God knows, there are plenty of men who need jobs in these parts."

Joelle waited, sensing that there was more information to come. When Zach didn't continue, she stood up. "I'm ready to see the windmi . . . wind machines."

Zach smiled at her. "Strictly speaking, a windmill is used for milling grain, not for generating electricity.

Technically my machines are wind generators, wind-driven turbines, wind plants or simply wind machines.''

"Should I be taking notes?'' she asked, following him out the door.

Actually, standing underneath the towering structure in the field behind Zach's house and watching the whirring blades split the air over her head, Joelle found she was really interested. "And you power all your buildings with this?''

Zach shook his head. "There's one behind the barn, too.''

"That's right. I didn't know if it was just a demonstration model or not. So you need two.''

"Two with twenty six-volt batteries and sixty two-volt batteries for periods of relative calm. Don't forget, the wind doesn't blow all the time.''

"Actually, I never thought this area was particularly windy.''

"It's windy enough, but there are better places in this country. Because wind power increases as the cube of the wind velocity, a little more wind means a lot more power.''

"But there's enough here?''

"Just enough to make it worthwhile.''

Zach explained how sites were chosen for wind machines and how wind velocity was measured so that output could be estimated. "The machines are inefficient, so we have to allow for that in our calculations. Every wind engineer dreams of creating the perfect machine that will be totally efficient, completely reliable in all weather and aesthetically pleasing, too.''

"And cheap?''

"Especially that. Right now, wind machines are impractical for most people. They're too expensive to make them worth buying."

Joelle was surprised to hear that piece of information. "Then why bother?"

"Because the situation is improving all the time. People like me are trying to harness the wind and make it pay. Eventually we will, and I intend to be one of the first."

Joelle decided that Don Quixote was an apt symbol for Windmill Charger's, Inc. It was obvious that a strong belief that he was doing something worthwhile motivated Zach's involvement in wind energy. His quiet idealism fit perfectly with the pattern of the man that was beginning to clearly emerge. Spontaneously she moved closer and on tiptoe, brushed his bearded cheek with her lips. "I believe that you will, Zach Smith."

They were both surprised by her impulsiveness. The woman who didn't like to be touched had taken a giant step. Zach's hands caught her waist, and for a moment they stood together staring into each other's eyes. Joelle knew nothing of him, of his past or of what was in his heart, but at that moment, she felt a union with him, a oneness that was uncanny. It's as if, she thought as his lips sought hers, it's as if this was foreordained, as if he's always been waiting for me.

Unafraid, her hands threaded through the brown waves of hair, exploring the slippery, shining texture with her fingertips. The feel of his lips was familiar, but today she relaxed against him as he kissed her, and the feeling of their bodies pressed together was unfamiliar and exciting. Joelle let her fingertips slide down his neck to feel the fluid muscles of Zach's shoulders and back. A shiver passed through him as she began to stroke her fingertips along his spine, and she smiled against his lips.

"So you like what you're doing to me," Zach whispered in her ear, his soft beard tickling her earlobe.

She did like it. There had only been one man in Joelle's life, there had only been one lover, and she had never excited him. Zach's response was so different from Tim's. Joelle felt desirable. "Yes, I like it," she said quietly. "I like it a lot."

There was much more that Zach wanted to do to her, but he sensed that anything else might scare her away. Let Joelle enjoy the feelings that she had just admitted to. And let her enjoy the fact that a man had just kissed her and she hadn't recoiled. *I wonder who the bastard is that's made her so wary,* he thought as he stepped back, putting his fingers under her chin to lift her eyes to his. Carefully he placed her fingertips on his knit shirt and over his heart, letting her feel the racing beat. "In case you needed more proof."

Joelle wasn't smiling. In fact she looked baffled as if she couldn't believe that she had done this to him. Slowly recovering her defenses, she drew her hand away. "Well, I should patent whatever I did. Do you realize how many people spend thousands of dollars a year at health clubs, just to get their heart rate above normal?"

Good for you, Zach thought. Through whatever crisis had brought her home, she had managed to retain the sense of humor that was reputed to make her such a popular performer. Smiling, he offered her his hand. "I have some business I have to attend to for the rest of the afternoon. I'd like you to stay and have dinner here, if you would. You can camp out in my house, read the newspaper, listen to records. Do all those things that civilized people take for granted.''

Joelle considered his offer. The spring was flowing now, and she had managed to make her own quarters habitable if not comfortable. She had been putting off making a decision about what she should do next, so there was no project waiting for her back home. An afternoon spent sitting on real furniture, in a real house. An evening spent with Zach. "Thanks. I'd like that. Would you like me to make supper?''

"Can you cook?''

Almost anyone can cook. Why would Zach ask her such a strange question? As if he were reading her mind, he interrupted. "Last time, you said you only make salads.''

"If I have to, if starvation threatens or someone holds a gun to my head, I cook. But I warn you, I only cook coal miners's food.''

They had reached the stairs up to Zach's porch. "Is that a unique cuisine?''

"When I was a kid," Joelle said candidly, "we ate lots of dumplings and biscuits and johnnycake. I learned to stew a squirrel before I was seven and butcher a deer before I was twelve. That's coal miner's food.''

"Times were hard, I know. But it's better than that now, Joelle. Coal miners make decent wages nowadays.'' Zach traced the lines of disbelief on her forehead with his fingertip. "It was too late coming, though.''

"There are a number of ghosts haunting the Pennington Alloy mine in Russell Creek who would heartily agree with that statement.'' Joelle watched Zach flinch, and again she wondered why he cared so much.

"Shall we skip the coal miner's cuisine tonight?" she asked.

"Let's cook dinner together," he said quietly. "Make yourself at home for now." With a wave Zach turned and headed toward the barn. When he was no longer in sight, Joelle climbed the steps and disappeared into the house.

Taking Zach at his word, Joelle enjoyed all the little luxuries that she had taken for granted until recently. She boiled water that came right from the faucet, marveling at how easy heating it was on a stove. She made a cup of hot tea that almost burned her tongue and then flipped through Zach's record collection, choosing to play a new album that a friend of hers had recorded and Joelle had never had time to listen to. With relief she noted that Zach didn't have any of her albums displayed on his shelf, and then with a spurt of professional pride, she wondered how his taste could be so bad.

The only sour note in the otherwise perfect afternoon occurred when she got to page three of the front section of the Pittsburgh paper, which she had found on Zach's kitchen table. "Folk-rock singing star missing," the headline read.

"I'm not missing," Joelle scoffed as she read the short article. "I'm sitting right here." The article nonetheless detailed the available facts about Jo Lynd's flight from civilization. Her manager and her agent were quoted, and Tim Daniels had been interviewed. Predictably the three of them had played her disappearance for all it was worth, feigning concern when Joelle suspected that none existed. Still, she was glad to see that no one was pretending that foul play might be a consideration. They had neatly put the blame on her heavy work schedule and her need for solitude, which was part of her image anyway.

Actually, Joelle had phoned her manager the night she decided to leave California. Calmly she had dictated her decision to his answering machine, telling him at the end that if he tried to find her, she'd fire him. She had just finished a grueling tour, and she wasn't scheduled to begin recording her next album for several months. There had been a couple of small performances that he would have to cancel, and numerous public appearances, but at the time, they had seemed unimportant.

Now he was using her decision to enhance her stature. Such was the nature of show business. Such was the way of life that had caused Joelle to run in the first place.

Tim's comments were also just what she would have expected. He came across in his interview as the concerned lover who was trying to put on a brave front for all the world to see. His carefully chosen answers only hinted at the pain Joelle's flight had cost him. Only he and Joelle knew how incongruous that was. She suspected that Tim, like the rest of the world, had only discovered her absence when her manager leaked the news. And if he had sought her out and found her missing, there were plenty of other women to keep him occupied.

Joelle rolled up the front section of the newspaper and threw it in Zach's garbage can, poking it under some other garbage. Perhaps Zach wouldn't associate Joelle Lindsey with the story in the paper, but the photograph that had accompanied the article had been unmistakably her. Time was running out. It would be only a matter of days before Zach saw another news item, talked to someone in town who remembered her or mentioned her name to Carl Trotter, who would surely know who she had become.

"A few more days." She just needed to be Joelle Lindsey for a few more days. It didn't seem like too much to ask. By then she would be strong enough to face whatever the results of her charade would be. And perhaps, if she was very lucky, when she told Zach who she was, it wouldn't matter at all.

CHAPTER FIVE

JOELLE WAS ASLEEP on Zach's sofa when he came into the living room late in the afternoon. Defenseless, she lay there, one arm thrown over her eyes against the light, unaware of his presence. Zach dropped down into a chair across the room and watched her sleep, wondering at the protective feelings he was developing. Asleep and vulnerable, Joelle stirred a powerful longing within him to shield her, to heal whatever pain she struggled with.

Zach had always felt these things for Jo Lynd. Now the real person, the Joelle Lindsey he had come to know, intensified such feelings a hundredfold. But then, his empathy, his concern were really not surprising considering their mutual past. What was surprising was the strong desire he felt for her, had felt for her since the day he first stood and watched her swinging a scythe.

Joelle Lindsey was a woman, lovely and desirable, and he wanted her. What an incredible irony. Not particularly religious, he still couldn't shake the feeling that some demonic force was having a field day. He was being forced to cope with the burden of a desire that would remain unfulfilled, slowly eating away at him for the rest of his days.

"Well, you look bleak." Joelle lifted her arm away from her face and stretched, unconsciously sensuous.

"Did a wind machine blow away or couldn't you find a squirrel for me to cook for supper?"

Unconsciously Zach gripped the arms of his chair, his knuckles whitening. "I was just watching you sleep, and wishing..."

Joelle sat up slowly, combing her fingers through her sleep-tumbled hair. "Wishing what?"

Zach shook his head. "Wishing that you'd wake up and talk to me."

"Here I am," she said, patting the sofa next to her. "Shall we talk about supper? I'm starved."

"I'm glad to hear that." Zach stood, but denied himself the seat next to her. "I think I'd better take a shower first. There's some Gouda in the refrigerator. It's not Russell Creek Cheddar but almost as good. Why don't you slice some and get crackers out of the cupboard over the stove? I'll be back in a few minutes."

Joelle watched Zach disappear up the stairs and wondered what was behind his pensive mood. She was used to moody men; they were the only kind she ever ran into, but she knew instinctively that Zach didn't fit into the same category. Something was bothering him.

When he came downstairs, his wet hair curling around his face and his strong, lithe body smelling of Ivory soap, Joelle silently offered him a neatly arranged plate of crackers and cheese, wanting to offer him much more. He was dressed in a cream-colored shirt and dark brown slacks. Evidently the shower had washed away some of his mood, because he smiled at her and stroked her cheek with the back of his fingers. "I could get used to you being here, doing this for me."

Joelle imagined, just for a moment, what it would be like to share everyday details of life with someone . . . with Zach. "It would be a new experience for me," she admitted. "But once you got to know me and I got to know you, we'd probably get bored, or we'd fight all the time."

"Now what kind of propaganda is that?" Zach asked, pulling her over to the little kitchen table to sit while he opened a bottle of inexpensive Burgundy. "Who told you that relationships end that way?"

"My eyes. My ears." And Tim Daniels, Joelle admitted silently.

"Was that how your parents' marriage was?" Zach set a wineglass in front of her, slowly pouring some Burgundy into it.

"Absolutely not."

She was so vehement, that Zach cocked an inquisitive eyebrow. "Then that should be your best example of what can be."

Joelle swirled the dark red liquid in her glass, watching the whirlpool she created. "My parents were crazy about each other. Were yours?"

His breath caught in his throat and Zach forced himself to release it. "No, they weren't. They aren't. They go their separate ways as much as possible."

"Then why are you so optimistic? And if you're so optimistic, then why haven't you settled down with someone?" Joelle took a sip and set her glass on the table, locking her fingers around it.

"My parents' marriage might not be the best, but I've seen enough good relationships to be a believer. I actually thought I might settle down a couple of times," he admitted quietly. "But every time I came close, I realized I was making the choice with my head, not with my heart."

"You're really an incredible romantic," Joelle marveled. "I've never met a man quite like you. Someday the right woman is going to walk into your life and you're going to sweep her off her feet and carry her away on a white charger."

"A blue pick-up truck," he amended.

"But that's part of your romantic mystique. I'm perceptive enough to notice that you're not a poor man, Zach Smith. Yet you drive a truck that really ought to be put out to pasture, and half of the time you dress like a sixties flower child."

"And I'm perceptive enough to notice that you live in a ramshackle springhouse and wear designer sportswear with the carelessness of the very rich." He covered her hands with his own. "Shall we continue this?"

For a moment finding out more about Zach and what must be an interesting life history almost took precedence over keeping her own secrets. Joelle ran her tongue over her lips and lifted her eyes to his. He was watching her, an expression very much like resignation settling over his strong features. Fear stopped her from satisfying her curiosity. They were developing a friendship that she was beginning to treasure. She did not want to jeopardize it. "I guess not," she conceded.

"Then let's talk about food."

Zach folded his hands in his lap and Joelle raised her glass to him. "So, what's for supper?"

"We've been invited out."

"I can't go." Her reply was so quick, so forceful that Zach couldn't ignore it.

"I know you're not anxious to meet a lot of strangers," he said, feeling his way to a suitable explanation, "but Jake and Carol are special people. You'll like them."

Jake and Carol were definitely better prospective dinner companions than Dorothy and Carl. "Are they from around here?" She began to swirl her wineglass again.

"No, in fact they're both from the Pennsylvania Dutch country. Matter of fact, Jake's from an Old Order Amish family."

"That's surprising. Don't they wear black and grow beards down to their belt buckles?"

"They don't have belt buckles, but they do have long beards and wear black. Jake left the church as a young man to marry Carol and become a mechanic. The Amish don't believe in modern machinery, and they don't believe in marriage outside the community. His family has shunned him ever since."

"How terribly unfair!"

Zach shrugged. "Who's to say? Jake knew what would happen, and he understands and accepts it. He made his choice. He wasn't afraid of change, and they were."

"Jake sounds interesting," Joelle said doubtfully.

"He and Carol still live very simply. No television, no record player. They're the most content people I know."

They sounded perfect. If Joelle wasn't safe visiting a family who lived without a TV or stereo, she wasn't safe anywhere, including Zach's kitchen. "Well, if I'm really invited, too, I'll come."

Jake and Carol rented a small farm off the two-laned highway to Taylerton. Joelle spotted the turnoff to the property when she saw the distant spokes of a wind machine whirring merrily in the light breeze. "Jake and Carol are exactly the kind of people anyone would want for parents or friends," Zach said as he pulled his truck up a steep hill into a clearing, where a small, freshly painted white bungalow stood. "They're one of the reasons I believe in marriage. You're going to like them."

Joelle did. Carol was plump with gray-streaked hair and a double chin that only served to further soften her cheerful face. She wore a starched white apron over a blue print dress, and Joelle suspected immediately that Carol was one of a dying breed of women who were not comfortable unless their aprons were firmly tied around their waistlines.

"Joelle, short for Jo Ellen?" Carol asked after introductions, as she shooed Joelle toward the front porch.

Joelle nodded. "I was named after my grandmother, but I was always called Joelle because Grandma lived with us till she died. She said as long as she was still breathing, she only wanted one Jo Ellen in the house." Joelle stopped for a minute, surprised at her own chatter, but Carol was nodding happily.

"Weren't you lucky to have your grandmother right there while you grew up?"

"Yes, I was," Joelle agreed, feeling an immediate kinship with the older woman who had put her at ease so quickly.

"My grandchildren are scattered hither and yon, but I make sure they see a lot of me. I get so much from them, and I have a lot to pass on besides." They dropped down into comfortable metal lounge chairs, and Carol handed Joelle a glass of sugar-laden iced tea. Zach and Jake had disappeared into a modest barn across the clearing from the house.

"Thank you for inviting me, Carol. I hope I'm not imposing."

Carol smiled. "Imposing?" She pretended to look Joelle over. "Now that you mention it, you are quite imposing. I haven't had such a lovely young woman sit on my porch since my oldest daughter was here this summer."

Joelle could actually feel herself blushing at the compliment. "Thank you."

"Now, tell me about you. Zach says you're from here originally. What have you been doing since you left?"

It was a polite question with no more than good-natured nosiness intended, but Joelle was momentarily at a loss for words. "Well," she finally started, "I lived in West Virginia for a while with my family, and then I went to California and worked in the Los Angeles area."

"Hollywood? You're pretty enough to be a movie star."

Joelle smiled. "No, I'm not an actress." She cast around for something to say that would not be a lie. "I worked for a recording company."

"Did you enjoy your work?" Carol took Joelle's glass and filled it to the rim with tea once again.

"At times, but it was quite a rat race." Joelle decided to change the subject. "How long have you lived here?"

"About three years. We were living outside of Lancaster, Pennsylvania, and Jake was working as a mechanic-fix-it man for the school system there. Jake's always been the handiest man you've ever seen, and he had a barn full of gadgets he powered with a wind generator he'd built. Zach heard about him, came to visit and hired him immediately. Now Jake gets to do what he likes best and gets paid good for it, too." Carol's pride was so palpable that Joelle could almost touch it.

"I know Zach thinks highly of Jake," Joelle said. "He thinks highly of both of you."

"Zach Smith is a fine young man. If we'd had a son, I'd have wanted him to be exactly like Zach."

They chatted comfortably until the two men came out of the barn and up to the porch to join them. Carol excused herself to see about dinner, refusing Joelle's offer of assistance. "Stay and chat," Carol said, waving Joelle back to her seat. "Everything's almost done."

"Would you like to see Jake's collection of gadgets," Zach asked. "I bet he'd love to show them to you."

Jake's gadgets took up half the barn. Self-taught at a price that had included exile from his own family, Jake knew more about electricity and how to use it than anyone Joelle could think of except, possibly, Thomas Edison. There were homemade hacksaws and drills, air compressors and electric forges. There were lathes, presses, grinders and battery chargers. Jake pulled switches, plugged plugs, manipulated electric cords, and like magic, machinery buzzed, lights came on and wheels spun dizzily.

"All of this works with wind power?" Joelle marveled.

"Jake's wind machine is homemade, too. Actually, some of the best ones are. We're incorporating some of his ideas in our plans for our own model. Jake's going to build it for us."

Jake was a quiet man whose brain seemed to whir constantly, like the blades of his wind machine. "I had a thought about gear ratios this afternoon that I wanted to discuss with you," he told Zach. Joelle listened patiently as the two men quoted formulas and used words that she couldn't even have guessed how to spell.

She was saved by Carol poking her head through the barn door. "Anyone hungry?"

The dinner was melt-in-your-mouth country cooking with a Pennsylvania Dutch flair. Joelle took one look at the heavily laden pine table and decided that she really didn't want to be a vegetarian anymore. Vegetarianism, like many other decisions of her life, had just crept up on her, made practical by a hectic schedule that rarely allowed her the time to eat a regular meal. She sat down at the table, listened patiently to the blessing and then said yes when Carol offered her a plate with roast pork smothered in tangy brown gravy.

There were boiled new potatoes, sweet-and-sour cabbage, pickled beets, homemade cottage cheese that didn't even resemble the store-bought kind in flavor, and finally, apple dumplings swimming in sweet cream. Joelle ate until she was sure that she could never eat again.

"So many young people are picky. It's a pleasure to see you eat, Joelle." Carol looked so pleased that Joelle was gratified that she had done such justice to the meal.

"I haven't eaten anything better in my life," she said with feeling.

Zach had tried not to pay too much attention to Joelle. It was safer if Carol and Jake didn't suspect how he was beginning to feel about her. But it had been difficult not to watch as she had bent, heavy hair swinging around her face, and made short work of a meal that a working man might have had difficulty finishing. Joelle was relaxed and happy, and Zach was so filled with the desire to touch her that his fingers tingled.

"You don't suppose," Joelle started to say, glancing up to see Zach staring at her, a quiet smile behind his beard. She stopped and smiled back, finally turning to Carol to begin again. "You don't suppose you could teach me to cook like this, do you?"

Joelle might as well have announced that she was really the Byler's prodigal daughter come home to stay. Carol was so delighted at the possibility of passing on some of her extensive homemaking skills, that she actually clapped her hands. Joelle stood and the two women cleared off the table, chattering about recipes and the best methods for selecting fresh vegetables. Jake and Zach watched openmouthed as they disappeared into the kitchen, not to emerge for an hour.

"Best thing that could have happened to either of them," Jake said, leaning back in his chair to light up his pipe. "Now about those gear ratios."

"Do you know, Zach, that was the first time that I've sat down and eaten a meal family-style in—" Joelle's hand waved futilely as if she couldn't even remember such a time. "In years," she said finally. They were in the truck, heading to the springhouse, and Joelle was happily content.

Zach was surprised that she was revealing so much. "You mentioned a sister. Don't you ever spend time with her?"

Joelle did spend holidays with her younger siblings on those rare occasions when she could get away, but when she visited they always ended up going out to celebrate. Actually, no one was fooled by their own lack of interest in coming together around a quiet family table. Inevitably memories would be exchanged, and the past was something they tried not to discuss. "I have two sisters and a brother, but I don't see them as often as I should.'' Joelle made a mental note to change that in the future.

The day spent with Zach and the evening spent with his friends had eaten away at Joelle's defenses. At that moment she had little desire to re-erect them. If he asks me more questions, I'm not going to lie, she decided. Even if he finds out who I am.

But Zach didn't ask her anything else, and the trip back to the springhouse was made in comfortable silence. At the end of Joelle's drive he swung the truck around and parked it, shutting off the engine.

The night had darkened to a cloudless wonder of stars and a moon that was almost full. Joelle put her hand on Zach's arm. ''Do you know what I'd like to do now?''

He turned, resting his elbow on the steering wheel. ''What?''

''I'd like to go back up to the top of the hill where you found me this afternoon and sit and watch the stars for a while. Would you come with me?''

Zach knew he shouldn't, but he was becoming used to his good intentions evaporating in Joelle's presence. How could he say no, when being with her was what he wanted most? ''Yes.'' He looked at her lightweight sweater. ''Will you be warm enough?''

''I think I'll run up and get a jacket.'' Joelle opened the truck door and climbed down. Zach watched her running through the trees up the path to the springhouse. She seemed to float, a moonlit vision, carefree and happy. At that moment all he wanted in the world was to keep her that way for the rest of their lives.

When Joelle returned, they climbed the hill, hand in hand, and found the blanket that she had left that afternoon. They sat as one, and Zach pulled her to rest against his shoulder, his arm encircling her. "Now, how did you know," he asked, his voice husky, "that this was the best place on planet Earth for watching the stars?"

"I've spent countless hours up here, doing just that."

"When you were a kid?"

"Yes, with my brother, Hoyt, Jr."

Zach stroked her hair. "What was he like?"

"Big. Funny. He was closest in age to me. We grew up fighting, but actually I worshipped him." Joelle stopped and a tremor passed through her body. Zach stiffened until he realized that she was laughing.

"Hoyt, Jr., would sneak up here late at night to have a smoke. One night I heard him leaving and I followed him up this hill. It turned out that he was collecting cigarette butts off the streets of Russell Creek and emptying them until he had enough tobacco to make a cigarette. Then he'd roll the scraps in cigarette paper that he swiped from our pa—Pa hid his tobacco, but not his paper—and Hoyt, Jr., would come up here to smoke them. Anyway, I caught him, and I promised I wouldn't tell if he'd let me come with him."

Zach stroked her hair back from her face. "And he did?"

"Yes. He was trapped. So we'd come up here together and we'd talk about our plans, our dreams. Even after he went to work in the mine, Hoyt, Jr., was still planning to be a race-car driver someday, and I was going to be..."

"What were you going to be?" Zach bent and rested his chin on the top of her head.

"A singer."

And she had succeeded. Beyond her wildest dreams. Zach held her a little tighter. "Hoyt, Jr., died in the mine explosion, didn't he?"

Joelle nodded, not surprised that Zach knew. Forty-five men had died; it was not hard to guess that Hoyt, Jr., was one of them. She pushed back the thought that if Zach knew that much, he also must know who she had become. "Yes. Do you know that the last thing he said to me that morning was that he'd be watching me? Of course, he didn't know that he was going to die, but for the longest time I thought that he was still looking after me, making things happen in my life."

"Did that make things easier?"

"I didn't feel as lonely, I guess."

Zach turned Joelle and pushed her hair back from her face. "And what would Hoyt, Jr., want for you now?"

"He'd want me to be happy." Hesitantly Joelle reached up to tangle her fingers lightly in his soft beard. "Do you know that when I've been with you, I've felt more relaxed, more content than I remember feeling since I was a child?"

"Only relaxed?" Zach bent to find her lips with his, brushing them lightly twice before he took them for a long, sweet kiss. "Still relaxed?"

"Not as much," she said carefully. "But I think I could grow to like this feeling, too." Clasping her fingers behind his neck, Joelle pulled Zach down again, opening her mouth this time for his warm invasion. She shut her eyes and relaxed against him, forgetting to be afraid or to think at all. More than anyone ever had, Zach seemed to sense her wariness, and he didn't push, didn't ask her to go where she wasn't ready. Instead he set a rhythm that she could follow, broadening the intimacies between them patiently.

When Zach lay back on the blanket, pulling her to rest on top of him, Joelle was ready to explore his body with her fingertips, outlining the firm muscles and flexing sinew. She sighed expectantly when he lifted her to unzip her jacket so that he could find the smooth skin of her back and trace it with fingers that trembled slightly. That she could have such an effect on him sent currents of delight through her system.

Together they rolled on to their sides, and Zach held Joelle against him as he began to explore her more intimately until finally his hand rested on her breast, bare under the sweater. She lay beside him, eyes tightly shut as he cupped the softly mounded flesh in his hand and let his thumb increase her excitement. His hand trailed to her other breast, and she shivered with pleasure. Instantly he stopped, withdrawing his hand from underneath her sweater. "Did I hurt you?"

Joelle was puzzled, then embarrassed. Finally she said, "Not at all. I think what I was doing is called 'responding.' "

Zach clasped her in a bear hug and laughed softly in her ear. "I'm sorry. Maybe I'm being too careful."

"I'm not going to fall apart over this," she assured him.

"I know," he said, "but I also know that you don't like being touched. I don't want to scare you away."

"There should be a compromise, though, don't you think?" Joelle sat up and rested her elbows on his chest, looking into his eyes, now amber in the moonlight. "If we continue at this pace, I'll be too old to enjoy it before we get around to being serious."

Quicker than Joelle had ever seen him move, Zach rolled over, pinning her beneath him. "Tap three times on my shoulder then if this gets to be too much, because I don't think you're going to be able to do too much talking." His mouth found hers, and Joelle gasped in delight as his tongue began to explore at the same time that his hand found the flesh it had so recently abandoned.

In a sensual daze, she moaned at his caresses, giving herself up to the sheer delight of his weight stretched over her. Zach's own excitement was evident, and she added to it by finding his back under his shirt, kneading his flesh with her fingers and with the palms of her hands.

"Joelle," he said finally, pulling away when she began to move her hips beneath his. "God, you're beautiful." He pushed up and off, moving to her side to stroke her breasts before regretfully pulling down the sweater to cover them.

Joelle opened her eyes, and behind the lingering excitement there Zach saw a glimmer of fear. He put his finger over her lips to silence her, tracing their contours before he pulled her up to sit next to him. "I know you're not ready," he assured her. "And I'm not, either, for that matter."

Joelle was surprised at his words, and she wondered what was keeping him from persuading her to make love to him. Perhaps she wasn't emotionally prepared for this intimacy yet, but it would have only taken a gentle shove to send her over the precipice of her own desire. "Well, it's good we agree," she murmured, not sure that she was telling the truth. The husky, musical voice carried her bewilderment.

"You don't know me," Zach explained. "I'm a stranger to you."

"No," she said, drawing out the word as if considering how to explain her feelings. "No, I feel like I know you as well as anyone I've ever met."

"We need to know more about each other before we make this kind of a commitment."

Joelle shook her head vehemently. "Please let it go for now."

Zach watched her silky hair swirl in the moonlight, and he sighed. "When you're ready then, tell me."

"You must think I'm...odd." Joelle watched as he stood, offering her his hand. She stood, too, and still holding the hand she had given him, he pulled her slowly down the hill.

"No, I think you're incredible."

At the door of the pick-up, Zach released her and they stood facing each other. "How much longer do you intend to stay?" he asked casually.

"I don't have any plans to leave right now. The crew starts work on the house next Thursday. I want to be here to supervise."

"There aren't any power lines coming up here."

"We never had electricity. Trying to sell me a wind machine, Smith?"

"We could work out a very interesting payment schedule," he said, pulling her close for a good-night kiss.

Joelle relaxed against him, reciprocating. "I've learned not to put myself into a man's debt," she said when she could talk, "but I might really be interested in a wind machine. Cash only, of course."

"We'll discuss it," he promised, turning to step into the cab.

"Thank you for this day."

Zach looked down at her. The moonlight silvered her hair and sparkled in her green eyes. His hand gripped the truck door handle spasmodically; he didn't want to open the door, instead he wanted to join her back on the ground. "My pleasure." He put his key in the ignition and the truck started with a quiet purr. "I'll see you soon."

Joelle stood back and watched as he guided the truck down the narrow driveway.

AFTER ZACH'S PARTING REMARK, Joelle was a little surprised when she didn't see him the next day. She wondered if she had scared him away. Alone again, Joelle felt her solitude close in around her. Dividing her time between fixing up her sleeping quarters and digging up what had once been her mother's vegetable garden, she kept busy. The fertile ground was soft and black under her fingertips, and as Joelle prepared it for late-spring planting, she wondered at her own actions. A garden was a commitment. Fixing the spring and repairing the springhouse and main house were property improvements, but planting a garden was different. A garden improved nothing except possibly her state of mind.

Still, Joelle continued to work the soil, finding that its healing powers were reason enough. And as she worked, she waited for Zach to come to her. Instead, her next visitor was Carol, who came bearing gifts of homemade bread and grape jelly made from the local wild-fox grapes.

Joelle greeted the older woman with genuine affection. "Welcome," she said as she opened Carol's car door and took the food so that Carol could stand. "If I had a house, I'd think this was a housewarming."

Carol stepped out of her car and laughed as she took the necessary time to examine her surroundings. "Zach wasn't teasing when he said this was primitive."

"A realtor would refer to it as a handyman's special."

"If a realtor would refer to it at all." Carol linked her arm through Joelle's. "Let's have the tour."

Later the two women sat on a blanket by the side of the springhouse and listened to the contented gurgling of the spring. "I like your ideas for fixing up the house," Carol said. "From what you've said about your family, there was so much life and love there once. It would be a shame to let the structure collapse. But I'd say you were just in time."

"It's taken me a lot of years to come back here."

"I'm glad that you did."

"So am I."

"Zach's glad, too."

Joelle considered Carol's words. "Zach's been a good friend."

"Well, I, for one am glad to see him reaching out to you. He's such a loner. Except for Jake and me and some of the other people who work for him, he keeps to himself. He needs what you can offer him."

Joelle pleated the blanket with her fingers. "I don't know what I have to offer him, Carol." It didn't seem at all strange to be discussing something so personal. Carol was so matter-of-fact and warm that Joelle felt as though they had always been friends.

"He needs what we all need. Someone to care about him; someone to make him realize just how special he is." Carol patted Joelle's hand. "You need that, too."

"You almost make me believe it could happen."

Carol laughed softly. "I'm living proof. If a plump old busybody like me can find happiness, it can happen to anyone."

Joelle laughed, too. "You deserve what you have. You'll have to tell me your secret, though."

"It's simple, really. You just have to face what's standing in your way."

The advice sounded strangely familiar. "That's the hardest thing in the world to do sometimes," Joelle said.

"Simple but not easy." Carol stood and stretched. "Listen to me giving advice to a beautiful young woman. I'm going back to my kitchen where I belong."

"I'm glad you came." Joelle stood, too, and the two women walked to Carol's car. "If you see Zach," Joelle said, trying to sound casual, "tell him I said hello."

"It's a nice walk to his house," Carol answered. "It might be good for you to stretch your legs."

"I might do that," Joelle conceded with a smile. She watched Carol drive away, and she understood that the visit had been more than a casual one. The older woman's message had been clear. It was time for Joelle to take the lead. Carol believed that Zach had made all the overtures he was going to make.

More days passed and one night, almost a week after she had last seen Zach, Joelle sat alone on the hillside, missing both of the men that she had shared that spot with. One was dead and the other seemed to be gone from her life as surely as if he had died too. She had come back to Russell Creek to be alone. She had needed to reorganize her life, rethink her priorities. The solitude she had found and the rich beauty of the countryside had given her back her health and the beginnings of peace of mind.

Now she needed something more. That something more took the form of a tall man with an auburn beard and brown eyes that melted her.

"Zach Smith," she said to the sky. "You're the first man in a long time to make me believe in possibilities. So where have you gone?"

The sound of her voice breaking the long silence was better than nothing.

"Did I scare you away? Did I insist one too many times that I needed my privacy? That I didn't want to be touched? Weren't you listening to what I was really saying, Zach?"

The soliloquy was useless: she did not want to hear her own words. The silence descended again. She counted the stars that were visible through the haze. As she watched through the long night, the sky slowly cleared and she lost count, marveling instead at the immensity of the universe and her own diminutive place in it. When the sun began to rise, streaking the gray canopy with fingers of shimmering light, Joelle stood and walked to the springhouse. Somehow her own doubts and fears had been put into perspective.

She slept until midafternoon, immersed in a deep slumber that allowed no dreams. When she awoke she washed in sun-warmed spring water and changed into pants and a matching tunic. The walk to Zach's house took only minutes.

ZACH AND JAKE were dismantling a portion of the wind machine behind the barn when Joelle found them. Quietly she took a seat on a split-rail fence that surrounded the area and watched them work. Zach had stripped to the waist, and although the air was pleasantly cool, his lithe body was covered with perspiration. He and Jake didn't talk, each seeming to know what needed to be done and what his own part in the job should be.

Joelle was fascinated by the graceful bending and lifting and by the unimpeded view of Zach's powerful muscles. His movements were so well coordinated that he seemed to be dancing, moving to silent music. Finally he turned around and caught sight of her, and Joelle watched his expression change from surprise to warm approval. He turned and bent again, finishing the task that he and Jake had set for themselves before he murmured something to Jake and pulled on his shirt. When Zach came toward her, Joelle saw that he was trying hard to cover the emotion that the sight of her had aroused.

"Joelle." He faced her and smiled a quiet greeting.

"Zach." Tentatively Joelle stretched out her hand, and Zach took it and held it between his. "I decided to come after you myself," she said, throwing polite precaution to the wind, "I couldn't stay away."

"You have no idea how complicated this is," Zach said, moving closer to push a strand of hair behind her ear.

"You told me once that I wasn't competing with another woman. Is that still true?"

Joelle watched as Zach nodded. "It's not another woman," he assured her.

"I think that's the only complication I couldn't handle."

Zach wanted to tell her that another woman would be simple in comparison to the real problems between them, but instead he stroked her cheek with the back of his fingers. He knew that coming to him had been an act of trust, a major step for Joelle Lindsey. If Zach rejected her, no matter how good his reasons, it would be destructive for both of them. And he didn't want to reject her. Quite the opposite.

"I'm glad you came."

"Well, now that I've come, I'm going to leave again," Joelle said, sliding down off the fence, her body brushing his. "You and Jake are very busy."

Zach nodded, desire flooding his body like a river rushing past a carelessly constructed dam. "We have to finish this before it gets dark. Will you come back for dinner?"

"No, I want you to dine with me."

"Roots and berries?"

"Something like that. Will you come anyway?"

"Is this a test?"

Joelle shook her head and Zach smiled.

"Okay, I'll come. What time?"

"Whenever you get finished. I'll be waiting for you."

JOELLE WAITED until Mr. Kincaid was done with a customer before she opened the door and went into the little grocery store. "Hello, Mr. Kincaid," she said with a smile.

"You still here, girl? I thought you'd take off long before this."

"No, I'm still on vacation." Joelle wandered the small room, reading labels on cans and checking the sparse supply of meat in the cooler. "Is this chicken fresh?"

"It's still cacklin'."

Joelle picked up the package and put it on the counter, choosing some fresh tomatoes and a can of green beans to go with it. A dusty bottle of barbecue sauce and paper plates and napkins joined the other items. "I guess that will be it."

"I'm glad you're still here. Never did tell anyone you was in town, but I've sure been tempted."

Joelle could see her anonymity drifting away in the tide of Russell Creek gossip. "I'll tell you what," she bargained. "Give me a couple of days, and you can tell anyone you like."

"They're gonna want to hear you sing."

"I guess I could give a concert on your front steps," she teased.

Mr. Kincaid pointed to a hand-lettered poster behind the counter. "How about at the Memorial Day picnic?"

Joelle read the poster. "The Russell Creek Improvement Society? You're kidding."

"Nope. Bunch of people are tryin' to make this town come alive again. Have you noticed all the cleanin' up that's been going' on?"

Joelle shook her head.

"This place was worse than dead a year ago. Then a bunch of folks got together over at the Presbyterian church and started meetin'. They made Pennington Alloy tear down all the houses that was fallin' apart. Got a fancy lawyer from Taylerton to take the company to court."

"Good for them!"

"Then they've been persuadin' folks that owns houses to start fixin' them up. Even made me paint my store."

"It's very nice," Joelle soothed.

"I didn't mind. Glad to see 'em takin' an interest in this town again."

"Where's all the money coming from?"

"I told you before, new folks movin' in, old ones found work in Taylerton and Awnsley. Russell Creek's becomin' a regular commutin' suburb."

Joelle held back her smile. "What about the picnic?"

"The Improvement Society wants to organize social events like we used to have. The Memorial Day picnic is gonna be held at that old beach on the river where you kids swam in the summer. They're chargin' admission. They're workin' on a fund to buy the old company store to use as a social hall."

"Pretty ambitious."

"Not so much. For once the company is bein' cooperative. They're willin' to sell the buildin' for peanuts."

"I doubt that they're being cooperative. Just smart. Who else would want the place?" She laughed at Mr. Kincaid's grimace. "Do you really want me to sing?"

"Think of the people who'd come."

"I'll give it some thought," she promised. "But you'd have to swear there wouldn't be any newspaper publicity. Just word of mouth."

"We could manage that." Mr. Kincaid bagged the meager groceries. "Gonna cook dinner for anyone I know?"

"My neighbor, Zach Smith."

Mr. Kincaid took a long time arranging the groceries in the bag. "You asked about him the first time you was in here."

Joelle had forgotten how every little bit of information was digested in a small town. She suspected that Mr. Kincaid's store was now the central information source for the people left in Russell Creek. All she had to do was show that she was still interested in finding out about Zach, and she would soon know his entire life history. It didn't seem fair somehow. She was refusing to share with Zach; it didn't seem right to pry into his background without being willing to reveal her own secrets. "I've gotten to know him since," Joelle said casually.

"He's a good man. Lots of folks hereabout don't like him, naturally, but he's proved himself."

Joelle knew that it was hard to be a stranger in a place like Russell Creek. She sympathized with the struggle Zach must be going through to be accepted. "I like him," she said.

"That says a lot, considerin'..."

Considering that she was famous and probably had her pick of men? Joelle hated to think about herself that way and she interrupted. "I hope this chicken turns out good. I haven't cooked in a long time. I've got to run now." With a wave and a goodbye she was gone before Mr. Kincaid could tell her any more.

CHAPTER SIX

IT WAS ALMOST DARK when Joelle lit a fire in the hibachi. She'd bought it in the Taylerton hardware store the day she had purchased her tools. Today she had forgotten to buy charcoal, but there were plenty of scraps of wood left over from her stairs-mending project, and she heaped them in the center of the grill along with her grocery bag and watched as they flared to life.

She had also forgotten to purchase a saucepan, although she had bought a can opener and eating utensils when she had shopped on the way to Russell Creek from Pittsburgh. In preparation, she opened the beans, deciding that they would cook fine in their can. Used to entertaining by picking up the telephone and calling a catering service, to Joelle the simple, impromptu barbecue seemed like a major undertaking.

Joelle was blowing on the wood scraps, trying to hurry them along, when she sensed Zach's presence. Looking up she admired his tall figure clad in fresh denim jeans and a Western shirt. ''I hope you're not starving,'' she said. ''The wood is burning nicely, but it'll be awhile before I can put the chicken on to cook.''

Zach crouched beside her, not offering to help as Joelle poked and prodded the fire. The wood had become glowing coals when he finally spoke. ''Watching you get such a kick out of simple things almost takes my breath away.''

Whatever doubts Joelle had entertained about Zach's interest in her disappeared entirely. "Having you so close has the same effect on me," she said, turning her face up for his kiss.

Zach drew back from the embrace finally. "If you don't put that chicken on right now, we won't eat tonight for sure." Joelle did as he suggested, arranging the can of green beans in the center of the chicken.

"Would you like to see what I've done with the springhouse?" she offered. Arms around each other's waists, they climbed the stairs and Joelle stood proudly as Zach complimented her on the changes she had made. Since he had last seen it, she had installed the new windows that she had ordered in Taylerton, and she had covered the insulation in the walls with weathered barn boards she had found neatly piled in a building that had once housed her grandfather's team of mules.

The little room was cozy with the glow of the kerosene lantern that Joelle lit. The warm, weathered wood and numerous mason jars filled with bridal wreath and fragrant mock orange from shrubs around the house transformed what was really nothing more than a shack into a home. "Do you know," Joelle said, her arms folded across her chest, "I've never been so proud of anything I've accomplished. The crew I hired to renovate comes tomorrow, but nothing they can do will seem as important as what I've done myself."

"I can understand that."

"When I was a kid, we had nothing but the basics, and I hated it. But for me, it's taken going back to the basics to make me feel, well, alive again."

"That's what a lot of the sixties and seventies was about," Zach said, coming to stand next to her with his arm around her shoulder. "All that bread baking and goat raising and vegetable growing was about learning to pay attention, to notice we were alive."

"I missed all that when it was in fashion," Joelle said, "although I certainly paid lip service to it, but I was...busy doing other things."

"Perhaps you didn't need those simple experiences then."

"I've certainly needed simplicity for the past few weeks. Sometimes the quiet's almost driven me crazy, and sometimes I've thought that if I didn't go somewhere or do something, that I might wake up the next morning and find I no longer existed. But it's been so good for me. I've been reborn." She leaned her shoulder against his shoulder. "And of course, you've saved me when all this solitude got to be too much to bear."

"Zach Smith, rescuer of damsels in distress."

"Just how many damsels have you rescued?" Joelle asked in pretended indignation. "I've never liked being part of a crowd."

"You stand out in any crowd, Joelle."

She was trying to understand why Zach's voice sounded so sad, when he pulled her toward the doorway. "It's time to turn the chicken."

"Who's cooking this dinner, you or me, Smith?" Joelle chastised him as she raced down the hill to flip the chicken before it blackened beyond recognition.

Zach disappeared into the bottom of the springhouse and came out with a bottle of white wine that had been chilling in the trough. "You were so mesmerized by your fire, that you didn't even see me arrive and slip this into the spring." He opened the bottle, pouring some wine into two paper cups. "To..." He stopped, hesitant to continue.

"To friendship," Joelle finished for him, lifting her cup to his.

They sipped wine and sliced the tomatoes, chatting casually about Zach's business and Joelle's renovations. Zach gathered some small rocks and made a camp-fire circle, dragging dead wood from a nearby fallen tree to make a fire. When the chicken was finally ready, they sat side by side on a log, and Joelle watched as Zach dumped the remaining coals into a bed of twigs, piling larger wood on top. In a few minutes they were enjoying a small fire as they ate their dinner, feeding their chicken bones and paper plates to the flames when they were finished.

"A simple meal, a simple cleanup," Joelle said, coming back from the fire to sit next to Zach again.

He didn't touch her, which seemed strange, and she waited for him to take charge of the conversation. When he did speak, she wished he hadn't. "I noticed you have a guitar."

Joelle stiffened, staring at the fire, knowing what would come next.

"I'd like to hear you play," Zach said.

It was a reasonable enough request. Anyone else would be flattered. Joelle was terrified. Obediently she climbed to the springhouse, her shoulders hunched with defeat. Thoughts tumbled one over the other, and she tried to push them away, tried not to guess what was behind Zach's request. She picked up the case and brought it down the steps, down the hill to sit once more on the log. Zach was crouching by the fire, warming his hands, and he didn't look at her as she snapped the latches on the case and strummed a chord, turning pegs to tune the instrument even though it was already in perfect tune.

"What would you like to hear?" Joelle asked finally, in a voice that gave away her anxiety.

"Anything you want to sing."

She shut her eyes and began to pick out the melody to one of the songs that she had written since coming back to Russell Creek. It was called, "Simplicity Blues," and it was about how easy, how romantic it is to live the simple life when you know that you have enough money in the bank to buy anything you want. Joelle liked the song, for it reminded her of the kind of music she had written and performed when she was sixteen, working in a Pittsburgh coffee house. It was completely different from "When I Come Home to You," her most recent hit, and she was proud of it.

Tonight, playing the song for Zach who still had not turned around, Joelle missed the entrance and had to begin again. She got through it, going on to another more sentimental song by someone else, and ended with one of Tim's songs, which was a standard part of her repertoire. Guitar across her lap, and pulse pounding in her throat, she waited for Zach to say something.

"Will you sing 'When I Come Home to You' now?" he asked, standing and turning slowly to watch her.

Silhouetted against the smoke and flames, Joelle couldn't see Zach's expression, and his voice was neutral. With a shrug, she set the guitar back in the case and snapped the latches. "I don't think so," she said. "I've done all the singing I want to do. You can turn on the radio for that one."

"You're much better in person."

Anger began to rise within her. "How long have you known?" Joelle asked, standing to join him at the fire. "Just how long have you had my identity figured out?"

"Since the beginning. I saw you standing over there and heard you chanting with that indescribable voice that's always sent shivers down my spine, and I knew right away." Zach turned and pulled her around to face him.

"Let go of me," Joelle said, pushing his hands from her shoulders. "Just what kind of a game has it been for you?"

"No game. You needed to be anonymous. I tried to give you what you needed. Then when I tried to talk to you, you refused to let me. Joelle—" Zach's voice broke from its neutral tone "—I've never wanted anything except to do what was right for you."

"And lying was right?"

"I never lied. You are Joelle Lindsey, as surely as you are Jo Lynd. I know only Joelle; it's Joelle I'm falling in love with."

"And tell me, Zach," she said, trying to digest his words. "If I wasn't Jo Lynd, too, would you be talking of love now?"

"If you weren't Jo Lynd, dammit, I'd have talked of love a lot sooner. I wouldn't have tried so hard to stay away; I'd have come after you. Who you are makes this impossible!" Zach turned back to the fire. "More impossible than you even know."

Joelle believed him. Suddenly all his moodiness, his withdrawals, made sense. She was Jo Lynd and he was Zach Smith. She was destined to fly back to California to live once more in the fast lane of the music world. Zach, on the other hand, was destined to stay in an almost abandoned mining town and run an alternative energy company that was never going to be listed in *Fortune 500*. Zach had seen the dichotomy between them, and he had retreated. He had cared enough about her and about himself not to want to hurt either of them. Joelle's anger drained away.

"Jo Lynd was created by a lot of people when I was too poor to say no and too young to know better." Joelle reached for Zach's hand, which he had shoved into the pocket of his jeans. For a moment she thought he wasn't going to respond. Finally with obvious reluctance, he linked fingers with her. "The Joelle you say you're learning to love *is* me. But I don't think I can be 'me' alone. Won't you help?"

"You don't know what you're asking."

Zach stared into the flames, but unconsciously he gripped Joelle's fingers tighter. There had been two secrets between them. Joelle was taking the news of her exposed disguise and trying to deal with it. But there was a more devastating revelation yet to come. Zach had expected her to be furious when she found out that he knew who she was. He had been banking on her anger so that he would have the courage to finish the story.

Instead Joelle's anger had passed swiftly, leaving her thoughtful and vulnerable. She was exposing more than her identity, she was telling him that with him, she was able to be the person she wanted to be. God, she was asking him to let that continue. The right words, words that wouldn't alienate her forever, would not form. All he could do was tell the truth.

"There's something else you have to know." He pulled his hand free from hers and turned to face her. "I've wanted to tell you this from the beginning, but I couldn't without telling you that I knew who you were. I've cared enough about you to give you your anonymity, and now I care enough about you to tell you who I am."

Her face was puzzled. "I know who you are. You're Zach Smith, a man I care about"

"I am Zach Smith, but I was born Zacharias Pennington-Smith. My father is the man who owned the mine where your father and brother were killed."

Forever after, when he thought about the next few minutes, Zach would remember the dancing firelight reflected in green cat's eyes. Nothing else was visible in them. Joelle had spent the years of her adult life learning to school her features so that the inner woman didn't appear for anyone to comment on. The rigid, self-imposed training stood her in good stead that night.

"I certainly do know how to pick men to put my trust in." Even to her own ears, the carefully voiced statement was incongruous in its lack of emotion.

"I wouldn't know about that."

"No, you wouldn't." She stepped back a pace to distance herself from him. "I think you should go."

"Talk to me, Joelle. Tell me what you're feeling."

"You can ask me that?" Her voice was still controlled. "One thing is certainly safe to say about you, Zacharias Pennington-Smith. You have unlimited gall."

"I'm no more just Zacharias Pennington-Smith than you're just Jo Lynd. Neither of us deserves to be put into categories."

"There's one big difference between us. You've known all along who I am, but I've never even suspected your real identity. It never occurred to me that you might only be telling me half of your last name. It never occurred to me that a son of Franklin Pennington-Smith would have the nerve to show his face in these parts."

"I should have told you on the first day I met you. But you took me by surprise." Instinctively Zach reached out to her, laying his hand on her shoulder. Joelle didn't move, she didn't even blink, but distaste swept across her features destroying her neutral expression. "You needed someone to care about you, and I found that easy to do. Still, Joelle, there was more than that to it. I knew if I told you who my father was, you'd never give me a chance. And I wanted a chance." Tentatively he raised his fingers to her cheek. "I'm the man you know. Nothing more, nothing less."

"You're not the man I thought you were." She stepped back to avoid his caressing fingers. "I would like you to go."

Zach dropped his hand to his side. They stood watching each other in the firelight. "Just tell me one thing then," he said finally, "and I'll go. If I had told you sooner than I did, or even later, would you have felt the same way? Is my parentage unforgivable in your eyes? Because if it is, you're not the woman I thought you were, either."

His words cut through her defenses like the clean, honed blade of a scythe. Anger, molten and destructive, raged through her. "You're not the first man who's made a mistake and then tried to pretend I was the culprit! Your father was the first, and there have been others since. I won't take your guilt and carry it for you. Get out of my sight Zacharias Pennington-Smith. I never want to see your lying face again."

"That's all the answer I need, isn't it?" He turned and walked up the slight slope to the driveway. Joelle watched his proud retreat. In a moment he had disappeared from sight. Her knees felt weak, and she slid to the ground, kneeling in front of the fire with her head in her hands. She didn't know how long she stayed there, but when she finally felt strong enough to stand, the fire had died down to faintly glowing embers and the stars were out in glorious display.

There seemed to be no place to go, nothing to do with her pain. Zach was gone and she was left alone with a sense of betrayal that was overpowering. It was too much to handle by herself and yet there was no one she could turn to. What friends she had were leading busy lives on the California coast. Instinctively she stood and climbed the slope to the driveway. Her keys were in the ignition of the Pontiac where she always left them. Sliding behind the wheel she started the engine.

ZACH SAT ON HIS PORCH RAILING staring into the darkness. His thoughts were the color of the night. They were formless, wordless, meaningless. In the midst of them he saw a bright spot of light. As he watched, a car slowed down in front of his house and then sped up again as it passed his driveway. He recognized Joelle's Pontiac.

He knew what she suffered. From the beginning they had been destined to bring each other pain. He watched as her lights disappeared back into the darkness. She had slowed down at the turnoff to his house. He held out no hope that she wanted to forgive him for his deception, but she had been tempted to communicate with him. That much he knew.

In a moment he was walking to the spot where he parked his truck, swinging up into the cab. There was too much left unsaid between them, and no more damage could be done. He decided to follow her, knowing that it was the only thing left for him to do.

Out on the blacktop he caught up with her quickly. If she recognized his truck, she gave no sign. Instead she drove as if she knew where she was going. They continued down the deserted road, their headlights the only sign of civilization as they rounded curves and dipped down over the sides of hills. When they neared the town of Russell Creek, Zach slowed, cruising noiselessly through the streets. There were lights here, and shadows of people moving in some of the houses. Russell Creek wasn't a ghost town. It was only a town full of the ghosts that had haunted him since he was twenty-one.

He was far behind her now, heading toward the Monongahela River and the abandoned mine that had become their mutual goal. Parking outside the tall chain link fence topped with barbwire, he got down from the truck and walked to Joelle's side. She stood quietly, her nose pressed against the gate. Beyond them was the weathered wooden building that was the entrance to Pennington Alloy #2.

There was no one else to offer her comfort. Fully understanding just how incongruous it was, Zach brushed a strand of hair from her cheek, which was wet with silent tears. "I know what you're feeling," he said.

"I've never cried for them before. I never could. Maybe that's why it's haunted me so all these years."

He had expected her anger, not her honesty. Reluctantly he dropped his hand. "Have you ever thought that all these years, while you've been suffering, that your pain has been shared with countless others? The tragedy touched so many. You've never been alone with it."

"I've felt alone with it." She turned a little. "I still do."

Zach nodded. "I've felt alone with it sometimes, too."

"It didn't have to touch you at all!"

"That's where you're wrong."

Joelle found herself responding to the sincerity in his voice. This was the man who had withheld his identity, who had destroyed her newfound faith in her ability to judge character. But how could she erect defenses when there were tears running down her cheeks? She was defeated before she even made the attempt. "Explain it to me. It won't change how I feel about what you've done, but I need to understand."

"I was in my sophomore year at the Massachussetts Institute of Technology when I learned about the mine explosion. I heard about it on the radio and it was a week before I could get in touch with anyone at home to talk about it." Zach leaned against the tall chain link fence and crossed his arms as he reminisced.

"Finally, my oldest brother, Isaac, called to reassure me that as bad as it sounded, Pennington Alloy couldn't be held responsible."

"And you believed that?" Joelle's tone was a mixture of scornfulness and sadness.

"Yes, I did." Zach's voice held no apology. He was telling the story as it had occurred. He could do no more than that. "I believed that my father was a man with a conscience. When the papers printed your mother's charges, I began to have doubts. Then the federal investigation concluded that Pennington Alloy wasn't to blame. I felt that our family had been vindicated. I flew home and appeared with Isaac and Jeremiah and my father and mother at the press conference."

"Holy and sanctified
God's chosen ones
The mine owner stood
With his trinity of sons
And he spoke...
In the voice of corruption."

Joelle intoned the words from the song that had made her famous, and for a moment Zach was quiet, remembering.

"It was two years later, three months before I graduated from M.I.T., that I heard 'The Voice of Corruption' for the first time. I remember that at first I just noticed the melody and the wonderful, husky voice of the young woman singing it. Then the words began to make sense to me. The song was very clever. No names were named, no fingers were pointed at Pennington Alloy, but everyone who could read a newspaper knew what the song was about."

"They were supposed to know."

Zach nodded and went on. "I graduated and went home to assume a position at Pennington Alloy. My father was furious about the bad publicity that 'The Voice of Corruption' was generating. He wanted to sue or retaliate some other way, but his hands were effectively tied."

Joelle still stared at the mine entrance. "Tim Daniels made sure of that. A whole battery of lawyers examined that song before it was ever recorded."

Zach's mouth was a grim line. "I'd never seen my father so upset. It was a facet of his personality that he'd never shown to his children. I began to wonder about his anger. And somewhere, deep inside me, I still harbored doubts about the mine explosion. After working at Pennington Alloy for a month, I began to realize that lots of things didn't quite fit together. I was given a top-level position. Every other male in my generation was struggling with decisions about the Vietnam War, but I was given an immediate deferment because we produced steel for the war effort. I began to see how much power my father had.

"One day I started to search hard for answers. I had access to any information I needed. I took notes, made meticulous records. But I had no real personal evidence, no eye-witness accounts of the way that Pennington Alloy employees were treated. So I went to my father and told him that I needed some time off. He wasn't happy about it. I think he suspected that I wasn't going to spend a month frolicking on the beach."

"What did you do?" Joelle faced Zach for the first time.

"I went to all the Pennington steel mills and I worked for a while in the Pennington Alloy coal mine #1 down in West Virginia. I found out exactly what I didn't want to know. When I went home, I presented my father with all the information I'd put together: the safety violations I'd seen firsthand, photographs of the way that Pennington employees were forced to live..."

"And you expected that to make a difference?"

"I didn't stay around long enough to find out if it did or not. I took my idealism and my guilt and I walked out of my father's office, never to walk back in again. I dropped Pennington from my name, roamed the country and eventually..."

"You came to Russell Creek. Was it noblesse oblige, Zacharias? The virtuous young prince working for good among the peons?" Joelle watched Zach straighten. She knew her words had cut deep. She was still feeling too betrayed to care.

"I owed it to you to finish the story. I wasn't expecting your forgiveness or your understanding."

"Listen, Zacharias Pennington-Smith. The tears were gone from Joelle's voice. It was low and controlled and intense. Each word was a swing of the scythe. "Can you hear voices on the wind? I can. The ghosts of my father and brother are here, between us. I've seen your father, but you will never see mine. He'll never hold his grandchildren, never know that I made a success out of my life.''

"Nor will he know that he raised a daughter who hangs on to the past to avoid living in the present.'' Zach's eyes reflected rather than absorbed the moonlight. His tone was equally as cold.

"You dare to criticize me?''

"I dare to challenge you. What happened here was a tragedy but that can't be changed. You did what you could to see that justice was done. And so did I. Neither of us can do more than that. Say your goodbyes to your father and brother tonight, Joelle. It's about time that you got on with your life, don't you think?'' Zach turned and started toward his truck.

"You have no right!''

Her words did not affect his purposeful stride or the pride evident in the way that he carried himself. Zach stepped into the cab of the truck and in a moment he was gone.

Joelle threaded her fingers through the chain link, rattling the fence in her fury. The metal clinking was the only audible sound in the quiet night except for the low keening of the wind. "Damn you, Zacharias Pennington-Smith!'' she shouted. "Damn you!''

Even the wind stopped. The night was perfectly still. Joelle was alone. Completely alone. She could not summon the ghost voices with which she had taunted Zach. Standing at the gate of the abandoned mine where her father and brother were entombed, she understood finally that they had gone to their resting place without her.

They were at peace. Only one grieving folksinger who refused to let go of the past still suffered.

JOELLE SAT ON THE STEPS of the springhouse and watched the crew of four men unload their tools from the panel truck with the logo, Penn Renovators, on it. Wearily she stretched and stood to walk down to meet them. She had come back from the mine in the early hours of the morning, but sleep had eluded her. She was exhausted, physically and emotionally. It was only when she had stopped pretending that sleep might come that she had gone to sit on the steps of the springhouse and spotted the procession of two trucks coming up her driveway. The men she had hired weeks before in Taylerton had come to begin the renovations on the farmhouse.

The crew's foreman, an older man with sandy, graying hair, was standing in front of the house, shaking his head. "When I talked to you last month, you didn't tell me the damage was so extensive," he commented when Joelle joined him. "And you didn't tell me you don't have electricity up here."

"Do you still want the job?" Joelle wasn't sure what she hoped he would say. She was too tired to care if they refused to work for her. It would give her the perfect excuse to pack her one suitcase and leave Russell Creek. The thought was tempting no matter what they decided.

"It's going to cost you a pretty penny. You might be better off to tear it down and start again."

"No!" She was surprised at the vehemence in her own voice. "Nobody's going to tear this house down. If you don't want the job, say so, and I'll find someone else to work on it. Money is no problem as long as you're fair."

"I'll have a complete estimate by this afternoon."

"Good." She turned to head back to the spring-house. It seemed peculiar to have the stillness of the farm broken by the buzz of men's voices, but the sound wasn't unpleasant. She had been alone too long. Even the sound of stranger's exchanging shouts and occasional curses as they explored the house made her feel more alive. No one had been here in such a long time. No one but Zach.

She passed the camp-fire ring he had constructed the night before. "I'm not going to forget who you are, Zach," she said out loud. "I'm going to go on with my life here. But you're the worst kind of fool if you think that life could include you now." Even to her own ears, her voice sounded less scornful than it should have.

CHAPTER SEVEN

"WELL, GIRL. You gonna sing for us this weekend?" Mr. Kincaid was neatly arranging groceries in Joelle's bag. In the three weeks that had passed since the crew began renovations on the farmhouse, Joelle had become a regular visitor to Mr. Kincaid's store. She no longer had to screw up her courage to drive into Russell Creek. She came regularly, stopping to talk with Mr. Kincaid and to get supplies. Every time he asked her if she was going to sing at the picnic.

Mr. Kincaid wasn't the only person who wanted her to sing. It was inevitable, with her frequent trips to town, that her identity would become known. It was surprising, really, that she had remained anonymous as long as she had. Mr. Kincaid had held his tongue, but eventually she had been recognized by other store patrons. Now when she walked through town, she was often stopped for friendly chats.

She was impressed with the way she was treated. The citizens of Russell Creek took her to their hearts like a long-lost child. Cronies of her father and mother fussed over her like proud parents, and people who she had not grown up with treated her like a welcome newcomer who just happened to be famous.

Joelle was surprised with the neighborly feeling in the little community. What she had seen as a bleak, depressing ghost town was really the home of warm-hearted people committed to bringing life back to Russell Creek. She found herself caught up in their dream. Somehow, singing for them didn't seem like too much to ask.

"Yes, I'll sing," she promised Mr. Kincaid, sweeping her grocery bag off the counter to rest firmly on her hip. "You can count on me. But remember, no publicity." The door behind her opened, and Joelle turned to smile at Mr. Kincaid's new customer. Her smile faded immediately. Standing in the doorway was the man she had not seen in three weeks.

Zach looked the same, although today he was dressed in dark slacks and a dress shirt, not his usual blue jeans. She had put him out of her mind, working hard to forget the way his eyes caressed her and his slightest smile sent warmth through her body. Today his eyes were opaque and there was no smile. They stood staring at each other and Joelle knew that he was masking his feelings as completely as she was masking her own.

"Goodbye, Mr. Kincaid," she said finally, not turning to look at the old man. "I'll see you at the picnic." She walked to the door and stood waiting for Zach to move so that she could pass through.

"Hello, Joelle."

She should have known that no matter what was between them, Zach would not be discourteous to her. He was first and foremost the well-bred Zacharias Pennington-Smith. She could be no less than the well-bred Joelle Lindsey, whose mother had always told her that being poor was no excuse to be less than a lady.

"Good morning, Zach." She waited for him to step aside.

"I understand you've started renovating the house."

"That's right."

"Planning to stay?"

She wondered how such a simple question could be so charged with meaning. "For a while." Up close she could see flickers of light in his eyes. Under his careful show of dignity was the man she had been so drawn to before she had learned his identity.

For three weeks she had refused to consider her own harsh reaction to his disclosure. She had avoided thinking of him by working hard on clearing and landscaping the yard around the house as the carpenters worked inside. In her quiet hours she had written song after song, singing sometimes until she was hoarse and the hour was so late that she fell asleep as soon as her head touched the pillow. She had filled her loneliness at the loss of Zach's presence in her life by making friends with the workmen and visiting Russell Creek. Now, quite simply, she realized that none of it had been enough.

"I'm glad you stayed," he said.

"Did you think your confession would chase me away?"

"I have more faith in you than that."

Joelle closed her eyes. When she opened them, Zach had moved around her, and she was facing an empty doorway.

MEMORIAL DAY DAWNED bright and clear with the early-morning sunshine burning off the night's lingering mist. Joelle worked until noon around the house. There was really very little left to accomplish. Although the house renovations would take at least another month, the yard was now a neat showplace of shrubs that Joelle had relentlessly tamed and a few beds of perennials that she had been able to rescue. Even her mother's vegetable garden was ready for planting. Hidden among the waist-high weeds and accumulated debris, Joelle had discovered rhubarb and asparagus. There were even a few raspberry plants that she had trimmed with the hope that they would produce again.

At noon she washed in the springhouse and changed into dark gold pants and a multihued cotton sweater. With nothing but her guitar to keep her company she set off for the picnic.

The beach where the picnic was to be held was half a mile from the entrance to Pennington Alloy #2. Officially the land still belonged to the company, but after years of disuse the community had reclaimed it. According to Mr. Kincaid, one night the fence obscuring the entrance to the beach had mysteriously disappeared. Now children swam in the river enjoying the cool water just as they had done when Joelle was a child.

The rocky beach had always been a favorite summertime meeting place. Today it was crowded. In fact Joelle was astonished by the number of people present. She had expected a handful. Instead she was confronted with dozens of cars parked up and down the road. Walking down the slope to the beach, she realized that there were fully seventy-five people on the shore and more were coming behind her.

A table had been set up to collect admission to the picnic. When Joelle appeared to pay her fair share, she was greeted with hugs and slaps on the back by everyone she came in contact with. If she had worried that her celebrity status would affect people strangely, she was put instantly at ease. Everyone knew that she was famous, but to all of them, both old and new citizens of

Russell Creek, Joelle was a local girl who'd made good. First and foremost she was one of them.

Several families invited her to sit with them, but Joelle chose to join Mr. Kincaid on a tattered wool blanket at the water's edge. The ladies auxiliary of the Presbyterian church had cooked enormous amounts of food, and Joelle bought a plate piled high with kielbasa sausage and sauerkraut and settled herself comfortably to watch the commotion around her. Two volleyball nets had been set up at opposite sides of the beach. By the slope leading up to the road, someone had organized an impromptu tug-of-war. Clusters of children waded in water still much too cold to swim in, and adults mixed and socialized, their daily cares forgotten.

For a moment Joelle pretended that she had never left Russell Creek and that some of the children on the shore belonged to her. It was a fantasy she rarely allowed herself. She would never sacrifice children to the demands of her career no matter how much she longed for them.

"This is like something out of another lifetime," Joelle mused out loud.

"Sure is," Mr. Kincaid answered. "Used to do this kind of thing a lot before the mine closed down. Folks was real friendly. Does my heart good to see they still can be."

Joelle smiled at the old man who had come to mean so much to her. "Everyone's trying. I wouldn't be surprised if today is a total success."

"I would." Mr. Kincaid pointed up the slope to a group of people coming down to the beach. "Here comes the real test of how friendly folks can be."

Joelle shaded her eyes with her cupped hand and followed Mr. Kincaid's finger. She saw Zach accompanied by Jake, Carol, Dorothy and a man whom she assumed was Carl Trotter. If she had allowed herself the luxury of thinking of Zach at all, she might have realized that he would come today. But she had continued to cancel any thoughts of him as they entered her conscious mind. Instead she had only acknowledged him in her dreams. And spiritual teacher notwithstanding, she had run from him every time he had appeared. Even asleep, she could not face her feelings about him.

"I gather from what you've said before that Zach isn't accepted well in Russell Creek," Joelle said carefully.

"That would be an understatement, girl. He's lucky some folks don't spit at his feet."

Mr. Kincaid's answer sent chills up Joelle's spine. "He doesn't deserve to be treated that way," she said, before she had a chance to think about her words.

"No. He don't. He's a good man. Ain't his fault he's got Pennington blood."

Joelle had no reply. Mr. Kincaid continued. "When he first came, weren't nobody who'd give him the time of day. Now there're folks who're warmin' up to him. The Trotter family, what's left of 'em anyway, thinks he's gonna make a real difference in the economy around here. And there are others who take him for the man he is."

"And the rest of the town?"

"Bad memories."

Joelle watched Zach's friends spread their blanket by the slope away from the water. They were on the edge of the socializing, and Joelle waited to see if anyone would approach them. Sadly she realized that the little group was being left strictly to themselves.

Zach was dressed in crisp blue jeans and a forest-green polo shirt that emphasized his trim build and wide shoulders. He was smiling slightly at something Carol was saying, and even from a distance Joelle could feel his quiet charm. Pulling herself back to reality, she realized that Mr. Kincaid had been speaking to her again. "I'm sorry," she apologized. "What did you say?"

"I said, in one old man's opinion, there's a lot of folks in Russell Creek who could learn somethin' from that young feller."

She wasn't ready to give in completely on the subject of Zach Smith. She might feel sad that he was being ignored, but a part of her was still too angry to defend him. "What exactly is there to learn?" she asked with irony in her voice. "To stay away from places you don't belong?"

"I expect better than that from you, girl." Mr. Kincaid tapped her on the shoulder and reluctantly she faced him squarely. "You ain't Hoyt Lindsey's girl for nuthin', Joelle. Your daddy was a fair man. If he was here, what would he say?"

"But he's not here, is he?"

"I remember once when your daddy was still livin'. We was all down at the Sportsman's Club, doin' what miners do best on Saturday night. There was this feller, a little banty rooster of a guy, that was always hangin' around your daddy. Nobody else could stand him, but your daddy never said a mean word to anyone unless they had it comin'. Anyhow, another guy, Skates Trimbaugh, decided to start pickin' on this little guy. Skates was a big, ugly miner, thought he was the toughest feller in Russell Creek. It weren't your daddy's fight, but the next thing I knew, your daddy was throwin' himself in front of the little banty guy, takin' his licks for him. Got beat pretty bad.''

Joelle couldn't answer.

"Anyhow, I've always thought that Hoyt Lindsey'd of understood why Zach Smith moved to this town to start his business. They're the same kind of men.''

The saddest thing of all, Joelle thought as she felt tears sting her eyes, wasn't that Mr. Kincaid was right. The saddest thing was that she had refused to realize the truth by herself. Caught up in the cycle of distrust that had begun with the mine explosion and had been perpetuated by other events in her life, she had condemned a man who deserved only praise for his actions.

"I don't know what to say,'' she admitted, swallowing the lump in her throat.

"You don't have to say nuthin'.'' Mr Kincaid stood. "I'm gonna get me some more of that good cookin'. Do you want anythin'?''

Joelle just shook her head. When she was alone, she turned to look out at the river. Regret for what she had done and for what she had lost by her own actions filled her body until there didn't seem to be room for any other emotions. Steadfastly for the past three weeks, she had refused to admit that she had been wrong. She had not allowed herself to think of Zach or what she had refused to forgive. Now a few sentences from a comparative stranger had opened the floodgates of her emotions. She was so shaken that she was incapable of trying to set things right. She knew that she could not face Zach. Not yet.

"Joelle?''

Joelle turned to find Carol standing beside her. "Carol," she said, a noticeable catch in her voice. "I'm glad to see you. Will you join me?"

Carol sat beside her and the two women exchanged long looks that were charged with meaning. "I've missed you," Carol said finally. "I've been hoping you'd come and see me."

"I'm sorry," Joelle said, reaching for Carol's hand. "I just couldn't."

"I'm your friend, too. Not just Zach's."

"I know that. I just didn't know what I could say."

Carol squeezed Joelle's hand. "You're used to handling your sorrows alone. It's so much harder that way. That's a trait you and Zach have in common."

"Has he talked about me?"

Carol shook her head. "It's what he hasn't said that's important."

They chatted about inconsequential things. Joelle told Carol about the house renovations and her vegetable garden, and Carol volunteered information about the best times to begin planting. Neither of them said anything else important, but when Carol left to return to Jake and her own group of friends, Joelle was certain that Carol knew exactly what she was feeling.

There was no peace after that. It seemed to Joelle that everyone there wanted to have a few minutes to talk to her. She was bombarded with offers to come for dinner, join the Russell Creek Improvement Society, attend one of the two tiny local churches. The total acceptance she received was nice, but she weighed it against the isolation of Zach and his friends, and she found that she could no longer bask in the warm glow of the townspeople's affection.

It was midafternoon when the Presbyterian ladies packed away what food had not been sold and an announcement about profits from the picnic was made. Combined with other fund raisers that had been held, the Russell Creek Improvement Society had finally reached their goal of two thousand dollars. The town had taken the first real step toward revitalization. No one held out any hopes that Russell Creek would ever be anything other than a tiny town in the middle of nowhere, but those people who had chosen to live there were now committed to making certain that it would be a town that had pride in itself.

When the excited buzz died down, the acting mayor of Russell Creek, an old man Joelle remembered knowing as a child, stood to announce that a special treat was in store for everyone. She listened quietly as he rambled about her accomplishments and her beginnings. He told a story about her childhood that she had forgotten. He confessed that he had heard her play the guitar in a junior high school talent show. She laughed along with everyone else when he said that Vicky Landry, baton twirler *extraordinaire*, had beat Joelle for first place that day.

When she finally stood and walked to the admission table, to perch on the edge of it and tune her guitar, everyone moved their blankets in a circle around her. She looked out on the expectant faces, and for a moment she wasn't certain that she was going to be able to get through the impromptu performance. These people were a part of her in a way that no one else would ever be. They were her beginnings, her roots. Silently she blessed them all.

She began with a song that she had recorded years before. It was one of a kind in her repertoire, a musical homage to family and love and home. She had written it when her baby sister, Rae, had turned eighteen; it had been a unique birthday gift. From there she performed selections of her hits, only stopping to retune her guitar and tell anecdotes about the songs. After a half-dozen selections, she volunteered to take requests.

The sun had gone beneath the cloud and there was a cool breeze blowing from the river. No one had moved except an occasional fretful child. There was a golden glow to the afternoon, a strong sense of peace and satisfaction that surrounded them all. Caught up in it, Joelle had temporarily put her feelings about Zach in storage. She knew that he was sitting on the edge of the crowd, along with his friends, and she had studiously avoided looking in his direction as she sang. She was uncertain how she was going to resolve her conflict with him, but the peace of the afternoon had woven itself into her soul and she knew that before the day ended, she would find a way to tell him that she was sorry.

She sang for another half hour, taking requests for songs that she had recorded and songs that were local favorites from the West Virginia hills. If she had given it any thought, she would have realized that by taking requests at all she was tempting fate.

Fate appeared finally, in the form of a man in his late forties who had obviously spent most of the afternoon drinking himself into an alcoholic stupor. Weaving perceptibly as he stood to deliver his request, the man's voice was slurred but plain enough to be heard by all. "'The Voice of Corruption,'" he said. "It's Memorial Day. What could be more fittin'?"

Joelle heard the low buzz through the crowd, saw the heads that nodded in positive response to his words. It had really been a miracle that no one had suggested the song before. Silently she cursed herself for allowing this to happen. Slowly the buzz died down and every pair of eyes on the beach was trained on her. She found herself searching for the one pair of eyes that she had so carefully avoided.

She found Zach. He was watching her, his expression veiled. He fully expected her to comply with the request. She had given him no reason to believe otherwise. And yet he sat there, his back straight, waiting for her to hurt him again. Not because he liked pain, but because he was a man who had the courage of his own convictions.

Joelle realized that she had been silent for too long. She broke Zach's gaze knowing that if she continued to look at him, she would not be calm enough to make her statement. Taking a deep breath, she stood.

"It's a funny thing about that song," she said in a voice that was clear and sharp enough to reach the edges of the crowd. "I wrote it when I was very young and badly hurt. I'm neither now. Maybe I said something that needed to be said, and maybe I didn't, but I can tell you this: no one here ever needs to hear that song again. There are better ways for all of us to remember our dead."

She tried to smile. "When I was a little girl and my daddy would get mad and whip one of us, we'd tiptoe around the house and wait for him to get over being angry. When he was calm again, he'd let us know it in a very special way. Daddy couldn't sing, but he could sure whistle. We knew it was safe to come out when he started whistling 'Amazing Grace.' To this day when I hear that song I feel like my daddy has forgiven somebody for something. Will you stand and sing it with me now?"

The crowd was buzzing again, and for a moment Joelle thought she was going to be the only person there singing the song. Then slowly, in groups of twos and threes, people began to stand as she strummed the introduction.

Amazing grace, how sweet the sound,
That saved a wretch like me.
I once was lost, but now am found,
'Twas blind but now I see.

Joelle listened to the voices swell. She watched some people shake their heads in disgust and gather their blankets to leave the beach, but the vast majority of her audience was standing to sing the familiar lyrics. She almost made it to the end of the song without crying, but as they repeated the first verse again, she felt tears run down her cheeks as she sang.

I once was lost, but now am found,
'Twas blind but now I see.

Afterward she accepted congratulations from those who came to thank her for her performance. More than one person thanked her for not singing "Voice of Corruption." More than one person told her that she had said what needed to be said.

When the crowd around her thinned out and people began to pack up, Joelle looked around for Zach. Finally she felt strong enough to tell him that she was sorry. The beach where he had been sitting was empty. Zach and his friends were gone.

JOELLE HAD BEEN LONELY before. There had been times during her weeks at the farm when she had felt that she was the only person left in the universe. But that evening, after sharing her feelings in front of the picnic crowd and soaking up the warmth of the little community, she felt lonelier than she ever had in her life.

There was a man for whom she was lonely, too. With her forgiveness had come the realization that Zach was more to her than a friend with whom she had just had a devastating misunderstanding. She missed their easy rapport and camaraderie. More than that she missed his touch, the sight of his powerful body, the indefinable essence of his masculinity that blended so perfectly with her own femininity.

She wanted to go to him and tell him how sorry she was, but she was frightened. Instinctively she knew that he would understand and forgive her; he was not a man to hold grudges. But what would she say when he told her he understood? There would be nothing left between them, except goodbye. And goodbye was not something she wanted to say again.

The night was pleasantly cool and fragrant with lilac blossoms. One of the workmen had made an oak swing for her. He had hung it the day that the porch had finally been declared safe to spend time on. Although the house was not habitable yet, Joelle was able to sit where she had often sat as a child and listen to the owls hoot in the darkness.

That night she swung for what seemed like hours, breathing the clean air and listening to the night sounds. She was so alert to her environment that she heard the distant crunch of footsteps long before she saw the shadow of a man in the moonlight. Joelle knew who it was.

"Zach? I'm over here."

He emerged from the shadows, his face illuminated by the glow of the kerosene lantern that she had set on the porch beside her to chase away her loneliness. He climbed the steps to stand in front of her.

She motioned for him to sit down, steadying the swing with her feet as he joined her. Then slowly, because she had to do something, she began to swing again.

"I wanted to come to you," she said finally. "I didn't know what to say."

"Coming would have been enough."

Joelle could hear the distance in Zach's voice. He had sought her out, but he was still keeping a part of himself remote.

"I was afraid," she admitted.

Zach was silent.

"I was afraid you wouldn't want to see me after the way I treated you." She turned and focused on his profile in the soft yellow light. "Can you understand that?"

He shook his head. "No matter what else has been true about our relationship, it should have been obvious to you right from the beginning that I was willing to put myself through a lot to be close to you. Frustration, rejection, pain..."

"I don't blame you for being angry."

"Disappointed is a better word."

"May I tell you I'm sorry?" She leaned forward just a little to watch his face as they rocked gently back and forth. "Will you forgive me?"

He didn't say anything. Instead he quietly began to hum "Amazing Grace."

Relief washed through her body. "'Twas blind but now I see,'" she sang softly when he finished.

They sat quietly for a few minutes as the swing soothed them. Already Joelle could feel the totality of Zach's presence in her life again. His forgiveness had destroyed the walls they had constructed, setting them both adrift in uncertainty. For a moment she imagined what it would be like if they had never had to face the problems between them. They would be lovers by now. Zach would know her body; she would have experienced the pleasure of his. He would be totally different from the one man she had known. Zach would give and give, taking his pleasure as he gave pleasure to her. Theirs would have been a union of souls.

"We were on the way to somewhere very special, weren't we?" Joelle asked. "Did you feel that, too?"

As he had been so many times before, Zach was surprised by her honesty. Joelle could cut through to the heart of a situation quicker than anyone he had ever known. She never spared herself the pain her honesty cost her. "Yes," he answered, "but all along, I knew what was between us."

"Did you hope it wouldn't matter?"

"Yes. I hoped."

"Star-crossed lovers," she said, her voice huskier than usual.

"Do you want to take on fate?"

Joelle stopped swinging and closed her eyes. After everything she had done, after her own betrayal, Zach still wanted her. Their problems were immense, their differences a wide gulf between them. But he was extending his hand to her telling her that they could challenge their destiny together.

"I'm frightened," she said quietly.

"So am I."

"Hold me."

Zach's arm came around her shoulders and he pulled her against his chest. His other arm encircled her and she was held in a terrifyingly warm embrace. Her loneliness melted into the mists of the night. She had needed solitude. Now she needed this closeness. More than anything, she needed this man.

"I can't make any promises," she whispered against his chest. "It's not ever going to be easy for us."

"I don't know what wind blew you here," Zach said after a long silence. "But I do know I'm tired of fighting." His hand traveled the length of her spine.

"Will you spend the night here with me?"

Not sure he was capable of a spoken answer, Zach sealed his assent with a kiss. In the weeks that he had not seen her, he had sometimes allowed himself the pain-pleasure of remembering what it was like to cover her lips with his own. Now he understood what a feeble alternative to reality memory was. He had forgotten how he could feel her kisses in every cell of his body, how he could absorb her being and allow himself to be absorbed. If he had thought that he could enter this relationship, keeping a part of himself safe and inviolate, he now knew that he had been lying to himself.

"Are you sure?" he asked when he could find the words. "I want it to be completely right between us."

"I'll just settle for right," she said, and Zach could see her slight smile in the flickering shadows. "I won't be selfish and demand 'completely.'"

Zach smiled, too, his eyes roaming the promising curves under her pants and sweater. "I think I can guarantee at least that much."

He stood and opened his arms, and Joelle stepped into them. For a moment they clung together, friends about to embark on a new journey. Then Joelle raised her head, stretching to place her mouth on his. They were no longer friends, not quite lovers. They existed in a void between two poles, a gray world of fear and anticipation. She tunneled her fingers through his soft beard, kissing him again, and this time the kiss caught fire.

"Tonight nothing else matters but us," Joelle whispered as arms entwined, they walked up the path to the springhouse.

"Tonight, nothing else will intrude," Zach promised, pulling her closer. "Tonight will be ours."

"Tomorrow, we'll talk."

"Tomorrow will be soon enough," Zach said quietly, willing himself to believe it.

CHAPTER EIGHT

JOELLE SET THE KEROSENE LANTERN on the floor, turning the wick low so that the upstairs of the spring-house was bathed in suffused light. Shadows flickered across the barn-board walls, projecting opaque carica-tures, and from the window, moonlight joined the man-made glow spilling liquid silver on the simple furnish-ings.

When she straightened she faced Zach, who was still standing just inside the doorway. His face was in shadow, outlined only by the softness of his beard and the thick wavy hair around his face. Having invited him, Joelle's courage faltered. Suddenly she felt her resolve softening, and she doubted she could continue to stand unaided. Leaning against the wall with her eyes fas-tened on the top button of his shirt, she waited for him to make the first move.

Zach closed the door, turning to snap the lock in place before he came to stand next to her. Joelle's hes-itancy was a physical barrier between them, so solid, so real, that if he reached out to touch her, he was certain that his hand would not pass through the wall she had erected. "Are you having second thoughts?" he asked, forcing himself to speak calmly. He sensed that she needed his patience, but his own need for her threat-ened to overwhelm him.

"No."

"Would you like to go to my house?"

"No."

Zach waited, hating the intrusion on the intimacy they had felt walking up the path together. "Would you like me to kiss you?" he asked finally, hoping to force a decision.

Joelle lifted her eyes, and the beginning of a smile was etched around her mouth. "I think that's how it begins."

"So I've heard," he said with a relieved rumble of laughter in his voice. Zach cupped her face in his hands and bent to take her mouth with his. She smelled of the outdoors, pine scented with a heady mixed bouquet of fresh country air and the newness of spring. Zach savored her taste, the feel of her smooth, freckled skin. He wanted to know all of her at once, experience completely the essence of Joelle Lindsey. Just the feel of her body so close to his, sent wildfire racing through his nervous system.

Pressing her against the wall, Zach began tracing the contours of her lips with his tongue. Joelle stood perfectly still, eyes shut and breathing disturbed, but she didn't open for him. With gentle persuasion he coaxed her with his tongue and with tiny bites and whisper-soft kisses, but still she stood, a wildflower refusing to bloom, a spring refusing to flow.

"I think you're supposed to press your body to mine and kiss me back," Zach said, pushing himself away from her. There was an unmistakable edge to his voice.

Joelle's smile had disappeared, and she lifted her slanted jade eyes to search his face. "I'm already a disappointment and we've barely begun."

Puzzled, Zach waited for an explanation, but she was silent. "Joelle, I can't read your mind," he said finally, shrugging his shoulders in frustration. "Tell me what you want."

"A miracle."

"I have none to offer."

She shook her head. "Not from you, from me."

More puzzled, Zach reached for Joelle's hand. It was cold, and he thought that her fingers were trembling slightly, although she had clamped them together. Leading her to the foam mattress, he sat, pulling her to sit beside him.

"Joelle, just because I've let you know how welcome you'd be in my bed, you don't have to feel obliged to do this." The words came with difficulty. He could feel his frustration build.

"You're being very generous."

Zach dropped her hand. "And you're being very hostile," he snapped.

He attempted to stand, but Joelle's slender fingers on his thigh stopped him. "I'm sorry. I don't feel hostile. I feel..."

Zach didn't touch her. "You feel what."

"Scared." Her voice was husky, and for a moment Zach wasn't sure he had heard her correctly.

"Do I strike you as the kind of man who likes to hurt women?" He shook his head as if to take back the angry words. "I'm sorry, now I'm being hostile."

"Zach, I know you'd never hurt me. I want this to happen. It's just that, as I said, I'm afraid you're going to be disappointed."

Zach was torn between taking Joelle in his arms and trying to sit patiently as they discussed the problem. He compromised by reclining on the narrow mattress, pulling her down firmly to lie beside him. When she was pressed stiffly against him, he began again. "Just tell me how you could ever think that disappointment was in the realm of possibility. I have never found anything about you to be disappointing."

"You've never made love to me."

Zach could feel anger leaping fiercely inside him. Not at Joelle this time, but at the man or men who had made her devalue herself so completely. He understood finally why she didn't like to be touched and why her acceptance of him was such a miracle. "No," he said as evenly as he could, "I haven't been that lucky yet. And when we do make love tonight, I won't be disappointed."

"How can you know that?"

"Because making love isn't a performance. It's something that happens between two people, hopefully two people who care about each other, and it's a giving and a taking. It's not a concert with an audience who's going to be angry if they don't get their money's worth."

Joelle flinched at his directness and tried to pull away, but Zach wouldn't allow it. He turned on his side and his arm drew her closer. "As long as I know that you want me, too, tonight will be good for me."

"I do want you. I just don't want tonight to drive you away."

It was such a clear statement of Joelle's desire to keep him in her life that Zach was overwhelmed with tenderness and, simultaneously, with fear. His anger drained away. He pushed the heavy sun-streaked hair from her cheeks and kissed the eyelids hiding vulnerable green eyes. "Tonight will bind us together," he said, hoping that it would be true.

"Tell me," Joelle asked, turning slightly to rest more fully against him. "How did an engineer become such a romantic?"

"I was born that way, much to the dismay of my family," Zach said, giving her a significant glimpse into his past. "How did a poet-songstress become so frightened of love?"

Her answer was a fully blooming kiss with her body pressed to his and her mouth open for his tongue to explore. Arms circling her torso, Zach brought her to rest along his chest. His hands began to explore beneath her sweater. "I want you to take the lead tonight, Joelle," he said softly, his breath warm against her ear.

Joelle shook her head, as if that much assertiveness was impossible. "Then let me know what you want," he offered as an alternative.

Drawing back just far enough to watch his expression, she shook her head again. "I don't know what I want."

Slowly Zach began to draw her sweater up her back and over her head. "Then, we'll have to learn together."

Joelle's skin was smooth, pliant velvet as he stroked her back, aching with the sensation of her small breasts pressed against his chest. He shifted her for a moment, unbuttoning his shirt so that when she lay on top of him again, the feel of her against his bare skin increased his pleasure a hundredfold. Joelle sighed softly, her warm breath moving over his shoulder in an unconscious caress. With self-control that he was delighted to find he still had, Zach rolled her far enough away so that his hand could begin to caress her breasts.

"We should get under the covers."

Trying hard not to cover herself with her hands, Joelle stood with him, letting her eyelids drop shut as she saw him drinking in the sight of her. "I know I'm too thin," she said sadly, needing to say it before he did.

Her slender body was too thin, but exquisitely formed, perfectly made in its fragile beauty. Zach wanted to throttle the man who had criticized her, and his fists clenched into granite spheres. Instead he forced himself to be calm, willing his hands to relax and each finger to uncurl. When they did, he put them on Joelle's shoulders. "You're beautiful."

"I'm a basket case."

"Yes, you are that." He smiled a little when her eyes opened to see if he was serious.

"And you don't really mind, do you?" she asked, surprised at his acceptance.

"I mind but I still want you."

As if she felt that she had passed an exam, Joelle's hesitation dropped from her like the clothes she discarded. When she stood in front of Zach, completely naked and shining in the golden lamplight, he could only stare. She moved to him for a long ardent kiss before she slid under the blankets and the heavy down sleeping bag.

She lay watching Zach undress, enjoying the sensuous revelation of each part of his body. Already he had made her more comfortable than she ever remembered feeling. His touch was gentle, yet it made demands she was beginning to think she could fulfill. As a lover he would be no different than he had been as a friend: considerate, attentive and warmly appreciative of everything she had to give. Of course, now there was an added dimension. The physical attraction that had blossomed since their first meeting would finally be resolved.

Anticipation glowed in every cell of Joelle's body, beginning to chase away the fears that she would not please him. She had fought against this need for intimacy with Zach Smith. There were still problems between them, problems they might never resolve, but their need for each other was far more potent than the ambiguous future they had before them. Fully conscious of what she was doing, Joelle forced herself to bury her concerns. They would not interfere with their night of love.

Zach was naked, and he joined Joelle underneath the blankets. Finally they were together with nothing between them.

Lying on his side, Zach began to discover the sleek lines of her body, stopping in the places where she liked it the most and where his experience told him he should. Although Joelle had said she couldn't tell him what she wanted, she responded to his movements as if she had been waiting all her life for him to show her the way.

Perhaps she had been. The act of love, which should have been instinctive and spontaneous, had never been that for her. Now she felt her mind disconnect from her body, drifting to a sweet oblivion as she became more and more attuned to the physical needs that had often been confusing and impossible to fulfill.

Zach's body was more than ready for her, had been from the first time he had seen her chopping weeds, but he forced himself to move slowly, taking the time to sensitize her warming flesh to his touch.

Hesitantly Joelle placed the palms of her hands on his chest, and then with cautious movements, she spread her fingers and raked them over the firm, hair-roughened flesh, stopping when inadvertently he groaned with the feelings sweeping through his body. Zach felt her shudder with pleasure at his response, and he turned and pulled her tightly against him to feel the full extent of it. "That's what you do to me, Joelle Lindsey."

She hid her face against his shoulder, letting her soft breasts caress his chest again as her hands moved to explore the long, flexing muscles, the bones and sinew of his torso. Finally she swept her hands over his abdomen to joyfully possess him. Zach shifted restlessly as her long graceful fingers worked a magic that was beyond his experience. Bloodstream singing with the force of his desire, he shivered helplessly as Joelle continued to weave a sensual spell that threatened to destroy his careful control. They moved together for long moments, their initial explorations intensifying to a new level of passion.

Zach was jubilant to see that she was as caught up in their lovemaking as he was. Careful not to uncover either himself or Joelle, he dropped his head, trailing kisses between and around her breasts. His tongue finally settled on the sweet, hard bud of her nipple, and he drew it into his mouth, reveling in the gasp of pleasure she gave.

"This feels so right," he whispered against her breast, taking possession of it again and nipping her lightly with his teeth. Joelle's skin tasted of the outdoors, fresh and clean, like cold, pure spring water that was heating beneath his caresses. Arms wrapped around her back, he lifted her against his mouth, drawing hard on her nipple as she writhed beneath him, her hands tangling spasmodically in his hair.

Joelle moaned his name, her body given into his keeping. Whatever hesitations she had expressed were disappearing under his expert hands. Zach was bringing her extraordinary pleasure, not taking his fill to leave her once again unsatiated and alone. He was giving. Giving pleasure, giving love, bringing life to a body that had only known casual, careless caresses and humiliation.

She wanted to give to him in return, not as a duty, but as a gift. Pleasure was to be returned; love was to be bestowed. "Tell me what you want," Joelle pleaded, unconsciously echoing his words.

"Everything you do gives me pleasure," Zach assured her, his voice coming as a rough endearment.

Joy burst around Joelle like a sunrise, and as she lifted to offer her other breast, Zach's hand found the warm home of her womanhood, his fingertips rotating to bring another gasp of pleasure and a slow sensual dance of her hips. "You're driving me insane," he whispered, completely immersed in the sight and smell and feel of the wraith's body moving beneath his exploring fingers.

When Joelle tried to draw him down to unite them, Zach resisted. "Not yet," he said, his fingers continuing their sensual torment.

"I need you, Zach" she pleaded, unconsciously making the appeal more plain with the slow thrusting of her hips against his hand.

"And I need you," he assured her.

Leaving her breasts, his mouth covered her smooth flat belly with kisses. He could feel the slow undulation of her hips beneath his bearded cheek, and he could sense the collapse of her self-control as he caressed her with his tongue.

"Show me you need me then," she moaned.

"I'm going to show you." Zach parted her thighs and his finger entered her softness, finding that she was warm and wet and waiting. She became almost incoherent with need, moaning his name as he brought her closer to the place she desired.

"Come to me," she pleaded finally, half sitting to pull him toward her. "Please, Zach."

Zach moved from Joelle's side, pushing her gently down as he positioned himself to enter her. For a moment he seemed to be denying himself the pleasure, anticipating their union until he could no longer control his need to have her body surround his. She was suspended in expectancy until, breath held, he thrust himself slowly into her, creating one expanded being where two had been before.

When he was deep inside, he lay quietly for a moment, gathering his self-control as Joelle became used to his body, now such an intimate part of her own. When he withdrew only to reenter a second later, she cried out, arms wrapped around his back, and clung with each movement. Each bit of space between them was too much.

Zach watched her struggle, struggling himself not to end the excrutiatingly pleasurable act before she could find fulfillment. There was nothing else he could do, only continue to thrust himself slowly into velvetized darkness and hope that it was enough.

Let it be enough for her, he unconsciously chanted to himself, afraid that if he failed her, left her alone to follow his own desires, that he would lose her forever.

Joelle gave into her body, flowing smoothly with the intensifying rhythm inside her. She could sense Zach's self-control and she trusted his wish to please her. The unbearable tension and the all-consuming pleasure built until she was sure that she would be torn apart. Just at the moment when Zach was sure that he could not hold back, Joelle cried out and clasped him harder, her body rigid with the force of a stormy release.

Feeling Joelle move beneath him, watching her expressive face as she found pleasure, sent Zach speeding toward his own. Collapsing afterward, his body encased in satisfaction, his legs entwined with hers, he rested on her slender body, and she buried her face in his neck. When he was able, he reluctantly moved away, wrapping his arms around her back to shift her so that they were facing each other. With hands that were still shaking, Zach stroked the damp hair back from her forehead and kissed every part of her lovely silken body that he could reach.

Joelle lay full length against him, her hands caressing his chest. She was bubbling inside, irritating bubbles that were demanding escape, and when she could hold back no longer, she erupted, finally letting herself shake with the laughter that was trapped inside. Zach listened to her laughter, and he smiled. There was a freedom, a spontaneity in the sound that he had never associated with Joelle Lindsey. He listened as the laughter was followed by a deep breath and then another, before he kissed her again.

"Now, was it that bad?" he teased her gently.

Joelle responded by biting down on his beard and tugging hard with her teeth. With a laughing "no fair," Zach resorted to washing her nose and eyelids with his tongue until she let go. Then he held her close again.

"Now, you must really think I'm a basket case," Joelle said, the remnants of the hour's wide range of emotions in her voice.

Zach couldn't tease; he knew that she was embarrassed by the intimacy of the past few minutes. Instead he said carefully, "I think that you're a very emotional woman who has never been able to share herself easily. And I'm very glad that I was here when you finally did."

"So am I," she said, reaching up to run her fingers over his face.

They drifted off to sleep that way, lamp still lit and Joelle's arm across Zach's chest, her fingers resting on his cheek.

The foam mattress with two bodies to weigh it down gave little comfort, and the room became chilled as the night wore on. Still, the lovers slept soundly, legs entwined and heartbeats synchronized.

Hours later, Joelle woke to find Zach sitting up beside her. "Anything wrong?" she murmured, hands pushing her hair behind her ears as she sat up to join him.

"Only that I'm taking up most of the mattress, and with our combined weight, it offers as much support as a sheet of newspaper. I thought maybe I ought to leave so that you could sleep in comfort for the rest of the night."

"I was sleeping in comfort until you sat up." Joelle said with a yawn. "What time is it?"

Zach felt around for his watch. "It's two."

"Don't go."

"Are you sure?" Watching her sleep, the moonlight intensifying her vulnerability, Zach had wondered if she would want solitude when she finally awoke. She had stepped over boundaries that night that were new and frightening. He had not wanted to pressure her.

"Oh, absolutely."

Joelle's voice was so relaxed, so unconsciously sensuous, that Zach smiled. "I guess I was worried for nothing."

"I guess you were." She lay back, starlight and moonbeams caressing the slim hollows of her naked body. Slowly, with graceful feminine appeal, she reached to bring him down on top of her. "Now that we're awake, I can think of something I'd rather do than try to go back to sleep."

This time Joelle set the rhythm, encouraging Zach until once again they were locked together in love. Their climb was a mutual one, fueled by the give and take of lovers who are becoming comfortable with each other. A shimmering eternity later Joelle sat cross-legged beside Zach, contentedly exploring his body with her hands and mouth.

"You're an incredibly sensuous woman," Zach said, his eyes half shut in delight. "You're everything a man could possibly want."

Joelle stopped, as if she was thinking about his words. "One man didn't think so," she said, averting his eyes as she snuggled back under the covers.

Zach was learning to accept the presence of his own angry feelings at the man who had played such cruel games with her ego. "Whoever he was, he's not worth the place you've given him in your life."

"I know that. But by the time I realized it, the damage had been done."

"Do you want to talk about it?"

"That's in bad taste, isn't it? Talking about an old lover to a new one?"

Zach ignored her. "It was Tim Daniels, wasn't it?"

"Does it matter?"

She stiffened and Zach soothed her, rubbing her back as he said: "Not to me. But it evidently matters a great deal to you.

"I'm sorry."

"Don't be. I'm not trying to invade your privacy. I'm just offering a sympathetic ear."

Joelle was quiet, and Zach was beginning to think that she had fallen back asleep, when she finally spoke. "Do you know anything about my beginnings in the music business?"

"A little. Tell me."

She sighed and settled herself more comfortably against him. "I was almost seventeen when I started working in a coffeehouse in Pittsburgh. I had run away from my uncle's house in West Virginia. My mom just couldn't afford to feed us all, and I knew she'd be better off if I left, so I hitchhiked north."

Zach imagined the sixteen-year-old Joelle Lindsey, alone and frightened, and he was frightened for her. "That was dangerous."

"I got one ride all the way to Pittsburgh with a bible salesman and his wife," Joelle said, soothing his unspoken fears. "When I got there, I walked through the streets, looking for a job as a waitress. I was tossed out on my ear every place I went. It started to get dark and I remember that I was terrified I'd have to sleep outside that night."

She shifted and propped her head on her elbow so that she could see him as she talked. "Finally I found this interesting little section of town, Squirrel Hill, and I ventured into a few places there. I was just about to give up and try to hitchhike home, when I saw a poster with a man playing the guitar in front of a hole-in-the-wall coffeehouse. I loved music, in fact I was carrying my guitar with me and I decided to try for a job just one more time."

"And the rest is history?"

"Not quite," Joelle said, stroking the worry lines from his forehead. "The owner was a guy named Artie Kapp, and when he saw me and heard my story, he couldn't say no. He told me that it would be unethical to refuse a miner's daughter who was carrying a beat-up old guitar. He fed me a ham sandwich and told me that he'd pay me to wait on tables and let me sleep in the back until I could afford a room."

"Nice guy."

"Actually, he was. He was a real family man, and he and his wife more or less adopted me. They'd always wanted children but never had been able to have any. I ended up living with them. Their friendship got me through what would have been a rough transition. When I think about what I could have gotten myself into, well..." Joelle's voice trailed off, and Zach tickled the end of her nose with a fingertip.

"So, you became a waitress."

"I was a pathetic little waif, and I think the customers felt sorry for me. Anyway, I made good tips, and I was even able to send money back home to my mother. My life was satisfying, but what I liked best was the music. I'd been singing at home for years, but I'd never heard a lot of the music they sang at the coffeehouse. Every night I heard new songs, and I wanted to learn them all."

"And one night," Zach interrupted, "the scheduled singer couldn't come and you went on for her at the last minute."

"No, it wasn't that easy. There was a talent night once a month, and after I'd been there three or four months, one of the other waitresses convinced me to sing. Artie thought it was funny. I was a daughter to him, not a performer. I went ahead anyway, and everybody liked me. The next month I sang again, and finally, after a few more months of that, Artie offered to let me sing in his late-night slot every night. He may have had parental feelings for me, but first and foremost he was a businessman.''

''That was a big step up.''

She laughed softly. ''Yes, but hardly anyone was there at first. I started at twelve on weekdays and one on weekends, after the place had started to clear out anyway. I didn't mind, I was just so tickled to be paid a little for singing.''

''What turned the tide?''

''Well, I developed a following.'' It still amazed Joelle that people had responded so well to her music, and for a moment she was silent.

''And then,'' she continued, ''Artie began to give me top billing twice a week. I was writing my own songs by that time, songs about coal mining and about becoming a woman. Folk music wasn't nearly as popular as it had been, but there were enough people who wanted to listen to make it worth Artie's while.''

Zach already knew the rest of the story, but he also knew that she was taking her time, trying to build up to something, and he prodded her to continue. ''How did you make the leap into the big time?''

''One night I was singing in the late slot, and there was a commotion at the back of the room. It was already pretty crowded, but the waiters brought in extra chairs and packed some new people around a table in the back. I was glad that so many people were there because I had written a song that I was singing that night for the first time.

She stopped. "It was 'Voice of Corruption.'" Joelle watched as Zach acknowledged the statement with a slight nod. "Anyway, I sang it that night. I'd been working on it since I was fourteen. There was a lot I didn't understand. I didn't understand why the room got so silent after I sang the song or why Artie wanted to see me in his office after my set was finished."

Zach hadn't heard this part of the story, and he forced himself to continue to lie there and listen.

"Artie was furious; he threatened to fire me on the spot. He said that he was a tolerant man and songs about society's injustices were all right, but never, never, was it all right to sit in a coffeehouse in Pittsburgh, Pennsylvania, and sing a song that slandered Pennington Alloy. He said I had betrayed him."

It was a measure of the new closeness between them that Joelle thought she could tell him this story, as involved in it as he was. "You must have been devastated," Zach said carefully.

"I was. Completely. I couldn't believe it. I had to keep that job, and Artie's friendship meant everything to me, but I knew that I couldn't stop singing the song, either. Can you understand that?"

Zach nodded again, his eyes shut.

"Artie told me that I was finished for the night and that if I sang 'Voice of Corruption' again, firing me would be his only recourse."

Joelle paused and sighed, reaching to run her finger under Zach's eyes and around the soft outline of his beard. "When I came out of his office, there was a big crowd outside the door. I couldn't move because one man was blocking my way. He introduced himself and said that he was Tim Daniels. I was so shaken, so dazed, that the name meant nothing to me.''

''Certainly you knew who he was.''

''Sure, I knew who Tim Daniels, the singer and composer, was, but I hardly expected to run into him late at night in a Pittsburgh coffeehouse. He told me that he liked my singing and wanted to know if I was going to sing anymore. I told him no, that I might not sing there anymore at all. There was this buzz from the crowd around him. I looked up and they were all looking at us with this collective look of awe.''

''So you figured it out.''

Joelle sighed. ''No, after I answered him, he said, 'Good, then you can come with me.' I was seventeen by then. Artie and Barbara, his wife, were always warning me that our male patrons might not have my best interests at heart. In short, I thought Tim was propositioning me. I asked him where he wanted me to go, and he said 'to California to record that song.'''

Zach tried to picture Joelle, heartsick and defiant, receiving such an offer. He caught her hand and kissed the work-calloused palm. ''Go on.''

''I asked him who he was again, and I'll never forget what he said, it's so typically Tim. He said: 'Come on, sweet thing, my records even sell in mining towns.''' She paused as if she was still remembering. ''Of course, I knew who that Tim Daniels was, I knew every song he'd ever written, but in person he was much smaller than he had seemed in fantasy, and I was in a state of shock. I found out later that it hadn't been an accident that he was there. He was visiting friends in town, and they had convinced him to hear me sing. Knowing Tim as well as I do now, I think he was really there to see if he could add another body to his female-folksinger collection.

"Anyway, I went to California, and I recorded the song, and for the kind of song it was, it became a hit."

Zach knew that so far the story hadn't been too difficult for her to tell, but he suspected that what she had been leading up to would be harder. "You and Tim became involved?"

Joelle stopped, as if to decide whether she should continue. "Zach, I don't think you want to hear about it."

He didn't. Already sensing what was to come, Zach wasn't sure that he could bear hearing the details. Protective instincts even stronger than he had suspected he possessed rushed through him, and he wanted to shield her from the pain of dredging up her past. "I'm not trying to pry, Joelle. Tell me what you want to. You don't owe me any explanations."

"I've never talked to anyone about this." Joelle hesitated again, and just when he was sure that she had decided to leave the past buried inside her, she began. "After I met Tim and went to California, he took over my life. I worshipped the ground he walked on. Anything he told me to do, I did.

"At first—" Joelle paused and took a deep breath "—at first it was like having Hoyt, Jr., in my life again. Tim took care of me. He taught me so much about the business. He critiqued my songs and gave me endless pointers on how to perform more effectively. But when I turned eighteen, things changed. On my birthday he took me home and decided he was going to make me a woman." She paused. "I had been so sheltered, first by my family, then by Artie and Barbara that I was blind to his intentions. I wasn't even sure what was going on until I was in his bed."

Joelle lay back, staring at the ceiling, and Zach lay beside her trying to fight the feelings rising inside him. "The bastard!" he said finally, his voice filled with loathing.

"He can be at times. Tim's domineering and totally lacking in patience. He was both those things that night. Of course, I was very young and terribly naive. In my eyes, everything that went wrong was my fault. Tim was my hero, and I tried for years to make up to him for my inadequacies."

"What inadequacies?" Zach was appalled that she still seemed to think that she was to blame.

"I was very inexperienced, and although some men would have loved that, Tim didn't. I expected too much. I wanted to be as special to Tim as he was to me. I was jealous of other women in his life, although he never pretended I was the only woman he slept with. Everyone around me was casual about sex, about relationships, and I was still operating on the same level I would have if I'd met and married a miner here in Russell Creek."

"Was that so bad?"

Joelle sighed, and her voice almost drifted away to nothing. "I was so far away from anyone I'd ever known, and I was so young. I didn't know what was right or wrong for me. I just started living one day at a time, making one decision at a time."

"And Tim Daniels?"

"Our careers took us in different directions, but when we were in the same place, he'd spend time with me. Tim cultivated the publicity about our relationship; it was good for his image, and it kept the other details of his life private. I knew that he didn't love me the way I'd grown up thinking a man loves a woman, but I hoped that eventually he would.''

"When did you realize the truth?"

Joelle heard the anger in Zach's voice, and for a moment she thought it was directed at her. "I don't know why I'm telling you all of this. You must think I'm an idiot.''

Zach pulled her against him sharply, "God no, I think that Tim Daniels is the idiot.''

Joelle put her face against his shoulder, lifting her head briefly to nuzzle his neck in what he knew was gratitude for his words. Then she continued. "I began to awaken to the truth a little at a time. Finally I confronted Tim with it and told him that I couldn't go on being his occasional mistress.''

"And it ended.''

"There was never anything real between us to end, Zach. When I confronted Tim, he just shrugged and said that was fine because I wasn't worth the time he spent in my bed anyway.''

Zach was so astounded by that final, ultimate cruelty that his hand tightened convulsively on her shoulder. "There's no word vicious enough for a man like that,'' he ground out.

Joelle covered his hand, and he relaxed it, realizing that he had hurt her. "He's not as black and white as I've made him sound,'' Joelle continued. "Tim hurt me badly, but he didn't set out to be cruel. He's careless. He lives for himself and his causes. There's nothing left over for anyone else. I was too young and immature to understand that.''

Zach understood her need to defend the man who had been so crucial in her life, but he only shook his head. "He took your innocence and gave you nothing in return."

"Tim gave me my career. Out of it, he got a lot of good publicity, it's true, but in his own way, he believed in me. He may have a character flaw, but he's not the villain he sounds like. I've had to come to terms with how much I let him get away with."

"You were a child!"

"At first, but I was twenty-four before I told Tim to hit the road."

Zach thought about her statement. Six years had passed since she had stopped her involvement with Tim Daniels. Yet the magazines and tabloids still pictured them together. "I've seen articles about the two of you since then," he said finally.

"Zach, who wants to hear that Cinderella and Prince Charming have gone their separate ways? Certainly not my fans. I don't actively encourage the publicity, but I don't discourage it, either."

"There's another reason isn't there?"

Zach could feel her nod against his shoulder. Finally she said: "Yes. It's kept men away from me. And for a long time after my experiences with Tim, I was sure I'd never want another man."

Zach drew in his breath softly. He had realized that tonight had been important for her, but he had not understood how important until that moment. "I don't know what to say," he said truthfully. "I'm glad I was here when you were ready to risk yourself again."

Joelle thought about how typical of Zach the comment was. He was glad that he was there when she had finally been ready for a relationship. He didn't see that *he* was the reason that she *was* ready. She challenged him.

"Now are you saying, Zach Smith, that on such and such a day, at such and such a minute, I became ready for a man, and you just happened to be the first one who came in sight?"

Zach laughed and pulled his arm out from under her, to lean over and place his mouth on hers. "That had better not be true," he said, beginning to draw away.

Joelle pulled him down once again and kissed him back. "I never felt less ready in my life than I did when I saw you standing there watching me chop weeds."

"Why? What brought you here?"

She shook her head, her hair spreading out like a gold-streaked fan on the pillow they shared. "Another story, for another time. I've talked your ear off." Joelle stroked his beard for a moment, searching his eyes in the dim light of the kerosene lantern. "Have I bored you?"

"You could never bore me."

"I'm going to have trouble getting used to that."

"Yes, I think you are." Zach sat up and blew out the tiny flame in the lantern. "It's time to go to sleep again."

Joelle moved her body close against him, and soon he could hear the even sound of her breathing. But sleep would not come so quickly for Zach. Joelle had shared so much of herself that night. There had been myriad feelings trapped by her image and her abortive relationship with Tim Daniels. She was hungry for the simple joys of relating, and she had taken giant strides tonight to begin healing the loneliness and self-distrust that had lived so long within her.

Zach lay awake, listening to the whisper of her breathing, and he was torn between joy and fear. Joy because the woman he loved had trusted him with her story and her body; fear because of the problems that still existed between them.

Joelle Lindsey and Zach Smith could be lovers and friends, but it remained to be seen if Jo Lynd and Zacharias Pennington-Smith would ever be able to bridge the gap separating them.

CHAPTER NINE

SUNLIGHT DAPPLED THE WOODEN FLOOR of the spring-house in the early morning when Joelle, curled comfortably on her side, opened her eyes. Stretching a hand over her head, she yawned, extending her long limbs to the other side of the bed only to contact warm, human flesh.

She had forgotten. Carefully she withdrew, turning as silently as she could to watch the man sleeping next to her. A dancing sun ray highlighted his face, warming the tanned skin and the strong, even features. His hair was rumpled, one lock curling across his forehead, and the face behind the attractive bronzed beard was peaceful. Joelle was filled with satisfaction. Waking next to Zach Smith, the man to whom she had given herself so fully, she was suddenly certain that she would never grow tired of this intimacy. And she was equally sure that she would never grow tired of him.

She wanted to stroke the chestnut hair away from his forehead and push her body into the circle of his arms. Instead she lay there watching Zach sleep and thought of the contrast between him and Tim Daniels. In all the years that she had been Tim's plaything, she had never awakened next to him in the morning. Tim was always gone by the time she got up, always off on a new mission or a new adventure. There had never been time for sharing, for comforting each other.

"Are you always an early riser?"

Joelle smiled at the question, giving in to the impulse to stroke Zach's hair. "How did you know I was awake? You haven't even opened your eyes."

"Your breathing changed; it woke me up."

"Talk about a light sleeper!"

Zach reached for her, bringing her body closer to his as his eyes slowly opened. "I'm not usually, but I seem to be especially sensitive to anything about you."

The morning air was chilly and Joelle realized that outside Zach's arms she had been cold but too happy to notice. "I was just watching you sleep. Did you know that you look like a man who is thoroughly pleased with himself?"

"I'm certainly pleased. But it's you I'm pleased with." And he was. Pleased that Joelle wasn't retreating from him or the intimacy they had established. Pleased that she was responding to his nearness and his touch as though the barriers between them were completely destroyed.

"I like waking up with you next to me," she admitted.

"And why is that?"

Joelle thought for a second, her brows furrowed in concentration. "Because you scare away the mice," she said in mock seriousness. "I didn't hear any scurrying last night at all."

With a whoop of laughter, Zach scooped her up, depositing her slender body in a sleepy heap on top of him and held her securely in place. "Perhaps you'd better think of another reason, too."

"What happens if I can't?"

"Any number of things too horrible to mention."

"Like this?" Slanting her mouth against his, she gave him the first kiss of the morning, their warm breaths mingling in the cool air, their hearts beating only inches apart.

"Exactly."

"I like waking next to you, because…because it's so right," she said for lack of a word more perfect. "It just seemed that you should be lying there." She slid back down beside him, when she felt his arms loosening, and she waited for reassurance that he felt the same way.

"I know. Last night when I made love with you, it was so new and yet I felt like I'd always been making love to you, as if you'd always been my lover."

"Is that because you've heard my recordings and knew about me from publicity about my career?"

Zach recognized the uneasiness in the question, and he rushed to abolish her fears. "I made love to Joelle Lindsey, not to Jo Lynd. I'm in love with you, Joelle, not your image."

They lay apart, their bodies not quite touching. The word "love" seemed to hover above their heads. Joelle instinctively shut her eyes, flinging one arm across them. "Zach," she said in a low voice, "you really don't have to tell me you love me. I'm not an inexperienced coal miner's daughter anymore; I grew up years ago. I accept the fact that men and women can be lovers and not love each other."

All her insecurities, all her regrets about the past and the problems between the two of them resounded through the words. Zach knew that they had been spoken to keep her safe and to keep him from leaving her.

He shifted to his side, winding a silky strand of Joelle's hair around his finger and tugging gently. "Joelle, I've never told a woman I love her before. There have been other women in my life, but I've never felt like singing at the beauty of waking next to one of them. I've been waiting for you.''

Jade eyes opened cautiously, her charcoal lashes vivid against her freckled skin. ''Please don't say that if you don't mean it.''

''I mean it.''

There was a past pain reflected in her eyes as she said. ''I hear you, but I'm having trouble believing you.''

''I understand that.''

''I'm not sure where I'm headed, what I'll do with my life. I'm not sure I can stay with you, Zach.''

''I understand that, too.''

Her long fingers reached up to stroke the softness of his beard. ''And you're not making any demands on me?''

''I have no right to ask anything of you.''

''Doesn't love give you that right?''

He bent to kiss her, their closeness hiding the sadness of his expression. ''Let's not talk about rights, Joelle.''

''But you haven't asked me for anything.''

Zach stroked her cheeks with his thumbs, searching the austerely beautiful face for more signs of the damage that Tim Daniels had done to her. ''Give me only what you want to. That will be enough for now.''

The tension around her eyes and mouth melted into one of her rare, breathtaking smiles. ''Then right now I have something to give you.''

''Could I be that lucky?''

''I was talking about breakfast.'' She tossed her head against the pillow and reluctantly Zach let her go, sitting up to swing his feet to the floor.

"You're going to cook pancakes and squirrel dumplings on the hibachi."

Joelle sat up, too, pulling the sleeping bag to cover her nakedness before she realized the futility of her latent modesty. Shyly she let the bag slip down as she reached for her scattered clothing. "I usually have crackers with peanut butter and apples for breakfast."

Zach made the face of a child who has been told that his mother is serving liver and onions for supper. "How about a western omelet with bacon and hash-browned potatoes on the side? How about a glass of freshly squeezed orange juice followed by a steaming cup of coffee with real cream?"

"Breakfast at your place, in other words."

Zach smiled. "My treat."

Joelle slipped her sweater over her head. "I know how busy your days are. You don't have to feel obliged to feed me."

"I don't feel obliged to do anything as far as you're concerned." He stopped and thought about his words. "That's not quite true," he amended. "We still have to talk about some of the things that are between us."

"Not on an empty stomach." Joelle slipped on the rest of her clothes and stood. "Feed me first and then talk to me over breakfast." She frowned at the serious expression on Zach's face. "Come on, Smith. What you need is to participate in my special morning ritual." She jumped up, energy surging through her slender body. She was suffused with joy over Zach's declaration of his feelings for her. She needed time to assimilate their closeness before they spoiled it with words. Everything was proceeding too quickly.

Zach stood and she watched him dress. His body was so beautiful, such a perfect contrast to her own. As she watched, Zach looked up and smiled as he zipped his pants. "Tell me about the ritual."

"I'd rather show you. Words just can't describe it." She took his hand and pulled him to the door. "Don't bother buttoning your shirt, though. You're just going to take it off in a minute."

"Why do I think I'm going to regret this?"

On the first floor of the springhouse the spring bubbled merrily through the stone trough. Hanging neatly on hooks were freshly washed towels and beneath them, on a makeshift shelf, was soap. "I told you I washed every day," Joelle said. "Tell me, in all those years of wandering the country, did you ever have a chance to take a bath in an authentic, primitive springhouse?"

Zach was smiling at the mischievous expression on her face. He knew he was glimpsing what she had looked like at age thirteen. "Never, and I don't intend to start now."

She ignored him. "There are several ways to do it. Everyone of them increases your blood flow and purifies your system. Why, if I could bottle the way you're going to feel in just a minute, I'd sell it and become a rich woman."

"You are a rich woman."

Joelle shrugged. "Details." She put her pinky in the water as if to test it for the proper temperature. "Ah. Perfect. Come see."

Zach stood steadfastly by the door. "At my house, there's a nice, warm shower waiting for me, for you, too, if you want one."

Joelle moved closer to the trough and wrinkled her forehead. "Now that's funny."

Zach was suspicious. "What's funny?"

"I've never seen that before." Joelle looked genuinely puzzled.

"What?"

She ignored him, seemingly absorbed in studying the bottom of the trough. With a sigh, he came to stand beside her, peering into the trough, too. "What do you see?"

"Your reflection!" With her hand cupped, Joelle splashed icy water on his face. When Zach opened his eyes and narrowed them to retaliate, she knew that he had declared war. "I couldn't help it," she apologized, backing slowly away as she tried hard not to laugh. "You were just so serious this morning. I thought you needed livening up." She watched as tiny drops of water trickled down his beard. "Zach, don't you dare!"

In a second she was dripping as Zach picked her up, turned her to face the trough and dunked her head in the flowing spring. She came up shrieking, trying unsuccessfully to pound him with her fists. In a second she went under again. This time she came back up with handfuls of water that she released on his head. He dropped her unceremoniously on the ground, and they splashed and dumped water on each other until they were both drenched from head to foot.

"Don't you feel wonderful?" she shouted between helpless giggles.

Zach's answer was a kiss. He pulled her dripping body close, forcing her back against the trough and took her mouth with his. Gone was the gentle man who had been so patient, so totally giving the night before. He ran his hands over her wet sweater, now molded to the slender lines of her body, snaking his hands beneath it to inch it up over her breasts. "Lift your arms."

Joelle did as she was told, caught up in the passion that had started as a silly child's game. In a moment she was shivering against him, slipping off his shirt with trembling fingers. He was cold, too, but their bodies together made warmth. "Are we going to take a bath together?"

"Afterward." Zach squatted on the floor, unzipping her pants and pulling them over her hips. In a moment she was naked with his face against her abdomen. He teased her with the softness of his beard brushing her sensitized flesh and with the feel of his lips. She tangled her hands in his wavy hair, leaning against the trough and moaning at his caresses.

When he undressed and came to her she had already escaped to another world, a world where touch and sound and smell take precedence, a world that lovers inhabit as they give immeasurable pleasure to each other. He lifted her slightly before he made them one. She leaned against the trough, responding to the rhythm he created inside her. She was dissolving with the magnificence of their union, weeping invisible tears at the beauty of each movement. She heard him say her name, over and over again in a litany. And as she felt her body rise and stretch to the heavens in a final shudder of fulfillment, Joelle heard herself tell Zach that she loved him.

Coming back to earth was easy. They made the trip wrapped tightly in each other's arms, and finally, Joelle whispered, "My legs are trembling."

Zach only held her closer, soothing her with his hands and his lips in her hair. For a moment they had been one. He had felt her flow into him like the bright, clear spring water flowing past them. Joelle had told him that she loved him. He wanted to hang on to that reality, but he couldn't. Real love was a mixture of many things, and one of them was trust. Real trust, if it came at all, would only come by slow inches.

He wanted to stand there holding her forever. Instead he laughed. "What you need," he said, "is a nice cold bath."

This time when they splashed and played in the water, it cooled the lingering heat of their lovemaking, and both of them relished the frigid baptism. Afterward Joelle dried Zach off with the reverence of a priestess worshipping idols in a pagan temple. With a fluffy blue towel she explored and adored every inch of his body and then stood silently as he did the same for her.

"Now that we're dry," Zach pointed out, "we can put on our nice wet clothes again."

"You forget, I live here. I have clothes upstairs that aren't wet." She scampered out the open door, and he heard her footsteps above his head in a moment. He stood looking at the spot where he had last seen her lovely, naked body before he finally bent and began to pull on his own damp clothing.

Joelle returned a few minutes later, dressed in a matching copper-colored blouse and pants. "Weren't you going to feed me?" she asked with a pretend pout. "For some reason, I'm famished."

"Then you'll have to stop distracting me." Zach joined her in the doorway and tucked her hand into the crook of his arm. "I walked over last night. You'll have to hike to my place if you want breakfast."

They walked along the driveway, and Joelle gathered wildflowers for a bouquet for Zach's table. The sun seemed brighter, the farm, one of nature's miracles. Everywhere she looked, something caught her eye. Snatches of a melody filled her head and she realized that she was humming. She didn't have to pretend anymore. She could hum; she could sing; she could talk to Zach about her life. She found herself wanting to tell him about Los Angeles and the doubts and fears that had ripped through her as she had made the decision to get out of the music world for a while. She hummed a little louder. Now there was time to really talk. She could take it slowly. Zach would be there to listen. For the first time in many years, she felt free.

THE DARK BLUE PORSCHE hugged the steep, winding road with the power and precision for which it was famous. The man behind the wheel barely noticed its performance, so intent was he on following the directions he had been given at the battered grocery store in Russell Creek.

His hunch had paid off. Jo had come back to the town where she had been born. It was the sort of sentimental gesture he might have expected from her. No posh island retreat, no chalet at a remote ski resort, only this godforsaken country where the silence and the emptiness ate away at you, leaving you full of questions that had no answers.

Tim Daniels didn't like not having answers. He pulled his hat down farther to shade his eyes from the morning sunlight and then tightened his hands on the steering wheel. If he had his way, in an hour Jo would be sitting beside him speeding back to Pittsburgh and from there relaxing on his jet to Los Angeles.

They hadn't been alone together for even a few hours in years. She had always needed more of him than he was willing to give. He had retaliated by giving her as little as possible. Now he wondered what all those hours traveling together might accomplish. He certainly knew what he wanted to happen.

Out of the corner of his eye Tim caught the Windmill Charger's sign and in the space of several seconds he had slowed to begin looking for his turn. It was an interesting twist of fate, he thought, that the son of Franklin Pennington-Smith now owned the property adjoining Jo's. The grocer had mentioned it as he gave Tim the necessary directions. Tim wondered how the discovery of her neighbor's identity had affected Jo.

He passed a big white farmhouse with various well-kept outbuildings, and then he saw the dirt driveway exactly where the old man had said it would be.

"Well, Jo," he said out loud as the car crept down the driveway with cautiously leashed energy, "let's just hope that a dose of your past has brought you back to your senses. Because I won't be able to stand much of this wilderness. Not even for you."

"IT SOUNDS LIKE SOMEONE'S COMING up the driveway," Joelle murmured against Zach's mouth. They had stopped at a curve to kiss before they came to the open road. Zach moved to the grassy edge and pulled Joelle to stand beside him. In less than a minute a dark blue Porsche appeared around a curve and stopped in front of them. At the wheel, wearing a denim hat with a protruding brim that didn't quite cover his wild mop of curls, Zach recognized Tim Daniels.

Zach had never been a particular fan of the charismatic folksinger with the smooth, mellow voice and the flamboyant, unorthodox life-style. There had always been something too contrived about both his music and his idealism to suit Zach's own tastes. After listening to Joelle's story of her relationship with Tim, Zach felt nothing but anger at this forced encounter. He had wanted her to have time away from the pressures of her life, time when she could believe in herself and her own value as a woman. Tim Daniels could destroy that time.

"Tim is nothing, if not resourceful," Joelle said quietly. "I should have known he'd find me." She turned to Zach, unconsciously gripping his hand a little harder as she heard the car door open, then slam shut. "I'm sorry."

"Well, sweet thing. So you're alive and well."

Joelle translated the tight grasp of Zach's hand as reassurance, although he said nothing. She turned to face Tim. "Yes, I'm fine. Why are you here?"

Tim leaned against the sleek hood of the Porsche, his ankles crossed and his hands folded over his chest. Joelle examined him, knowing that Zach was doing the same. Tim never seemed to change. Joelle knew that he had recently passed his fortieth birthday, but he still had the same arrogant, boyish appeal he had always had. His dark curls hung over his forehead, his eyes, almost black, were snapping with intensity. "Is that any way to greet an old friend, Jo?"

They had been many things to each other, but never friends. She waited stoically for a better answer.

"I was worried about you," he finally said with a half smile. Tim examined her with the same thoroughness she had shown him. The differences he saw were surprising and definitely appealing. She had lost the gaunt, ascetic look that had often made him feel a twinge of guilt when he looked at her. That feeling of responsibility for her had simultaneously angered and confounded him. The most surprising thing about her, however, was the way she held on to the hand of the man standing beside her. Obviously Tim's visit was going to be more challenging than it had first seemed. His smile broadened. He liked challenges.

Joelle continued to wait. She understood that it was going to take some time to find out the real reason behind Tim's appearance. She had known him too long to think she could force him to reveal his motives before he was ready. "I don't suppose you could leave and pretend you never found me," she said finally.

Tim shook his head. Joelle felt Zach's hand tighten around hers. She could feel his anger, and she turned slightly to face him. "I have to talk to him, Zach. I'll take him back to my place."

Zach had stood quietly beside her, watching the flickering expressions cross her face. If he had, for one moment, been jealous of the man leaning against the Porsche, the curious mixture of feelings reflected in Joelle's eyes had cured him. Now he could not leave her at Tim's mercy. "Come to my house," he offered quietly. "I'll fix breakfast for all of us. You can talk in privacy when I go to work."

Tim stood erect and stepped closer. "It doesn't look like Jo's going to introduce us. I'm Tim Daniels." He didn't offer a handshake.

"I know who you are." Zach faced him squarely. He forced himself to control his animosity. "I'm Zach Smith."

Tim shook his head in disbelief. "Russell Creek's a very small town. I stopped at the grocery store to get directions and got the town's history, too." The old grocer had only neglected one part of the story. He had not mentioned that Jo was sleeping with Zach Pennington-Smith. Tim guessed it was a fairly new development.

Joelle interrupted. "You can turn your car around at the end of the driveway. Then turn right on the black-top. Zach's house is the first one you come to." She started to move around the car. "We'll see you there in a few minutes."

"I can give you a ride."

"No, thank you." She continued down the drive-way, still gripping Zach's hand in hers. Behind her, she could hear the rumble of the Porsche's engine.

"Thank you for letting me talk to Tim at your house, Zach."

"I didn't want you to be alone with him."

Joelle thought about his words as they walked. "Over the years I learned to deal with his particular brand of bullying, but it's never been easy. It will be nice to have you nearby."

"Will you think so when he makes a point out of my parentage?"

Joelle didn't answer until they reached Zach's mail-box. The Porsche had passed them with a honk min-utes before. "We're going to miss our chance to have that heart-to-heart talk over breakfast," she said, stop-ping after they'd turned into his driveway. "So let me just say something now. The name you were born with doesn't make any difference to me anymore. It never should have, and it never will again. You're Zach Smith, and I respect you for being that man. Last night couldn't have happened if I didn't."

"And what happens when the part of me that is still Zacharias Pennington-Smith shows itself?"

She wrinkled her forehead. "Then I guess we'd bet-ter hope that the part of me that is still Jo Lynd isn't around to see it."

The silence between them as they walked up the driveway was an uneasy truce.

Tim was sitting on the porch, his feet propped on the railing and his hat pulled down over his eyes. Joelle recognized the posture; it was Tim doing his best to show that he was "just folks."

"Why don't you sit out here with him," Zach suggested, "and I'll get breakfast started." He disappeared into the house, and Joelle took the chair next to Tim's. She waited.

For long moments the only sounds were the birds and distant shouts from the barn. "I remember when you were seventeen," Tim said finally. "Even then you could wait longer to break a silence than anyone I'd ever met. It was one of the things I found so intriguing about you."

Joelle was wary. The words were as close to a compliment as anything Tim had ever said to her. Briefly she wondered what he would have thought if he had heard the flood of feelings and anecdotes she had revealed to Zach the night before. There had been no silences to break. "Why are you here, Tim?"

"That was one of the other things that intrigued me. When you did talk, you always went straight to the point."

"And you never did. Still don't."

"I always like to understand my environment before I explain myself."

"How long do you expect it to take this time? I don't plan to spend my day gaining your confidence."

Tim pushed his feet against the rail and started his chair rocking. His arms were folded across his chest. "Now, that's a part of the new Jo Lynd, isn't it? I remember a time when you didn't mind spending any number of hours with me.''

Joelle sighed. ''Your memory extends further back than mine does then.''

''Your memory is selective. You remember only the bad. I remember it all.''

''See if you can work your way toward the point of this discussion.'' Joelle put her hands behind her head, forcing herself to relax.

''Relentless, aren't you?'' Tim gave a short, unamused laugh. ''First, a few questions. What's your relationship with Pennington-Smith in there?''

Joelle shut her eyes. ''None of your business.''

''Wouldn't the tabloids have a field day if they made the connections I made when the old man at the store was telling me all about Russell Creek?

''It's not the news story of the century, Tim. Don't bother leaking it.''

Tim decided to confirm his suspicions about the nature of her relationship with the man inside cooking their breakfast. ''You're safe there. Why would I want our adoring public to know you're sleeping with another man?''

''Because you have the moral strength of a starving hyena.'' Joelle kept her voice placid and unconcerned. ''If it suited you in any way, you wouldn't hesitate to leak that story or any other.''

Tim stopped rocking. So he had been right. He sidestepped. ''When did you get so self-righteous?''

It was the first thing he had said that morning that penetrated her defenses. Pointing out her faults in a kindly, parental tone was one of his finer tricks. It took Joelle precious seconds to combat the guilt she felt because of the grain of truth in his words. She knew Tim realized that he had scored. He would try again.

"Not self-righteous," she finally countered, "self-confident and aware. Fully aware of what you're trying to do. I just don't understand what your motivation is yet."

"You cut your hair. It's not much of a disguise, you know. And it was so sexy the other way."

Another trick: trying to throw her off balance. "I like it," she said simply.

"It's very sensible looking. Is that what you wanted, Jo? For everyone to think you were being sensible? A real-life, down-to-earth coal miner's daughter?"

"I thought that was the quality you appreciated best about me." The humor inherent in Tim's words temporarily annihilated her caution. She smiled. "I was the token real-life poor person whom you rescued for all the world to see. Now what good would I have done you if my father had been a professor at Harvard?"

He let his eyes flicker over her body. For a moment bad memories were tangible in the air between them. "Perhaps in some other ways you would have done me more good than you did."

Joelle knew that he was playing to win, pulling out all the stops to gain control. At one time his subtle innuendos would have made her cringe. But not anymore, especially not after her night with Zach. She had forgiven herself for her inadequacies years before. Now she finally understood that there were no inadequacies to forgive. Not hers, anyway.

"Do you ever regret the way you use people?" she asked quietly.

Tim's laughter wasn't forced. The ease with which it came was answer enough. "Who used whom? I took you out of a dirty little coffeehouse and made a super-star out of you. What did I get in return?''

''I could make a list. At the top would be 'good pub-licity.' But let's not continue this. I believe most of it has been said before.'' She stood. ''I'm going to see if Zach needs any help. Let me know when you're ready to talk about why you came.'' She was through the door be-fore he could reply.

Tim settled back in the rocker. There would be time to say what he had come to say. For the present he had accomplished enough.

Joelle stood in the hall. ''Zach?''

He was in the kitchen putting finishing touches on their breakfast. Joelle walked to the doorway, thoughts of Tim drifting away as she watched the man she had spent the night with move with masculine grace around his kitchen. ''Can I help?''

Zach looked up and their gaze caught. Are you all right? his eyes asked her, and hers answered, yes, I'm fine. He smiled reassuringly and Joelle felt her own lips turn up at the beauty of their communication.

''Everything is just about ready. Why don't you but-ter the toast,'' he said out loud.

Joelle stood beside him at the counter enjoying their casual camaraderie. She wanted it to continue; she wanted to shut out Tim's presence, but all too soon the three of them were seated in Zach's dining room eating breakfast.

Tim seemed to be enjoying the built-in tensions of the situation. ''Is this part of the new Jo Lynd? Seems to me you never had anything except black coffee in the mornings.''

She wanted to ask him how he knew since he never had stayed around long enough to see what she ate.

Wisely she held her tongue, shrugging casually as she reached for another slice of toast.

Tim turned the conversation to Zach. "Tell me what you do here."

Zach explained succinctly what kind of business he operated. To Joelle's surprise, Tim seemed genuinely interested. He was knowledgeable about energy, and he asked enlightened questions that seemed to surprise Zach, too. This was Tim at his best, she thought, watching the two men together.

No matter what she had finally come to feel about this man who had been her first lover, she could not condemn him totally. As she had told Zach the night before, Tim was not as black and white as he had sounded when she related the story of their relationship. His personal life was a sad shambles, but on a broader level, he was concerned and caring, talented and intelligent. She wondered if he would have matured differently and been capable of more genuine emotion if he hadn't become such an enormous success so early in his life. She understood, from experiencing the pressures of her own career, just how difficult it could be to remain a thoughtful, moral person when you were drowning in a sea of adulation. She had not always succeeded, either.

Some of what she was thinking must have shown in her face because she saw that Tim was looking at her, and for just a moment, his sharp features softened. "Whatever you've been doing here, Jo, I think it's agreed with you. You look good."

"I feel good."

"It shows."

Zach watched them. No one could sit in the same room and miss the palpable tensions between them. No matter how much Joelle denied it to herself, there was still a strong link between her and the man who had been her mentor. Zach analyzed his own feelings. He wasn't jealous. Joelle's feelings for Tim were obviously ambivalent. He wanted none of that for himself.

And yet it was still difficult to feel completely secure. Tim had been there during some of the most important moments of Joelle's life. They had shared enough so that there would always be a bond between them. Zach knew Joelle for the warm, giving woman that she could be. She was very capable of giving second chances. He only hoped that she would not fall prey to Tim Daniels again.

CHAPTER TEN

"I'LL TAKE CARE OF THE DISHES," Joelle told Zach. "I know you have to get to work."

"Will I see you at lunchtime?" They were standing at the kitchen sink after clearing off the dining room table. Tim was back in the rocking chair on the front porch.

"I don't know." She set the plates in the sink and turned so that she and Zach were face-to-face. "That depends on Tim."

"Just be careful."

Joelle was touched by his concern. Standing at the kitchen sink, a most improbable place, she experienced a new wave of desire for the man who could be so supportive and so wonderfully sexy at the same time. Giving in to her impulse, she wove her fingers through his brown waves and stretched to kiss him. "Last night was wonderful," she whispered against his mouth.

"And this morning?" He was playing with her bottom lip, nibbling and sucking until she was sure he planned to drive her crazy.

"Equally wonderful." She broke away reluctantly. "Don't worry about me. I'm fine."

"He can be quite a charmer when he wants."

She heard the warning and further behind it she heard the unvoiced fear that she would be taken in by Tim Daniels again. "You're just going to have to trust me."

Zach put his hands on her shoulders. "I'm sorry. I have no right to act this way, do I?"

Joelle wanted to tell him that he had all the right in the world, but she couldn't say the words. They smacked of commitment and promises. She could make no promises. "You're allowed to be human, Zach. You're such a frightening paragon sometimes, I'm almost glad to see that you worry, too."

Yes, he was worried. More worried than he could begin to express. Instead he smiled. "If you only knew what goes on inside me, you'd wonder how you ever thought I was a paragon." He pulled her close for a quick hug and then released her. "If you're not here at lunchtime, I'm not coming after you. Come to me when you're ready to talk." He turned and in a moment he was gone.

Joelle took her time washing the dishes and straightening the kitchen. When everything was done and she realized that she could no longer avoid Tim, she folded her dish towel and went out to the porch. This time she sat on the steps, back propped against the railing.

"This is quite a place," Tim said conversationally. "I almost feel as though I'm in a time warp. It's so peaceful. Reminds me of some of the farm communes I visited when I bummed around between concerts in the sixties."

"It is peaceful. But Zach's a hardworking businessman. He combines his sixties idealism with eighties ambition. He's one of the few people I've met who can pull it off."

"You think you're in love with the guy, don't you?"

Joelle didn't miss the patronizing edge to his question. "I thought you didn't believe in love?"

Tim was surprised they had come so far, so fast. "I know that you believe in it. You always did. You were such a romantic child."

"And you were always so good at putting me down for it." Her voice betrayed no emotion; it was a simple statement of fact.

"Too good at it." Tim stopped rocking and watched her intently. He wondered if she had any idea what he was feeling at that moment.

Joelle thought she knew every one of Tim's tricks, but his answer spun her into a place she had never been with him. Tim never admitted to being wrong. She wondered if she had misunderstood his meaning. "You always had a real talent for going straight for the jugular. You knew where I was vulnerable."

"I had no patience with your romanticism. I wanted no part of love and daydreams. My energies were consumed elsewhere."

"I grew to understand that finally. But I was a slow learner." Joelle couldn't take her eyes off Tim's face. There was something there that she'd never seen before.

He was sitting forward in his chair now, his eyes snapping with passion, his brow furrowed. "If you were a slow learner, it was because I never told you the rules or admitted my feelings."

"Did you ever feel anything other than a certain possessiveness about my talent?"

He hesitated. Joelle could see that finding the right words was difficult for him. Tim never had trouble discoursing about anything. She watched in fascination as he struggled.

"You were so young. You were trapped in a world you knew nothing about with no one to guide you, except me. In my own way, I tried." He stood and came down the steps to stand across from her. He wanted to reach out to her, but he knew better than to push too fast. "I couldn't give you half of what you needed. I was perpetually angry at myself because of it. And I was angry at you for making me feel the way I did."

Joelle was wary. She understood that they were no longer playing the game that had been the only way they had previously related. For the first time in the history of their relationship, Tim was expressing real emotion. "I'm not sure I want to hear this, now," she said. "I'm all grown up. I don't care anymore."

"I need to say it. Will you let me?" His voice carried his frustration. Even now, Tim couldn't be patient.

Somehow, his impatience lessened the tension for Joelle. He was the same old Tim, not a stranger. She nodded.

"The first time I heard you sing, that night in Pittsburgh, I knew I wanted you. You were so lovely, so talented, so wistful. You were also a kid." "Kid," came out as an accusation and Joelle smiled a little as Tim ran his fingers through his wild curls.

"I couldn't help that," she reminded him.

"And I couldn't seem to help the way I felt. You tortured me. When I was with you, you drove me crazy and all I wanted to do was get away. When I wasn't with you, I'd think about you constantly. It was madness."

"I never knew."

"When you turned eighteen, something snapped inside me. I will always regret the way I treated you after that. You deserved more."

"Yes, I did."

They were both silent for long moments, neither meeting the other's eyes. Joelle was awash with the pain of the betrayal she had felt so many years before and with the realization that Tim had suffered for his behavior, too.

"If you regretted it, Tim, why didn't you just try to treat me better?" she asked, finally breaking the heavy silence. "I worshipped you. I would have forgiven you anything." To her dismay, she heard the slight catch in her voice.

Tim knew he had gained ground, but he was beyond the point of cynically pushing his advantage. For a moment he could only be honest. "You scared me to death. I didn't have room for what you were offering me. You would have slowed me down. And yet I couldn't stay away, either. Dammit, Jo, even if I knew that I was hurting you I couldn't leave you alone. I began to hate myself for it, and that made me angry with you."

"Just once. Just once if you'd given me even a tiny hint that you cared about me as something other than a good publicity gimmick, I would have waited for you. I was that vulnerable." She finally met his eyes. "But at the end, you were a complete bastard. You gave me the courage to send you on your way."

"That's exactly what I was trying to do."

Joelle searched his eyes. No one on earth knew Tim Daniels better than she did. She looked for signs that he was telling her this story as a way to get something from her. She could detect no insincerity. Only self-blame and the beginning of the peace that comes after a confession.

"Tim, do you expect this to make a difference between us? It's been six years since we shared anything at all. My feelings for you died a very painful death. They can't be resurrected."

He took a deep breath and tried to regain his emotional footing. "I don't know what I expect, Jo. I'm forty years old. I have a satisfying career; I have causes I believe in to dedicate myself to. I have women who are more than happy to meet my needs and people to talk to if I want to talk. I've got it all. But there's been something missing since you walked out of my life."

"There can't be anything between us again."

"Because of Zach Pennington-Smith?" Tim shook his head slowly. This he could deal with. "I thought we had an improbable future together, but what kind of future do you have with the son of the man who killed your father and brother?"

"Now we're going to play dirty, right?" Joelle stood to go back into the house. "If you've said what you came to say, perhaps you'll leave now."

Tim grabbed her arm and his fingers held her tightly enough to bruise her flesh. "Jo, just what do you think you're doing? Maybe you've forgiven this man for his parentage, but he is who he is. Forgiving him won't erase that. Come back to California and forget Zach Smith before you suffer because of it."

"Let go of me." She waited until Tim dropped his hand before she spoke. "You lost your right to give me advice years ago."

The words sent a surprising shiver of pain through his lean body. He pushed on. "I have another reason for wanting you to come back."

"Let's have it." They were standing only inches apart. This close Joelle could see the new lines that the years had carved around Tim's eyes.

"I want you to do a concert with me. Equal billing."

In all the years of their tenuous relationship, Joelle and Tim had never shared a concert. Once, at the beginning of her career, he had called her out of the audience and asked her to sing a song with him. She had been well received, but Tim had never asked her to sing with him again. Even then she had understood that the competition was too keen for him.

"Why?" she asked. "We've never performed on the same program before."

"It's a benefit for world hunger. If we do it together, it will be a sellout."

"It will be a sellout without me," she said. "It's been awhile since you've done a big concert. Your fans will go crazy."

"I want to do a recording, live-in-concert. We don't always appeal to the same audience. With both of us on an album, the proceeds will go sky high."

"I'm not sure my recording contract . . ."

"It can be worked out. I checked." He stood quietly and watched the conflicting emotions flicker across her face.

She didn't want to be tempted. It was a neat trap, though. Too neat. Tim was appealing to her social conscience as well as her performer's ego. One concert was such a small price to pay for the huge successes of her professional life. And world hunger—she had known what it was like to be hungry herself. "I'm not ready to leave here yet," she said quietly.

"I can take care of the details for a while. You'd have to be back in L.A. at the end of June to start rehearsals."

She could already feel the crazy rush of L.A. and the music world beginning to buzz around her. Once back in the thick of that life-style there would be no time to meditate or stare at the stars or feel Zach's arms around her. There would barely be enough time to eat or sleep.

"That gives you a month," Tim prodded. "You're committing yourself to one concert. That's all. Just one."

"I'll think about it if you'll tell me one thing."

"What?"

"Did you plan to soften me up with your confession just so that I would agree to this?" She held his gaze.

"No." Tim was angry, and Joelle thought it was probably genuine.

"I don't know whether I can trust you, but I'll think about it. Where can I reach you?"

"I spent last night in Pittsburgh with friends, but I want your answer in person. I'd hoped I could stay at your place tonight."

"You have no idea what you'd be letting yourself in for at my place. And I guess a motel's out of the question. You're too easily recognized." The obvious solution was distasteful, but she could think of no other. "I'll ask Zach if you can stay the night at his house. Just one night, though. I'll give you my answer tomorrow."

"Believe it or not, I'm not so enchanted with the local countryside that I'd want to stay longer." He smiled a little. "Especially if you're coming back to L.A. soon." He moved closer.

"Don't get any ideas, Tim. If I come it's because I want to do the concert."

His smile widened a little. Tim smiling was Tim at his most attractive. Joelle remembered why, once upon a time, she had been so much in love with him. In a way he had been right when he said that she remembered only the bad. It had been easier that way. But there had been good times, and there were parts of Tim that were human and warm. She reminded herself that there were also parts that were not.

"I mean it Tim," she cautioned. "Perhaps we can be friends, but nothing more. I don't even want a hint of publicity suggesting that there's anything between us."

"I don't control the media. But I won't issue statements you don't approve." He stepped closer until there was little room between them. "Tell me you'll do it now, and I'll go. Think of the unpleasantness it will save Pennington-Smith and me." He reached up and casually fingered a lock of her hair to remind her what they had once been to each other. "Two of your lovers under the same roof could be awkward."

"You're no less a bully when you're trying to be charming than when you aren't." She shook her head to dislodge his hand and then stepped down to the ground. "I'll ask Zach if you can stay here tonight. But don't push your luck with him—or with me, either." She started down the path to the barn to seek the comfort of Zach's arms. He was a port in the storm that was Tim Daniels.

Zach was sitting on the sofa in his office, the last building she tried. He was alone, just the way she had hoped he would be. Without contemplating the wisdom of her action, Joelle threw herself into his arms. He barely had time to open them to receive her.

"I'll murder him." Zach's voice was ice-cold with anger. "What did that bastard do to you?"

She was half sitting, half lying on his lap with her head against his chest. She couldn't talk; she had just gone through an emotional wringer. "Just hold me," she managed to say.

He did, with arms as sure and strong as anything she had ever known. Her body curled naturally against his, and she listened to his heart as she gained control of her thoughts. When she could, she moved to sit beside him on the sofa. Just the day before she had put this man totally out of her life. Now she was running to him with her troubles as though they had been long married. It was impossible to miss the significance of her own actions. He was more than a lover, more than a friend.

"Shall I murder him now?" This time, when he spoke, Zach's voice was calmer. Holding her, he had forced himself to control his anger. "No. For once it's not really Tim's fault." She leaned her head on his shoulder, not yet ready to give up the welcome physical contact. "He just threw me a curve."

"Do you want to talk about it?"

She wasn't sure what she could say. "He tried to be honest about his feelings. That alone was enough to disorient me."

Zach didn't have to guess what those feelings were. "He's in love with you, isn't he?"

Joelle's eyelids drifted closed. "He doesn't believe in that word. But I guess Tim loves me as much as he'll ever love anyone."

"I'm not surprised. You're very easy to love."

She wiggled against him until his arm was around her and she was half turned against his chest, her hand stroking the side of his neck in gratitude. "So are you."

Zach understood that her words were reassurance. "And Tim?"

"Tim is not easy to love, although I guess there's a part of me that's never stopped caring about him. But I feel absolved."

"From what?"

"I know now that I wasn't responsible for the failure of my relationship with him." She put her fingers to Zach's lips to stop the flood of protests. "No, you're not a woman. You may never understand. We're programmed to believe that if we don't satisfy a man, it's our fault, no matter how badly we're treated. As a little girl I'd hear stories of miners my daddy knew beating up their women, and somehow, no matter what those men did, someone would point out that the woman was at fault. She didn't keep the house clean enough, or she didn't try to stay attractive for her man, or she tried to be too attractive to someone else's man. You can't grow up like that and not wonder..."

"Is this the same woman who made a tour of the country giving part of the proceeds of her concerts to help shelters for battered women?" Zach stroked her hair, and his soothing touch took the sting out of his words.

"Who better? You've got to understand what can happen to women in order to want to fight for justice."

"And now you understand a little better what happened to you?"

"Yes."

"Where do you go from here?"

Back to Los Angeles? She couldn't think about that yet. But she had to tell Zach about her pending decision because she knew Tim would if she didn't. "Tim wants me to do a concert with him in L.A. It's a benefit for world hunger."

Zach tipped her head back so that he could see her eyes. "What did you tell him?"

"I told him I'd give him my answer tomorrow."

He reminded himself that he had no rights to her. There had been no commitments made. But if that was true, why did he want to shake her for considering Tim's offer? Something of his thoughts must have appeared on his face because Joelle seemed to understand.

"If I go," she said, "it will be because I want to do the concert. Not because I want to be involved with Tim again."

"When would you leave?"

"At the end of June."

Thirty days. Only thirty days that he could count on. Thirty days of love and lovemaking. Zach was beginning to realize that thirty thousand days with Joelle wouldn't be nearly enough. "What will you do with the farm when you go?"

"I haven't made any decisions about anything. I have to have time to think." She trailed her fingers up his neck to stroke his beard, then smoothed them around his eyes. "I hadn't planned on leaving quite so soon."

Zach couldn't find the words to release her. "I hadn't planned on you leaving so soon, either." Without a conscious signal from his brain, he bent the few necessary inches and covered her mouth with his. He struggled to keep the kiss casual, but it hinted at the desperation he felt. Thirty days were nothing when he had waited a lifetime for this.

When they parted, Joelle's eyes were sad. Zach knew that her decision had been made already, even if she was denying it to herself. "Where is Tim staying tonight?" he asked, brushing her hair back from her cheek.

"Can he stay here, Zach? I know it's a terrible imposition."

"Better here than at your place."

She laughed softly. "Can you imagine Tim taking a bath in the springhouse?"

"No, and you'd better not invite him to, either." Zach kissed the tip of her nose. "Will you stay for dinner?"

"I could take him to Taylerton to eat. That way you wouldn't have to put up with him any longer than necessary."

"The two of you would cause a riot. You must know that after your performance at the picnic yesterday, all of southwestern Pennsylvania must be aware that you're here. Soon the news will hit the papers and probably the national press. No more anonymity, Joelle. People will be on the lookout for you. If they see Tim too . . ."

"I wish things were different."

"Since they can't be, stay here for dinner."

"All right." She rose and flashed him a lovely smile. "But I plan to make it up to you if I can just think of something I can do to please you."

"Any more comments like that and I'll need CPR." Zach stood, too, and watched her move gracefully to the door. "Are you going home?"

She nodded.

"By yourself?" He hated himself for asking.

"Yes." She stood in the doorway for a moment, shaking her head. "After last night I'm surprised you'd be worried." She smiled again and blew him a kiss. "I'll see you tonight."

Zach reminded himself that they had thirty days together as he watched her close the door. Perhaps by then he'd be used to the lonely feeling he got whenever she stepped out of his life.

DINNER WAS A SIMPLE CASSEROLE and salad. Zach came back from his office just in time to prepare the meal before Joelle joined them. He had not wanted to spend any more time alone with Tim Daniels than was necessary.

The conversation was pleasant enough and the three of them ate quickly, obviously having no desire to linger over the food. Joelle felt as though she would drop from exhaustion. After her talk with Tim she had gone back to the farm and thrown herself into the renovation project. The roof's constant leaking had rotted much of the house's floor, and the crew had torn it out to replace it with heavy, solid-oak planks. Joelle had spent the afternoon helping. It had been therapeutic, and although she had a suspicion she may have set the project back a day or two, the experience had been worth it to her.

They carried coffee out to the porch, and Joelle told the two men about her day's accomplishments.

"The floor's going to be beautiful," she said. "The crew salvaged it from an old mansion in Taylerton that was being torn down. It's inches thick and lustrous. Better than anything we could buy that was brand new. When it's in, the worst of the work will be over with."

"How does the house look to you?" Zach asked. "Is it beginning to seem like home?"

"Not really." Joelle leaned her head against the back of the rocker and shut her eyes. "They've torn out walls and opened it up. It used to have tiny rooms, but I didn't want to keep it that way. It's basically the same shell, but a different house. The kitchen will be modern now with lots of south-facing windows. If I decide to live there, I'm going to have them build a greenhouse addition." She opened her eyes and smiled at Zach. "You'll have to give me advice."

"If you live here?" Tim's voice was incredulous. "Don't tell me you're thinking about staying here, Jo?"

"I've spent thousands on the house, Tim. It wasn't a sentimental whim."

"What could living here possibly offer you?"

"Peace, freedom, happiness."

He snorted. "That sounds like a hippie chorus from *Hair*. Aren't you being irresponsible?"

"To whom am I responsible?"

"You have an adoring public. You owe them for the success they've given you. Your songs can make a difference in people's lives." Tim was so sure of himself, and Joelle marveled at his unshakable faith in his own infallibility.

"That might have been true once, but not anymore." Joelle stood and walked to the railing, turning to face the two men. "What difference did 'When I Come Home to You' make in anybody's life, Tim? And what was your latest hit? The song sold a million records, but I can't even remember the title. We both sold our souls to the devil, only I realize it and you don't."

"Sainthood does not become you."

She ignored his sarcasm. "I'm not pretending I'm any better than you are or even that either of us has committed any crimes. I let the little decisions slide for years. Bit by bit fame seduced pieces of my soul until I wasn't sure I had one left. Coming back here made me realize that I could still be the person I wanted to be."

"Don't try to tell me that you've been miserable being a superstar. I see what a charge you get when you perform. When the crowds scream themselves hoarse, it does something to you, just like it does to me. You haven't hated being rich and famous." Tim stood and reclined against the railing beside her. For a moment it was as if Zach wasn't even there.

"No, I haven't hated fame. But I've begun to hate the things I've done to stay famous."

"What things?"

"Changing my music, my image."

"You couldn't stay a virginal coal miner's daughter singing protest songs forever. People change. What they want are changes."

She sighed. "Precisely. And what I want has changed. I want to go back to singing songs that mean something to me, songs I write myself. Not protest songs but songs about real life, real feelings. I can't write those songs in L.A., but I can write them here." Joelle looked directly at Zach and smiled.

"What made you leave L.A. in the first place?" Tim was watching the softened expression on Joelle's face. He didn't like it. Now was the time to take the offense.

She drew in a sharp breath and exhaled slowly. She knew immediately that Tim had picked up her tension at his question. "I just realized I needed a change."

"And what made you realize it?" His voice was silky and persuasive.

Tim knew her reason. Joelle hadn't known that he did, and she hadn't understood what he was leading up to. Now it was too late to turn back. She tried anyway. "This is no place to discuss it, Tim."

"On the contrary. This is just the place." He turned to look at Zach. "Has Jo told you what made her leave L.A?"

Zach's expression was neutral. "Joelle owes me no explanations."

"Oh, I think she does this time. Ultimately it concerns you and your family." Tim turned back toward Joelle. "If you haven't talked to him about why you disappeared into the night, what does that say about the kind of relationship you can expect to have?"

Joelle didn't have an opportunity to answer.

"I'm not going to let you bully her," Zach said quietly.

"My relationship with Jo is our business," Tim said, drawing himself up to his full height.

Zach stood and stepped toward him just as Joelle placed herself firmly between the two men. "Stop it," she said. There was a primal tension in the air. Two healthy male animals were prepared to battle for their female. "I don't want to hear any more of this. Zach, will you walk me home?"

She could see Zach force his hands to relax. They were no longer clenched into fists, but his body was still taut with anger. "Please?" she asked again.

He nodded. Joelle slipped her hand in his and began to pull him toward the porch steps. In a minute the darkness had swallowed them. Tim Daniels stood on the porch staring into the night, a faint smile on his lips.

CHAPTER ELEVEN

THERE WAS A FINE, WISPY MIST covering the moonlit landscape. Joelle thought of English moors and old movies about Sherlock Holmes as they walked quietly down the road and turned into her driveway. She also thought about Tim's words, and she wondered if she and Zach would ever be done with secrets.

When they reached the springhouse she dropped Zach's hand and tentatively put her arms around his waist. "Are you angry with me?" she asked.

"No." Zach let his fingers tangle in her hair. Even in the dim light he could read the concern in the jade eyes searching his. "I was just trying to figure out how I'm going to spend the night under the same roof as that arrogant . . ."

She put her hand over his mouth, shaking her head. "I got you into this, I'll get you out of it. It's simple. Stay here with me."

As much as he wanted to stay with her, the thought of leaving Tim Daniels alone in his house was unpleasant enough to make him refuse. "I can't."

"Compromise. Spend part of the night with me and go home later when Tim's already in bed."

"I have a feeling he'll be waiting up." Zach smiled at her wrinkled brow. "But that's a good idea. Only it will be hard to leave you before morning."

"I loved waking up with you today. There was a very special intimacy about it." She rose on tiptoe and sought his mouth. "I could get used to it quickly," she murmured.

"Move in with me." Zach felt her surprise in the sudden rigidity of her body. He covered her mouth and kissed her until she softened against him again. "Until your house is ready to live in, Joelle. Come live with me. We can wake up together every morning."

The idea was more appealing than anything she could imagine. Zach's strong, wonderful body cuddled against hers all night, every night. Waking together, going to sleep together, dreaming together. They would share stories, thoughts, feelings. They could make love whenever they chose; he would be there to kiss and hug and laugh with.

"There must be some disadvantage to it," she mused out loud. "There has to be some reason I should think twice before I say yes."

Zach hadn't expected her immediate acquiescence. There were reasons why living together wasn't a good idea at all. He was surprised that they hadn't yet occurred to her. He smoothed her hair back from her face. "It will make it harder to say goodbye when you leave at the end of the month," he warned, wishing that he didn't have to voice the concern.

"I haven't said I'm going."

"But you are, aren't you?"

Zach had known her answer before she had admitted it to herself. It was like him to be that sensitive to her feelings. "I have to go," she said quietly. "The concert is something I want to do for my career and for myself. It's a chance to put some of the pieces of my life back together."

He couldn't answer. Instead he continued to stroke her hair.

Joelle closed her eyes. "There's another reason why we shouldn't live together. There's still a secret between us."

"That can be taken care of easily."

"Not easily, Zach. I didn't want to hurt you any more than I already have."

"Must you always take responsibility for pain? I should have told you right away who I was. You felt betrayed. I was wrong, too." Zach grasped her hand. "Come with me. I know a place where everything human seems insignificant."

Joelle let him pull her along through the yard of the house and up the path to the hill where he had almost made love to her weeks before. Mist had settled in pockets around them but at the top of the hill, the grass was still dry and they sat together quietly counting stars.

Joelle searched for the right place to start her story. "I'm sorry you had to witness that scene with Tim," she said finally. "But maybe it explained a little of why I had to leave L.A. and come here for a while."

"A little."

"Are you religious, Zach?"

"In my own way."

"My parents were very religious people. My grandfather's folks were snake handlers in West Virginia."

"Is that the cult that picks up poisonous snakes to prove their faith in God?"

Joelle nodded. "I never saw anyone do it, but my parents would talk about it sometimes. A great-uncle of mine was killed by a copperhead during one of their rituals. My parents wanted us to understand about faith, even if they didn't agree with what had happened. It was important to them that their kids have the same values that they did. There was one thing my daddy used to say to me over and over again that's really colored my life."

Zach reached for her hand and covered it with his.

"He'd say, 'Joelle, your soul is your own. No one can take it away from you unless you let them. Now sometimes, people lose their soul all at once, but most of the time they lose it in bits and pieces until it's gone and they don't even know it.'"

"A wise man."

"You would have liked my daddy." She squeezed Zach's hand. "I've never forgotten his words. Maybe you just hang on to things that your parents said when you lose them early like I did. But I've always thought that statement was true, no matter what the reason. Anyhow, for years after Daddy died, I tried to live by his wisdom. I wanted to hang on to my soul. All of it."

"You told Tim tonight that you felt you'd begun to lose bits and pieces of your soul."

"It was seduced right out from under me. It was always the little decisions I let slip right by me. Sometimes I was just too tired to care, sometimes I just shut my eyes to what was going on. I started singing songs I was uncomfortable with, cultivating an image I didn't like. I avoided the usual traps of drugs and casual affairs, but I didn't avoid letting myself get exploited for more fame and money."

Zach thought about her words. Joelle had come from a rigidly traditional background. Because of it, she judged herself more harshly than anyone he knew. Almost as harshly as he judged himself. "Could you be exaggerating your sins?"

Her mouth lifted in a half smile. "Well, I've come to see that they weren't as devastating as I thought they were the night I left L.A. I had just finished a long concert tour. I was totally exhausted. I'd been living on coffee and cold pizza for weeks."

"The glamorous life."

"It has its moments, but long tours aren't glamorous. They're grueling and painful." She stopped, realizing that she was killing time to avoid telling Zach about the party that had brought everything to a head.

He seemed to realize it, too. "What made you decide to leave, Joelle? And what does it have to do with me?"

"I met your father."

Zach was silent. Waiting.

Joelle forced out a long breath. "I was invited to a party the night after I came back from tour. Usually I would have slept for a week, but Tim called and insisted that I go with him. I was too tired to argue, and it was a gala, star-studded affair. I knew the publicity would be good.

"Tim disappeared immediately after we arrived. I didn't care, I'd come to expect that from him, but I needed somebody to hold me up that night. There were several men who kept trying to volunteer for the job. I spent the first part of the evening trying to fight them off.

"The party was the worst of its kind. All glitter and noise and fake laughter. Everywhere I looked people were making fools of themselves. Those who weren't drunk were sniffing coke. The music was too loud, the house was too crowded. It was just more than I could bear.

She paused as she remembered. Then she continued. "I went outside to get away from the bedlam. There were lots of people around the pool but farther away, in the gardens, it was almost deserted. There was only one other person there.''

"Franklin Pennington-Smith."

Joelle nodded. She felt Zach drop her hand. "I didn't know who he was. I'd seen him once on the news when I was a teenager, and after that a few times in the newspaper. But he'd aged considerably. I had no idea it was him.

"He was very polite. A real gentleman. Of course he knew who I was right away. I suspect he had even known that I was invited to the party. All I knew was that he seemed to be the only sane person I'd met that night. We talked for a while. I was impressed with his voice." She gave a small laugh. "Quite an irony after the title of my song, don't you think? But he had a deep, rich voice that I found very calming after all the noise inside. I was finally beginning to relax.

"He told me he was quite a fan of mine, that he'd followed my career for years. I was delighted, not because I needed the ego boost, but because he was such a decent kind of person. I was glad to see I still appealed to people I could actually like. I found myself telling him about my tour. He seemed genuinely interested. Then I asked him what he did for a living.''

"And?"

"He seemed truly surprised by my question. 'You really don't know who I am,' he said. Then I asked him his name.''

Joelle could feel Zach's tension. She hurried on. "He told me who he was. He was watching me to see how I would react." She turned a little so that she could see Zach's face. "You would have to understand my state of mind to know what discovering his identity did to me. It was the final straw. I was face-to-face with the enemy, and I hadn't even realized it. But worst of all, he had assumed that his identity didn't matter to me. No one would have assumed that years ago. But my image had changed so much, there didn't seem to be any question about my reaction. He assumed I'd be sophisticated and blasé."

"Were you?"

She shook her head. "I don't even remember leaving the party, and I don't remember much of what I said to your father. I went home, packed my suitcase and called my manager. The next morning I stopped by my hairstylist on the way to the airport and had her cut my hair so that I wouldn't be so easily recognized. I hopped the first plane to Pittsburgh. A week later I met you."

"The son of Franklin Pennington-Smith. You must have felt surrounded when you finally found out who I was."

"It doesn't matter anymore."

"You're kidding yourself."

"No, I'm not. You see, there was something more than just anger and embarrassment at making such a stupid mistake. I was always sure that the difference between right and wrong, good and evil, was clear-cut and easily detected. Meeting your father that way not only made me question my own image, it made me question all the stereotypes I'd always believed in. Meeting you has done the same thing. I've never met anyone I could respect more than you, Zach."

"There's so much between us, Joelle. We may be foolish to keep fighting the odds."

"We have a month together as Joelle Lindsey and Zach Smith. The other parts of us don't have to intrude at all. We can forget I'm Jo Lynd and you're Zacharias Pennington-Smith. We can just be who we really want to be.'' Joelle put her hand on Zach's shoulder. ''It's what I want most in the world.''

Zach knew she was closing her eyes to reality. He could do no more, himself. He had come to realize that there was very little he wouldn't do for the love of this woman. ''A month,'' he said.

She relaxed visibly, and then they reached for each other at the same moment. The hill, which had always been a special place for Joelle, became a special place for them both.

IT WAS HOURS LATER when Zach opened the front door of his house. The lights were still on downstairs, and he went through the rooms, flicking on switches and straightening up. He found Tim in the kitchen.

The two men eyed each other silently. Finally Zach gave Tim a curt nod. ''Is there anything you need before I go up to bed?''

''I want to talk to you.''

Zach walked to the refrigerator and pulled out a can of beer, holding it up to offer it to Tim. Tim nodded and Zach tossed it to him, taking another for himself. He shut the refrigerator door and leaned against it as he popped the tab. He waited.

''What are your plans for Jo?'' Tim was sitting at the table, tipping back in his chair.

''Joelle makes her own plans.''

''In some ways she's still surprisingly naive. She can be easily led.''

Zach thought of the woman he had come to know so well. She had overcome overwhelming obstacles to gain fame and then turned her back on everything when she realized that she was no longer the person she wanted to be. She had endured solitude that would have driven most people insane, risked a love affair and tried to face up to her past. This was not a woman easily led. He smiled a little as he sipped his beer. "Perhaps that's just one of the many things you don't understand about her, Daniels."

"I've known her since she was seventeen. I understand everything about her."

"No, in your arrogance, you only think you understand." Zach took another sip. "You came here, offered her something that you thought she couldn't resist and expected her to fall groveling at your feet. You got quite a surprise, didn't you?"

"She'll do the concert."

"I wasn't talking about the concert."

Tim lifted an eyebrow. "What were you talking about, then?"

"You offered her yourself. Years ago when she thought she needed you, you wouldn't have given her a broken fingernail. Now when she's found someone else, you're all sentimental and misty eyed. But she wasn't buying any, was she?"

Tim was surprised that Zach knew about his conversation with Joelle, but he didn't show it. "I didn't tell her anything that wasn't true."

"But you underestimated her. She's beyond needing your love. You used a sledgehammer on her ego for years, but she came out of it intact." He took another sip of his beer. "She's quite a woman. Much more than you deserve."

"Let's talk about what she deserves. Does she deserve a man who has to hide in a two-bit mining town because he's so ashamed of who he is?"

"That's up to Joelle to decide, isn't it?" Zach examined the man across from him. He was impressed with Tim's ability to find a person's Achille's heel. The fact that Joelle had survived her relationship with this man was even more miraculous than Zach had imagined before. "I intend to let her make her own choices."

"She's going to come to L.A. to do the concert."

"Yes, I'm sure you're right about that. But one concert is not the point, is it, Daniels? She has a whole lifetime after that." Zach finished his beer and threw the can in the wastebasket. "I fully expect her to spend that lifetime with me."

"Here? You're asking her to give up everything for a lifetime of sleeping in your bed? That's what it is, you know, nothing more or less." Tim waited just long enough for his statement to make an impact before he delivered his final twist of the knife. "She's always been remarkably inhibited. If she's lost some of those inhibitions with you, she's probably so grateful she can't think straight."

Zach understood what it meant to see red. His vision blurred, his hands clenched into fists. He was seldom angry, never furious. Now he wanted to tear Tim Daniels to pieces, slowly and thoroughly. He could feel his body tensing to spring. "Get out of my house, Daniels," he said in a low voice. "Leave a number where she can reach you and get the hell out before I strangle you."

Even Tim could see that he had gone too far. He stood, leaving his half-empty can of beer on the table, and left the room. Minutes later Zach heard the roar of the Porsche. He moved then to see what direction the car was going. It was heading in the direction away from Joelle's, toward the highway to Pittsburgh. Tim had taken him seriously. It was the only good judgment he had shown that night.

JOELLE WALKED UP THE DRIVEWAY to Zach's house and noticed immediately that Tim's car was gone. The front door was unlocked and she stepped inside to look for Zach. He was not downstairs, and on a whim, she climbed the steps, looking for his bedroom.

She found him, asleep in the biggest room at the end of the hall. He looked completely exhausted, as if he had battled mysterious forces all through the night. The bed showed signs of having been through a tornado, covers tangled and half on the floor.

Noiselessly she turned and went back downstairs. She was in the process of flipping her first batch of pancakes when she heard his footsteps. ''I hope you have something to put on these, Smith,'' she said without turning around. ''We always used real maple syrup at home. My father tapped the trees around our house, and my grandmother had mother boil it down in big kettles. I used to think nothing should be that much work. Now I'm not sure.'' She turned to face him to find that he was almost on top of her. ''What are you doing?''

Zach reached around behind her to turn off the heat under her skillet. ''Getting ready to carry you upstairs to make love to you on a real bed.''

''Before breakfast?'' Her voice was an octave higher than usual.

''I guarantee everything will taste that much better.''

IT'S JUST AS WELL we didn't eat first,'' she said much later, lying peacefully in the crook of Zach's arm. ''You never would have made it up the stairs with me if I'd eaten even one pancake."

"Clark Gable made it look so easy in *Gone With the Wind*." Zach buried his face in her hair.

"Vivian Leigh was six inches shorter than I am."

"But not a pound lighter." Zach ran his finger over the slender curves of her hips and waist. "You have gained weight, though. You look healthy, and happy, and . . ."

"Satisfied?" she supplied. "Especially satisfied."

"I was going to say beautiful." He tasted her mouth and the satin-smooth skin of her neck.

"I want to move in today. Am I still invited?"

"Yes. Did you think I'd change my mind?"

"I have eyes. You and Tim had a fight last night. His car is gone." Joelle put her hands around Zach's waist and pulled him down to lie beside her.

"What makes you think we fought?"

She gave a short laugh. "I know Tim. Remember? He tried to provoke you, you took the bait. The only thing I don't know is if you came to blows. Did you?"

"No."

"And after I foisted a most unwelcome guest on you and then left you to fend for yourself, you're still willing to have me move in with you?"

"I'm going to help you pack."

"It will take two minutes."

"Then I'm going to tell your carpenters that they're to take their time finishing your house."

"They'll like that."

"And then, once I've got you where I want you, I'm going to make wild, passionate love to you every day until your brain is a quivering bowl of chocolate pudding."

"I can't wait." She trailed her hands up his back and cupped them behind his neck. "There's only one thing," she whispered seductively, pulling his mouth to hers.

"What's that?"

"Do I get to eat breakfast first? I'm starved."

"Anything your heart desires."

"Anything?"

"Mmm."

"Then perhaps I'd better rethink my priorities."

JOELLE WAS SETTLED at Zach's house by nightfall. Her clothes hung neatly in the closet beside his, her underthings fit neatly in one of the drawers in his dresser. She had hummed all day as she made the transition.

At five o'clock Zach had come up to the house, given her a big welcoming kiss and then headed back to the barn. He and all of his employees were working overtime, trying to get a big order ready to ship. He told her to make herself some supper, that he would be back in a couple of hours.

It was just the excuse Joelle needed to try her hand at cooking something more complicated than pancakes. When Zach returned at seven-thirty, the house was fragrant with the aroma of chicken simmering in broth with spices. He paused in the doorway, the carefree domesticity of the experience pouring warmth through his body. He could hear Joelle rattling around in his kitchen, and for a moment he could not bear to face her. Every thoughtful, spontaneous thing she did put her stamp on his quiet existence. He was sure that she had no idea how much lonelier he would be when she left than he had ever been before.

"Oh good! You're back." Joelle came out of the kitchen her khaki jeans decorated with smudges of flour. "I was just coming down to the barn to see how much longer you'd be. Did everything go all right?" She stood on tiptoe to kiss his cheek, holding her body away from his. "I'll cover you with flour," she explained. "I've got dinner all over me."

Zach pulled her close anyway, and he felt her relax against him. He couldn't seem to find the strength to let her go. "We finally got the order off. I didn't expect to have dinner waiting for me."

"You didn't think I'd let my man starve, did you?" She tried to pull away, but Zach held her tight. "You might starve anyway," she warned. "Now that you're home I need to put the dumplings on."

"Authentic coal miner's fare? Not only do I get dinner, I get dinner with a theme."

"You'd better watch the sarcasm or next you'll get authentic California vegetarian tofu burgers on sprouted barley bread." This time when she stepped back, he let her go. "We can eat in about fifteen minutes."

"That will give me time to take a shower."

"I'll have dinner waiting."

The meal was surprisingly good. "It tastes just like my mother used to make," Joelle said after the first bite. "Cooking must run in my genes."

"Actually, cooking is all over your jeans," Zach commented with a smile. "If you keep this up, I'm going to ask Carol to make you an apron."

"Wouldn't she love that? I'm going to go see her tomorrow and visit for a while. Maybe I could hint." Joelle rested her chin on her hands, which were folded over the steaming bowl of dumplings. "Doesn't this feel strange?"

Zach knew exactly what she was referring to, but he wanted to hear her feelings about it. "What?"

"Sitting here like this. Eating together, talking about what we're going to do tomorrow. I wonder if I'd ever get used to it." She bent her head and her hair swung forward over her cheeks. She pretended to examine the table. "This is more than just a place to stay until my house is ready."

The flashes of Joelle's vulnerability were coming much more often. Zach understood that so much had been locked inside her that now, even with the inherent risks, she was letting him see the real woman underneath the self-confident and aloof exterior. He loved her more for it; he also knew that the bond between them was strengthening. No matter what he had told Tim Daniels, Zach was not sure if that bond would keep them together or only cause them both more pain when they parted. He was vulnerable, too.

"Tell me about your house in Los Angeles." He could tell she was grateful that he was tactfully changing the subject.

"Let's play a guessing game," she challenged, picking up her fork to resume eating. "Tell me what you'd expect."

It was an intriguing invitation. Zach considered her question as he finished his dumplings. "All right," he said finally, sitting back to finish the Chablis she had poured with the meal. "I'll bet you live on a canyon somewhere, out of the city. You have lots of land around your house and it's not landscaped, just very natural with trees and native shrubs. The house is redwood, of course, and very contemporary with glass and views and decks. Your furniture is sleek and functional and expensive and the art on the walls is modern.'' He shut his eyes as if he were a medium in a trance. ''Ah, I see it now, there's one, no, two Picassos and a Dali.''

''Go on.'' Joelle was finished eating, too, and she sat back to enjoy his conjectures.

''You have no animals, but the security people who take care of you use two gigantic German Shepherds who wag their tails whenever they catch sight of you. You have a hot tub outside on one of the decks, and at night when you're alone you step outside and go for a long soak.''

''Why'd you stop?'' Joelle asked after a long silence.

''I'm hopelessly entangled in the image of you alone and naked in a hot tub.''

''Somehow I don't think you're imagining me alone,'' she said dryly.

''Now who's trying to read minds?''

She wanted to touch him. Sitting across the table from him was not good enough. She rose and went to stand behind him, massaging his neck with her fingers. ''Have you finished?''

His answer was a contented groan.

''Shall I tell you how wrong you are?''

He groaned again.

''I live right in the city surrounded by houses that make mine look like a shack. I have about two acres of land and a fence that I couldn't scale if I was standing on your shoulders and you were standing on a stepladder. My house is stucco and designed to, quote, 'breathe, with the landscape,' unquote, whatever that means. The architect was a crazy man.''

''You don't like it?''

"No, I bought it because it's centrally located, in a good neighborhood and easy to forget when I'm on tour. I have a wonderful Japanese gardener—my very favorite person in Los Angeles—who has put in outrageous, exotic plants everywhere I look. My swimming pool resembles a travel ad for Tahiti; I'm afraid that one day I'm going to step out of my hot tub and one of his man-eating vines will finish me off."

"Ah, your hot tub."

"Do you have any idea how much it costs to keep a hot tub hot?" she chided. "Couldn't be done with wind power."

Joelle dug her thumbs into the back of Zach's neck and rotated them slowly. She could feel him melt under the steady pressure.

"Inside my house, everything is painted white. I hired a decorator whom a friend recommended, and when I came back from an overseas tour, my house was permanently suspended in a cloud. White walls, white furniture, white rugs. I even have a picture by some maniac in New York entitled, *White on White on White*. Every time I walk through the front door, I want to spill something just to get some color in the place."

"Why don't you change it? Joelle, what are you trying to do to me?" Zach's last question was a gasp.

"It's just a massage, Smith. Calm down." She laughed softly at the shudder she could feel rippling through his body. "Why didn't I change it? I think its my working-class background. People don't throw away perfectly good furniture and rugs. You don't paint walls unless they're filthy. I'm not home enough to get anything dirty or to use up the furniture. When I finally do smudge something, my housekeeper cleans it up immediately. If I live to be one hundred, everything will still look brand new and completely sterile.''

"Sell it, furniture and all, and move."

"To a canyon?"

"Here." Zach stood and turned, pulling her tightly against him. "There's nothing sterile about this environment. You can support yourself giving massages."

"A massage parlor in Russell Creek? That's certainly one way to rev up the local economy."

"I'll keep you well supplied with business." He tunneled his hands through her sun-streaked hair and covered her mouth with his. Her response was immediate and completely sensual. It was difficult to believe that they hadn't always been lovers. She moved against him like liquid desire, knowing instinctively how to provoke him, how and when to call forth his deepest passions.

"Am I ever going to stop wanting you?" he asked when she was half-undressed and they had found their way to the living room couch.

"I hope not. God, I hope not," she said, her body blending into his like the cool mist blending into a cloudy night.

Zach watched her half-closed eyes as he brought her to the place where now she could so easily go. He watched her go wild beneath him, as finally he sought his own nirvana.

"Am I ever going to stop wanting you?" he whispered.

CHAPTER TWELVE

"THE FLOOR'S IN, Zach." Joelle had spent the day at her house watching the carpenters nail the final boards to cover the sturdy, new floor joists. Now she was telling Zach about the progress that had been made. "The roof's on, the floor's in, they've replaced the porch and torn down walls. They've put up new wallboard and ceilings. It's a house again."

"It's not livable, is it?" Zach asked. Joelle had been living with Zach for two weeks, and even though they teased about her moving back to her own place when it was finished, both of them knew that she wouldn't.

"Definitely not. They still have to sand and seal the floors and paint. Then there's all the trim to take care of. I told them to take their time. It could be quite a while before it's livable."

"Too bad." His lips turned up into a smile framed by his beard. "I'll just have to put up with you, won't I?"

"I guess." Joelle was sitting on the sofa in Zach's office, watching him work. She had come to distract him, and she could see that she was succeeding admirably. "It's almost five-thirty," she chided. "You work too hard."

"I can see it's hopeless to think you'll let that continue."

She pouted playfully. "It's going to be a beautiful night. I want you to take me out."

"Where shall we go?" He listed the choices. "We could drive around the countryside, park and neck. Or we could drive around the countryside, park and neck. Or we could drive..."

"I understand. Stop!" She leaned back and played with a lock of her hair. "I want to go on a real date. Here we are, living together for all the world to see, and you've never taken me anywhere."

"I just offered to. What do you think the local teenagers do on a date?"

"They drive their daddy's cars into Taylerton or Awnsley, they eat fast food, go to a movie."

"Park and neck."

She put her hands on her hips. "Afterward. I give in. We can park and neck afterward. But first you have to take me out and spend at least five dollars on me, or I won't be easy."

Zach closed his account books and stepped around his desk. "You think I'm made of money, woman?" He advanced menacingly. "First its fast food, next you'll be demanding sit-down fare at the diner, after that appetizers and dessert at Enrico's."

"Enrico's?"

"The finest Italian restaurant in Taylerton. Manicotti for $5.98, veal scallopini for $7.50"

"My mouth is watering."

"MacDonald's or nothing."

"We could neck a little first."

"Enrico's is sounding better."

"We could even neck a lot."

"Appetizers and dessert it is." Zach lunged at her, kneeling between her knees. "Why didn't I meet anybody like you when I was a teenager? My seductions were never this satisfying."

"I'll bet you were a heartbreaker. All those Pittsburgh girls just fell at your feet." Her head fell back as Zach's hands began to possess her. Her reaction to him had become more intense with time, not less, as she would have expected. Now he merely had to look as though he planned to touch her for her bones to begin dissolving.

"I didn't live in Pittsburgh as a teenager. I went to a military school in eastern Pennsylvania. There were no girls there to fall at my feet." His mouth found her neck, tormenting her in the places he knew she liked best.

She was surprised by his disclosure, filing it away to ask him about when he finished what he was doing. "I'll have to refantasize where you got all this expertise," she said. "I had you pegged as the Romeo of some plush, private school."

"Are you admitting you have fantasies about me?" he teased, as he pulled her close and then twisted until they were lying face-to-face on the sofa.

"Silly, isn't it, when I have the real man so close." She opened her mouth as they kissed, seeking his tongue. He held her tighter. "Now, that's just a sample of what you'll get, after dinner," she said pertly, taking advantage of his laughter to pull away and stand before he could grab her. "I'm going to get dressed for our first date." She stopped. "What does the well-dressed Russell Creek adolescent wear on a date?"

"Something provocative."

"I'll see what I can do."

Half an hour later she was ready to go. She was wearing the only dress she had brought with her, a simple designer original that emphasized her slender curves more than it had two months before. She decided that she was lucky the weight she had gained had settled in appropriate places. The dress was jade silk with a soft, draped bodice and a trim skirt slit discreetly up one side.

She brushed her hair, regretting for the first time that she had cut it. The practical, attractive style was wonderful most of the time, but there was nothing to do with it on special occasions. She solved the dilemma by wearing large gold earrings and subtle eye makeup. She was finally satisfied with her appearance.

Zach had showered and changed in the bathroom. He was waiting for her downstairs. "Well, what do you think, Smith?"

"I think I should change again, then we should drive to Pittsburgh and have a late dinner at one of the restaurants on Mount Washington overlooking the city."

"Another time. Taylerton will do tonight. Cheap Italian sounds perfect."

"You might as well wear one of your albums around your neck, you know. You look very much like Jo Lynd tonight."

She raised her hand to her head. "I thought my hair was a good disguise."

"It emphasizes your features. You won't fool anyone." Zach continued to drink in the sight of her. "I think you're beautiful when you're up to your knees in mud or up to your elbows in dumplings, but seeing you like this is eye-opening."

"I'm the same old Joelle Lindsey."

"I don't think so." He didn't feel like smiling, but for her sake, he tried. "Are you ready to sign a few autographs?"

"I can't hide forever. If I'm going to spend time here, the locals are going to have to get used to me."

Her answer was unexpected. He couldn't even begin to hope it meant anything important. "Then let's go."

"My car or your truck."

"My car."

She was surprised. "I didn't know you had a car."

"You're going to love it." He took her arm, dismissing thoughts of her other identity. She might look like Jo Lynd, but she was still Joelle Lindsey, the woman he held in his arms every night.

Outside, he guided her to one of the outbuildings she hadn't yet investigated. "My garage," he said, folding back a series of hinged doors. Sitting inside was a thirty-year-old Mercedes that had been lovingly cared for.

"Zach, it's fantastic!" Joelle tentatively stroked the gleaming, pearly-gray exterior. "Wherever did you get it?"

"It was my grandmother's. I used to help her chauffeur polish it when I'd visit her. I learned to drive in this car, made out with my first girl in this very back seat one summer."

"Ah, the expertise!"

He laughed. "When Grandmother died, she left it to me in her will."

"Did you drive this all over the country when you were exploring and working at all those different jobs?"

"No, my brother Isaac kept it for me, along with the furniture I have in the parlor. Isaac understood that eventually I'd want to reclaim part of my heritage."

"He was wise."

"Isaac's a good friend." Zach walked around to the passenger side of the car and opened the door for Joelle. "Shall we go?"

Joelle didn't want to admit it to Zach, but as he expertly pulled the luxurious car out of the old garage and turned it in the driveway, she was stung with guilt. She would never have characterized herself as a selfish person, but now she realized how little she had asked Zach to share of himself. She had told him intimate details of her own life, but she had asked him little about his own past. They had talked about his business, his likes and dislikes, but never about his roots and beginnings.

She understood why. She had not been ready to hear about the Pennington-Smith family. Now she realized that by not asking, she had cut herself off from a large part of Zach. To know the man, Zach Smith, she had to know the boy, Zacharias Pennington-Smith. She started with something simple. "I've been wondering why you and your brothers ended up with such wonderful Old Testament names."

"We were named after some our ancestors who helped settle the three-rivers area around Pittsburgh. It wasn't too much of a trial for me, I was always Zach to my friends and Jeremiah was Jerry to his. Only Isaac couldn't manage a nickname."

"Tell me about Isaac," she said, turning to watch him as the car ate up the miles to Taylerton.

He seemed pleased at the question. "Well, he's my oldest brother. He's forty-two, but looks about thirty. He takes extraordinary care of himself, works out at a gym four times a week, eats whatever food is considered healthy at the moment. Isaac always sleeps exactly eight hours every night. Not a minute more or less."

"Sounds stifling."

"He's not, though. He's funny and warm. Isaac figured out early just exactly what was expected of him, and he did exactly that."

"No more or less." Joelle was getting the idea.

Zach nodded. "Then he did what he wanted with whatever he had left over. He's my father's pride and joy because on the surface Isaac is everything my father wants him to be."

"And your father doesn't see beneath the surface?"

"I'm not sure what my father sees."

"So what does Isaac do?"

"He's a vice-president at Pennington Alloy."

"Oh."

"You asked."

She had asked. Obviously all questions were going to lead back to a subject she wanted to avoid. She could stop now, or she could continue taking risks. She remembered how pleased Zach had looked when she had asked about Isaac. She plunged on.

"What about your other brother?"

"Jeremiah? He's forty. I grew up watching him battle it out with Isaac for favorite son. He's a good man, but he was a rotten kid, eaten up with ambition."

"That's heavy."

Zach smiled. Joelle didn't often lapse into California slang. It always delighted him when she did. "No heavier than any other family, I guess, but there was an empire at stake. When Isaac and Jeremiah realized it was big enough to share, they became friends."

"Too bad J.R. and Bobby didn't realize that about Ewing Oil."

"I don't believe it. You watch *Dallas*."

She blushed and the rose color seemed to connect all her freckles into a unified whole. "I tape it on my video recorder and watch it whenever I get the chance. Then I root for the bad guys like everyone else in America does."

"They're all bad guys."

"How would you know, Smith?"

"I watched it once. It was too evocative of my childhood to watch it again."

"*Dallas* only had two brothers, and look what happened to Bobby," Joelle mused. "The Pennington saga has three. Why weren't you battling it out with Isaac and Jeremiah?"

They were on the outskirts of Taylerton, and Zach was too busy maneuvering the Mercedes through traffic to answer. Finally he pulled up under a flashing red sign showing a chef flipping a pizza. Enrico's. He got out of the car and came around to open the door for Joelle. "I'll ask them to seat us in the corner. The bar's dark. We can wait in there until a table's available."

The bar was like nightfall, and they settled at a small table away from the modest crowd with a bottle of cheap California Burgundy. "Enrico's best," Zach apologized.

"No different than the quality I get at home," Joelle teased. Then she thought about what she had said.

"At home in California? Or at home at my house?" Zach asked softly.

"Your house. I think of it as home already." It was silly to feel shy after all they had shared, but Joelle had trouble meeting Zach's eyes.

"It's more a home now than it's ever been," he said, taking her hands.

"We're good together, aren't we? Good lovers, good friends. I like white meat, you like dark. I like pajama tops, you like bottoms. We both like music . . ."

"You make it, I listen to it."

"See? We both like star-studded evenings and misty Pennsylvania springs."

"Simple people and Russell Creek Cheddar."

"Enrico's," she said, pulling a hand from his to gesture around the room.

"Being quiet together."

"Yes. Perhaps that's the best part of all." Joelle favored Zach with a magnificent smile. "It's been wonderful."

He pulled back a little. "It's not over yet."

"Of course it isn't." She was surprised at Zach's defensive posture. "Anyway, tell me why you let Isaac and Jeremiah fight for something that belongs to you, too."

Zach forced himself to relax. He was pleased that she was picking up the conversational thread of their discussion in the car. He chastised himself for overreacting to the past tense in her statement. "I was the black sheep of the family. Right from the beginning everyone knew I was out of the running."

Joelle refilled their glasses. "Tell me why."

"I was a dreamer."

"That's not the same thing as a black sheep at all."

"It was in my family. At first, no one really cared. My father had two hardheaded sons who were already battling for control. I was quite a bit younger, an accident I think, and it was easiest just to let me do what I wanted. When I approached junior high school age, they took a good look and were shocked at what they saw."

"You're not exaggerating?"

"Afraid not."

"Were you such an awful child?" Joelle stroked Zach's beard for a moment. "A hellion?"

"Not at all. I had a bumpy record at school. I hated memorizing facts and refused to study for tests, but I loved theory and abstract thinking. Everyone else was learning lists of countries and capitals, I was busy making detailed globes out of flour and water and giant balloons.''

"You were brilliant. They were ordinary."

"I was in trouble. My father decided I needed toughening up so he sent me to a very strict military school. You've heard of places like it I'm sure. If your nickel doesn't bounce on the bed after you've made it, you have to run ten laps around the track."

Joelle shivered at the bleakness of the image.

"Anyhow, obviously it was only destined to make things worse. I didn't fit in; I was an outcast. Then physics saved me."

"Physics?"

Zach smiled at the disdain in her pronunciation of the simple word. "Yes, physics. I loved it. I understood things that my teachers didn't even understand. I mystified everyone. Suddenly I had a talent. When my father heard, he was so grateful I wasn't a failure, that he pulled me out of the military academy and sent me to a prep school that specialized in the sciences. I finished my last year there. It was wonderful. Finally I was considered a real person."

There was no self-pity in the story. Zach told it as though it had happened to someone else. Joelle couldn't understand his lack of involvement. "Weren't you angry at the way you were treated?"

"I'd had time to develop a good sense of myself before I was sent away. I realized that I wasn't to blame. Later I was glad that somehow I was able to please my family, but I wouldn't have changed myself to do it, even if I could. Luckily it just happened on its own. When I graduated from college and started working for the research and development section of Pennington Alloy, we all began to realize just how much my abilities could add to the company. Of course you know how short-lived that period was.''

''I think all that changed you more than you admit.''

''How?'' Zach sipped his wine, watching Joelle try to put her thoughts together.

''It prepared you for Russell Creek. You've had to face a lot of rejection there, just as you did as a teenager. But you have this unshakable inner core that makes you keep right on going. That's something most people don't have any reason to develop.''

''That's probably true. But I'm also my father's son.''

''How so?'' Joelle hated to think that Zach was anything like his father.

''I see what I want, and I go for it.''

''Your methods are different.''

''Mine are more well thought out than his. My father misses a lot of what goes on around him. He decides what he wants and he lets someone else take care of the details. I take care of my own details.''

It was as close to a defense of Franklin Pennington-Smith as Zach had ever made. Joelle was silent, thinking about his words.

''Mr. Smith, we have a table for you, now.'' A pretty young woman with a black ponytail came to the table to deliver the message. She smiled at Zach, turning to glance at Joelle. The glance became a stare. ''Aren't you?''

''Yes, I am,'' Joelle acknowledged, ''but I'd like to keep it a secret if I could. Will you help?''

Sandwiched in between Zach and the young waitress, Joelle walked through the bar into the restaurant, where she was seated facing a corner with her back to the door. "This is perfect," she thanked the waitress. "I'll be glad to sign autographs when I'm finished eating if you can just keep everyone away till then. Okay?" She smiled at the young woman.

"Certainly, Miss Lynd. Boy, is my mom going to be surprised when I tell her." Her ponytail swayed back and forth as she left the table.

"How does it feel to be continually recognized when you go out?" Zach asked as they studied the menu.

Joelle tried to decide between the manicotti and the lasagna. "Well, it's a funny thing. Sometimes I'm spotted immediately, and sometimes no one ever notices me. It depends on whether people are expecting to see a celebrity or not." She decided on the lasagna. "I came to Taylerton a number of times when I first arrived, and no one ever figured out who I was. I wore sunglasses and a scarf over my head, but mainly it was because no one expected me to be here."

"Now they do."

"Unfortunately yes. But I couldn't stay in hiding forever."

"The article in the *Taylerton Times* didn't help."

There had been a feature article about Jo Lynd's meteoric rise to fame and an account of her appearance at the Russell Creek Improvement Society's picnic in the newspaper the week before. Joelle knew that it was only a matter of time before a reporter showed up at Zach's front door or at her farmhouse. "Reporters have to make a living, too. I've learned how to handle them."

Their waitress returned, bouncing with excitement. "I have a surprise for you," she said after she took their order. "Listen." The jukebox in the bar had been playing a series of polkas guaranteed to provide the restaurant clientele with exuberant spirits. Now Joelle listened to her own voice drift through the air.

"Thank you," she said trying to smile. "That's very nice."

"I hate this song," she told Zach after the young woman had gone to get their salads. "I hated it when I first heard it, hated it when I recorded it and I hate it every time someone plays it now. The message is so negative."

"When I come home to you, there'll be no more denying,
No cheating, no lying,
When I come home to you.

When I come home to you, I'll be a woman who wants you,
No memories will haunt you,
When I come home to you.

But for now, I'll just spend my time
Making love to strangers,
Drinking wine.
But for now, I'll just pluck the rose,
And where it withers,
Another grows.

When I come home to you..."

"There won't be any more 'When I Come Home To Yous' in my life," Joelle said. "I'm not going to sing anything I don't like again."

"What are you going to sing in your concert with Tim Daniels?"

The song had ended, and Joelle visibly relaxed. She waited to answer Zach while the waitress set their salads in front of them. "I told Tim I'd do a medley with him of all our biggest hits. But after that, I'm going to introduce my new songs. I'm finishing up the program. Tim is beginning it."

"I'm surprised he let you go last."

"He wasn't pleased. But I told him I wouldn't sing if he didn't."

"I'm glad you stood up to him."

Joelle toyed with her salad. "Zach, you don't think I can handle Tim, do you?"

"I think handling Tim is more dangerous than handling rattlesnakes in the West Virginia hills. They can only kill you. Tim can destroy you."

"He won't because I won't let him."

Zach shook his head. "You described him as domineering once. I never thought that word was so anemic until you applied it to Tim Daniels. He's much worse than domineering."

"You're going to have to trust me."

Zach set his fork down. "I don't have any choice, do I?" He heard the anger in his voice and berated himself silently for exposing so much of his inner turmoil.

"What's this about?"

He could be honest, or he could brush it off. He opted for the latter. "I just don't want you to have to deal with Daniels. That's all."

Joelle knew he wasn't telling the truth. "I don't believe you."

"And I don't want to talk about it." Zach's words were clear, his message even clearer.

Joelle shrugged. It was as close to a fight as they had come since they had begun living together. "Suit yourself, Smith. I thought we were beyond secrets."

"There are no secrets, only things you don't want to see."

"I thought you didn't want to talk about it."

"I don't."

Joelle tossed her fork on the table. "It was inevitable, wasn't it? It's been too good to be true. Now we're fighting like an old married couple!"

The disgust on her features cut through Zach's anger, and he was smiling in spite of himself. "Is that so bad?"

She was surprised by the tenderness in his voice. She peeked at him warily. "I don't know. What do you think?"

"I think I like it. See? We survived. We're still together, still friends. I still want to take you out on some country road and neck. If we can't get angry at each other occasionally, who can we get angry at?"

"I could never get angry at Tim. He'd laugh and walk out and I wouldn't see him for months."

"I'm not Tim Daniels."

"And I'm not the same woman I was then." Joelle smiled and took Zach's hands. "I was on my way to making important changes in my life when I met you, but knowing you has made it so much easier. I'll never forget that, Zach."

"This sounds curiously like goodbye."

"We still have almost two weeks."

"Somehow, when you start thanking me for what I've done for you, it sounds as though you're about to hit the road." Zach withdrew his hands. "Here comes our order."

Joelle was mystified by what she saw as Zach's over-reaction to her words. They ate their dinner in silence. She was hurt that he was refusing to share his feelings, but she understood that whatever those feelings were, they ran deep. She would have to wait until he was ready.

Their waitress kept Joelle's identity a secret through-out the meal, but when Joelle and Zach were finished and sipping coffee, it came time to pay their dues. First Enrico himself was introduced, then the other staff. Eventually the restaurant clientele was alerted, and be-fore long Joelle had signed three dozen autographs. She was wary of the crowd at first. She had been in situa-tions with fewer people that had gotten completely out of hand, but Enrico was a wonderful, burly man who kept the group of admirers under strict control.

When they were finally able to escape, Joelle and Zach made their way to the Mercedes. Once they were in traffic again, she began to relax. "Well, that wasn't too bad," she said, wondering how Zach had liked his initiation into superstardom.

"It was a zoo."

"It was nothing. Once I went out to dinner with my band when I was on tour. I don't even remember what city I was in. Anyhow, someone spotted me and the en-tire restaurant descended on us. It was a mob scene. It's funny how people will act when everyone else is acting the same way. They were grabbing my silverware, even the food off my plate. The band kept them from rip-ping my clothes to shreds, but someone got a handful of hair."

"Is it worth it to you?"

"My mother always told me not to look a gift horse in the mouth. There are probably thousands of people out there with better voices than mine. But I'm the one who made it. It would be the height of foolishness to feel sorry for myself.''

Zach pulled the car into the right lane and turned into a drive-in movie. ''I don't want another repeat of the restaurant scene. If I take you to the movies, it will have to be here.''

Joelle studied the sign. ''*Gidget Goes to Hawaii*?'' Did it just get to Taylerton?''

Zach tickled her neck. ''It's a beach-movie revival. See, the second feature is *Beach Blanket Bingo*.''

''I'm either too young or too old to appreciate it.''

''You know what the other choice is, don't you?''

''Park and neck?''

''Exactly.''

''I don't know...you haven't spent any money on me tonight.''

''It's not my fault Enrico said the dinner was on the house.'' Zach wrapped his fingers around the back of her neck and pulled her closer. ''Make up your mind. In a minute we're going to be trapped in line here. Once I pay for the movies I'll make you stay for them both.''

''Park and neck it is.''

He gave her a sample of what was in store for her before he backed out of the lot.

The spot Zach chose was on a bluff overlooking the Monongahela. There was no beach to speak of, only water and the twinkling lights from a town across the river.

''Would your grandmother approve of what you're about to do in her car?'' Joelle teased as Zach gathered her in his arms.

''She'd say, 'Zacharias darling, just remember that you're a Pennington, and a Pennington always acts like a gentleman even when he's doing things a gentleman shouldn't do.' "

Joelle tried to laugh, but Zach's mouth made short work of it. Neither of them wanted to rush to a conclusion. There was a nice warm bed at home for that. They played and teased and experimented like two well-bred teenagers on a date. Finally they reached their frustration limits and leaned back on the seat, arms wrapped around each other, as they waited for their hearts to beat normally again.

"Let's pretend," Joelle said.

"What shall we pretend?"

"Let's pretend we're in high school, going steady, and we just got back from the senior prom." She settled herself more comfortably against him.

"What would we talk about?" Zach thought for a moment. "It will depend on who we are. Who are we?"

"Well, I'm just a local girl, and you? Who do you want to be?"

"A local boy?"

Joelle nodded her head. "You're too well mannered to be just anyone, though. We'll make you the son of the mayor of Taylerton."

"I'm on my way to Penn State, then."

"And I'm trying to get you to elope before you leave so I can go with you."

"Yes, let's do it."

"Wait a minute. You're supposed to stutter and stammer. You don't want to be boxed in when you should be sowing all those wild oats. You're supposed to say, 'Darlin' it just wouldn't be fair to you, havin' to work to put me through college like that.' "

"I'll try." He cleared his throat. "Darlin', marry me right away so I can get you in my bed."

"You just can't seem to get it right, Smith." Joelle gave a pretend sigh. "You're supposed to say..."

"Marry me, Joelle."

It took her a full ten seconds to understand that Zach was serious. "You mean it, don't you," she said with genuine surprise in her voice.

"Yes, I mean it. I want to marry you."

"Why?"

"I want to live our lives together, have children together, grow old together. I want to wake up every morning and shove you back to your own side of the bed, just like I've had to do for the past two weeks. I want to..."

"I get the picture." Joelle put her fingers over his lips. "I didn't realize that you were a glutton for punishment."

Zach stroked her hair. "What's that supposed to mean?"

"Didn't tonight give you some small idea of what it would be like to be married to me?"

"Tonight's been wonderful. Being with you is wonderful."

"It's wonderful now, but what would it be like when the honeymoon is over? You don't want a wife who can't go to the grocery store without being mobbed. You don't want a wife who's out of town for months on end. You want to have children? So do I. I've always loved kids. But how am I going to be a good mother and tour the country at the same time? Even if you were free to live where I have to live, you'd hate Los Angeles." Joelle had not consciously allowed herself to imagine marriage with Zach. But during their weeks together, she had collected reasons why marriage between them was impossible. It had been a way of building her own defenses. Now she was trying to help him build his.

Zach's answer was silence.

"I don't ever want to make you unhappy, Zach, but marriage is impossible. Can't you see that?"

"I can see that you think it's impossible." Zach set Joelle gently away from him and turned the key in the ignition. The engine was the only sound to break the stillness.

Once home, Zach came around to Joelle's door and politely held it open. On the porch, she could no longer stand the wide gulf between them. "Talk to me," she said. "I'd rather fight than have you suffer by yourself."

"I misunderstood what was happening between us. I won't again." Zach put his key in the lock and opened the door.

"What did you misunderstand?"

"I thought you loved me."

"I do."

Zach was waiting for her to pass ahead of him, and as he turned, she could see the raw emotion in his eyes. "I do love you. You weren't wrong about that," Joelle said, putting her hands on his shoulders. She felt him stiffen, and she went on. "Come inside, let me make us some coffee, and we'll talk this through."

"No coffee. Just talk."

"Zach, love has nothing to do with this. I love you."

"But not enough to marry me."

Joelle followed him into the living room and took a seat on the sofa. Zach stood by the fireplace.

"Love's a circle, Zach, not a continuum. There's not some magical point where I realize I love you enough to overcome all the myriad obstacles in our way. I could change who I am for you, or you could change who you are for me, but it wouldn't work.''

"We could compromise. There are a thousand ways we could take care of the differences between us.''

"And there are a thousand ways that those compromises might not be good enough.''

"You're afraid to try, aren't you?''

She was afraid to try. She didn't know anyone in show business who had made a successful marriage. If a friend married another performer, the excuse when they divorced was that their careers had been too competitive. If they married someone outside the business, the excuse was that no one outside could understand the pressures a performer was subject to. "I guess I believe in marriage. If I failed at it, I'd never forgive myself.''

Zach was trying hard not to let his pain at her rejection get in the way of understanding Joelle's feelings. "Tell me why you think we'd fail.''

"You want to marry Joelle Lindsey, not Jo Lynd. I'm both people. You want to marry the coal miner's daughter, not the superstar.''

"I haven't asked you to give up your career.''

"And you wouldn't. But it would be between us. Even if you could travel with me sometimes, you'd hate the craziness of touring. What would you do if I had to stay in L.A. for months at a time? Could you leave your business to come with me? Would stolen weekends be enough?''

"We'd find a way to manage if you wanted to.'' Zach shook his head at the obvious sorrow on her face. "Joelle, don't eat yourself up over this. I think I knew what your decision would be before the question was even out of my mouth. You said it before. We're star-crossed lovers. Taking on fate is a risky business.''

She stood, fighting for poise. "Do you want me to leave?"

"God no. That's the last thing I want."

They were facing each other, yards still separating them. "Can we pretend this didn't happen?"

Zach tried to smile. "No, but we can adjust to it and go on with our lives. We still have two weeks together." Those words had never sounded so final to either of them.

"I want to make some changes in my career," she said tentatively, "I plan to spend time at the farm. That's why I renovated the house. We can be together then."

"No." The simple word was an explosion. "Two weeks or a lifetime. Nothing in between."

"I don't like ultimatums."

"And I don't like being fed crumbs under the table." He watched his words sink in.

"Is that what I was doing?" Joelle asked softly.

"I want a real relationship. I'm not interested in less. Not even from you."

"Is there someone next in line?" She hated the question, but she wanted the answer.

"Did you think I made a list of available women and put them in order from one to ten? I don't fall in love that easily."

"Neither do I." She stepped closer. "I'll never forget you, Zach."

"Somehow that's not much consolation."

"Are you sure you don't want me to leave?"

Zach closed the distance between them, scooping her up against him. "Joelle, what I really want to do is drag you upstairs and make love to you until you beg me to let you stay."

"You'd regret it always if I did," she said against his chest.

"And what regrets will you have to live with?" he asked as he lifted her face for his kiss. "I can always tell myself that I reached for what I wanted. What will you tell yourself, Joelle?" His mouth brushed back and forth over hers. "What will you make yourself believe?"

She didn't know. She gave herself up to his mouth and his hands and to the nagging sensation that something about her decision made no sense at all.

CHAPTER THIRTEEN

FOR THE NEXT TWO DAYS Joelle looked for signs that Zach was angry with her for refusing his proposal. But whatever emotion he felt, he kept hidden. They still made love, took long walks and laughed together. On the surface nothing had changed, but both of them were more guarded about showing their feelings. If the first two weeks of June had been spent sharing and growing closer, the last two seemed to be destined to be spent drawing apart.

Joelle stayed at her farm during the day, helping the workmen or working on songs in the springhouse, which she had turned into a rustic studio. She had purchased a comfortable couch and armchair and an antique pine desk. Carol had come to visit on a Monday and then returned Tuesday with bright, striped curtains for the windows. Joelle's decorator would have been appalled, but Joelle loved the changes. The place lacked only one thing: electricity.

The house lacked the same. The kitchen and the new bathroom were supplied with running water from the springhouse. All that was needed was electricity to light the house and back up the wood heating system, which would be installed at the very end of the renovation. The crew had wired the house, installing sockets and switches. Now Joelle had to decide how to get power to the house.

The local electric company offered to do the work for an enormous fee. Even more enormous was the cost of a wind machine adequate enough to do the job. In addition, Zach now seemed reluctant to install one for her.

"It doesn't make sense," he told her one afternoon when he had come to see how the renovations were taking shape. They had toured the house and the spring-house-studio, and they were sitting on the front porch. "You aren't going to be here enough to make the investment worthwhile. A couple of weeks a year hardly makes it worth installing such an expensive piece of equipment."

"Money's not a problem, Zach. And I'm not enthusiastic about having power lines all over my property." She leaned back against the railing and watched his profile. The sunlight brought out the red highlights in his hair and beard and touched the warm tan of his skin. She never tired of looking at him.

"Maintenance is a problem, though. You won't be here to keep an eye on things. It's not as simple as calling the electric company and asking them to turn off the power while you're away."

"Could you keep an eye on it for me? Or one of your employees? I could pay to have it . . ."

"No."

Zach turned so that Joelle couldn't see his face. It seemed an appropriate thing to do, she thought. His words had also been a clear signal that he was leaving her behind. "I miss you," she said quietly. "I'm always going to miss you."

He ignored her words. "If you want my advice, I think you should install a solar hot-water heater and a wood stove to cook on as well as to heat the house. You can use kerosene lamps for light. Later, if you think you're going to spend enough time here, you can decide about electricity.''

''You don't want to put a wind machine over here because it's too much of a connection with me.'' She sat up again, pushing her hair over her ears. ''When I leave, you want to forget I ever existed.'' Her tone was accusing.

''When you leave, I'm going to go on with my life.'' Zach's voice betrayed nothing. ''I'll check on your property, just as I always have, in exchange for using some of your land for my demonstration models. But I won't come over here on a regular basis and fuss around in your house for you. That's asking too much.''

She bit back her angry words and tried to lighten the tone of their exchange. ''What kind of businessman refuses a big sale?''

''One who's trying not to mix business with pleasure, or with pain.'' Zach stood, jamming his hands in his pocket. ''I've got some work to do this evening. I'll see you back at the house later.''

The message was clear to Joelle as she watched him walk through the yard, which was now a lush green carpet of grass. They could not talk about what was happening to them. The subject was forbidden, just as other subjects had been forbidden throughout their short and stormy relationship. Zach Smith had blown into her life like the wind that he struggled so hard to harness. In a short time he would be gone again, and her life would be as still and stagnant as it had been before. The ending had been inevitable. Zach was right. Discussing it didn't help. Nothing helped.

AFTER THAT THEY WERE CAREFUL not to put themselves in situations where they would have to unveil their feelings. Joelle sang some of her new songs for Zach, but only the ones that had nothing to do with him. Zach worked longer hours than before, but they still had quiet evenings together. If they couldn't talk about their feelings, the time they spent in passionate lovemaking was enough of a reason to stay together until it was time for Joelle to go.

Although he had refused to install a wind machine for her, Zach did agree to sell and install two wood stoves, one for the kitchen and another airtight model to heat the rest of the house. The renovators constructed an attractive heat-proof barrier to protect the wall and floor, and they cut the necessary holes for the stove-pipe chimney. On the Saturday before she was scheduled to leave, Zach and Jake loaded the stoves on Zach's truck and drove to Joelle's house to put them in.

For Joelle it was a bittersweet moment. The day before she had said goodbye to the workmen who had labored so long and so hard on her house. They had been craftsmen who felt pride in their work, and the house was now a monument to their painstaking care. They had taken a dilapidated ruin and made it a home to be proud of. Now, installing the stoves was the final step.

"What can I do?" Joelle asked, when the truck pulled up in her driveway. She had walked over earlier to make sure that everything was ready.

"I'll let you know," Zach said.

Jake got out to guide the truck to Joelle's front porch, and she stepped back and watched the complicated maneuver. An hour later, after the kitchen stove had been installed, she finally had to admit to herself that her help was not needed. Jake and Zach were a team. If they gave her a job to do, it was only to humor her.

She had invited Carol and Dorothy to join them at lunchtime, and she busied herself taking the lunch she

had packed and other picnic supplies up to the hill.
When she came back to the house, it was to find Jake
alone.

"Zach forgot a piece of pipe. He went back home to
get it," he said, his head almost swallowed by the
yawning opening of the stove. Jake continued to busy
himself making minute adjustments, and Joelle went
out on the porch to wait.

Carol arrived first. Zach had warned Joelle not to
pack too much for lunch. From experience he knew that
Carol would bombard them with food, and true to
form, she did. Joelle wondered what the designer who
made her stage clothing was going to say when he discovered the extra pounds she had gained. Today's lunch
alone was destined to add another inch somewhere.

"Dorothy called me at the last minute and said to tell
you that they can't make it. She's not feeling well,"
Carol said with a huge grin.

"Is that good news?" Joelle took the heavy hamper
out of Carol's hands and set it on the front porch.

"She's pregnant. Just told me today. Carl's got her
in bed with her feet up. She says he's acting like Desi
Arnaz in a rerun of the *I Love Lucy* show."

"I'll have to drive by and see her before I go."

"So you're still planning to leave." Carol flopped
down on the porch swing, and Joelle sat on the steps
facing her.

"Yes."

"We're all going to miss you."

Joelle smiled at the woman who had become such a
good friend. No one Joelle had ever met had been less
impressed with her fame. In Carol's eyes, Joelle sang
for a living just as Jake built wind machines and Dorothy typed invoices. Everyone did his part in making the
world a better place. In her eyes, everyone was equal.

"I'll miss you, too. I'll be back from time to time, though. I think of Russell Creek as home now."

"Home's wherever you are, honey. If you designate this one spot as home, you'll feel like a stranger everywhere else you go."

"Don't you feel more at home some places than others, though?" Joelle asked. "You came here from eastern Pennsylvania. Don't you miss your family and friends there and the life you had before you pulled up roots?"

"I might, if I didn't have Jake." Carol thought about her words. "I guess for me, wherever Jake is, well, that's my home. Oh, I miss Lancaster and my life there, sometimes, but we've carved out a new life here. I never would have met Zach or you, Dorothy or Carl, or that funny Mr. Kincaid if I hadn't come to Russell Creek. This is home now."

"If you're right, then all the time and money I've spent making this house come alive again was just a gesture."

Wisely, Carol didn't interrupt. She understood that Joelle was thinking out loud.

"I wanted a home, and so I came back to the only home I've ever known and rebuilt it from the ground up." Joelle closed her eyes. "Was it for nothing?"

"You had to face your past. There was nothing wrong with clinging to your roots for a while. But in the long run, if you keep on clinging, they'll give way and you won't have anything."

"I never get it right. I try to make a home for myself in the darndest places," Joelle said after a while.

"I'm an old woman and I was raised in a culture that valued home and family and marriage. I can't change my beliefs. I thought that you and Zach could find happiness together, but if that's not to be, I know you'll find your place in the world eventually, and so will he." Carol swung back and forth. "I can't help but wish it were different," she added finally.

"There's too much separating us." Joelle opened her eyes and tried to smile. "Love's not always enough."

"Enough love is."

"Enough love?"

"Sometimes I think that's the one thing my generation forgot to teach yours. We wanted so much for you. We went through a depression and a terrible war, and we wanted more for you than that. We taught you to go after what you wanted, to enjoy yourselves without guilt and to be freer than we ever were. But we forgot to tell you that sometimes you have to compromise. Sometimes you have to take a risk and suffer the consequences. Sometimes you just have to love enough to keep on trying when trying is crazy."

Carol laughed softly. "But then, what do I know? I'm just an old woman who hasn't seen much of the world. And I worry more than I should about the part I do see."

"But you're speaking from your own experience," Joelle said. "You and Jake faced tremendous odds against you. Obviously you think it was worth all the suffering."

"Jake's the one who suffered, not me. He'd have to be the one to tell you if it was worth it."

"It was." Jake came out on the porch and leaned against the door. "Worth every bit of it." For a moment he stared off into the distance. "I didn't want to leave my people. I still miss them, as ornery as they were. But if I hadn't done what I did, I'd have wondered all my life where Carol was, if she was happy." He turned to Carol, and his look was a caress so intimate that Joelle felt its power from across the porch. "Besides," he continued, "I knew she was the best cook in Lancaster County. What kind of man would pass up a temptation like that?"

"One with a smaller stomach," Carol said with a wink. "And speaking of food, weren't we going to have a picnic?"

Joelle had to give herself a mental shake. She felt as though she needed a month just to digest all of Carol's homey wisdom. "Zach's not back yet. I wonder what's keeping him?"

"I'll drive over and see," Jake volunteered.

"No. I will," Joelle said, rising. "I'll walk over and ride back with him. I bet I'll meet him partway. Will you two be all right here for a few minutes without me?"

"Fine. You go ahead. We'll nibble on deviled eggs while we wait."

"Don't eat them all." Joelle waved as she made her way up the driveway.

The walk to Zach's house was just long enough to begin sorting out some of the things Carol had said. As Joelle turned into Zach's yard, she wondered if her friend's words really applied to her relationship with him. Was it just a question of life-style compromise or were there deeper problems she couldn't identify still lurking beneath the surface? Perhaps it was simply that she didn't want to take on the risk of a marriage that had so much going against it. Or perhaps there was more.

She was almost up to the house when she saw the strange car parked beside Zach's truck. Obviously he had been sidetracked by the visitor who was probably a potential customer. Now that the summer had begun, Zach's business was at its peak. In addition to increased orders, there was a steady trickle of people interested in wind power who found their way to Zach's to see his machines and discuss their own needs.

Joelle wouldn't have considered interrupting if she hadn't known that Carol and Jake were at her house waiting. She glanced at the car again. It was a sleek white Lincoln with Pennsylvania tags. Hopefully it belonged to someone who lived close enough to visit again. She opened the door and entered the front hall. Certain that Zach had taken his guest to his office, she decided to call his business number and ask him what she should do about the picnic. Instead she heard voices in the living room.

She had already made enough noise to announce her presence. Knowing that Zach would wonder who was there, she went to find him.

He and his guest were sitting on the sofa, talking earnestly in low voices. She stood in the doorway for a moment absorbing the scene. The man was familiar, although it took her precious seconds to identify him. It was only when she noted his resemblance to the man she loved that she recognized Franklin Pennington-Smith.

She wanted to retreat, to leave and not come back. Neither of the men had looked up. They were so involved in their conversation that they didn't realize she was standing there. She stood watching them, knowing that if she turned and walked away, they would notice her. She was trapped. Finally she cleared her throat. It was not to call attention to herself, although it served that purpose very well. She did it to try to dissolve the lump that was forming beside her vocal cords, a lump made of a decade and a half of tears and anger.

"I came to see what was keeping you." Her voice sounded normal. It was a surprise.

Zach nodded his head. "I thought you might." He stood and his father stood, too. "Joelle, you've met my father." He nodded to the man standing beside him.

"Oh yes. I've met your father."

"Won't you join us?" Franklin Pennington-Smith asked.

"I don't think so."

"Please stay, Joelle." Zach's eyes locked with hers. "He's here to talk to us both."

"We have nothing to say to each other."

"I have some things I'd like to say to you," Franklin Pennington-Smith said.

Joelle admired the deep, rich voice at the same time that she shook her head. "You're a man who's used to getting what he wants, aren't you? Tell me why I should play your game."

"Because it concerns you and my son."

She was curious to know just how much he knew about her relationship with Zach. She dropped into a chair across the room from the sofa and folded her hands in her lap. "I may be the first citizen of Russell Creek who's been given an audience with the owner of Pennington Alloy #2. I guess I'd be a fool to turn it down."

"I delivered the deed to the company store to the president of the Russell Creek Improvement Society today," he said quietly. "That makes you the second citizen to be given an audience."

"Am I supposed to thank you? They paid for it."

"I didn't come to talk about that."

"I'm sure you didn't." Joelle's words were bitter, but her tone was flat and emotionless. Weariness settled over her whole body, and she could not even find the energy to try and read Zach's expression.

"You're not going to make it easy, are you? I didn't manage to get through with this when the occasion arose several months ago," Franklin Pennington-Smith began.

"Get through what?"

"An apology."

"Save your breath." Joelle pushed her hair off her face with one hand in a distracted gesture. "Apologies come cheap, Mr. Pennington-Smith. Life doesn't."

"Neither does guilt or years of self-blame."

"I'm going to have a lot of difficulty feeling sorry for you."

"Joelle, put aside your hostility for a minute." Zach's voice cut through the tension in the room. "Let him say what he came to say."

"Who are you to tell me what to do?" she shot back at him, anger overcoming reason.

"The son of this man." Zach stood and came toward her, bending to put his hand under her chin and raise her eyes to his. "And the man who loves you enough to want you to be finished with hatred. You've put so much behind you. This is the last step you have to take."

"I lost my family!"

"And I lost mine."

"What are you saying?" Her voice was for his ears only.

"I've known for some time that I was letting past bitterness color my life. When you found out who I was and rejected me because of it, I realized that I could never escape my identity. Then I began to realize that I didn't want to escape it."

"I don't want to hear this."

"You have to." He removed his hand, but his gaze still held hers. "Over the past month my father and I have reconciled most of our differences. I've agreed to work for Pennington Alloy as a consultant. Father is retiring at the end of the year and Isaac is taking over. I'll be working directly with him.''

The cold hand of betrayal squeezed Joelle's heart. ''All the time I've been living with you? All that time you've been making these plans without telling me about them?''

''I thought a time would come when you'd accept me for who I really am and we'd be able to put our pasts behind us.''

''That time will never come!'' She spit out the words that sealed the end of their relationship.

He straightened. Joelle recognized the proud posture. Even now, he would not give up his dignity. Only the expression in his brown eyes signaled the sorrow he had felt at her words.

''You said once that the real problem between us was that I wanted Joelle Lindsey without wanting Jo Lynd. But the irony is that you always wanted Zach Smith without wanting Zacharias Pennington-Smith.'' His hand brushed her hair. ''For your own sake, listen to my father now. You'll never be whole until you can come to terms with his.''

''It won't make a difference,'' she said coldly.

''Not between us. But it might make a difference for you.'' He touched her hair again as though his hand was drawn to the gold strands of its own accord. ''I'll go tell Carol and Jake where you are.''

''I'll be gone when you get back.''

His hand fell to his side. ''Then goodbye, Joelle Lindsey,'' he said gently. ''May you have all the happiness you deserve.''

Joelle refused to look at Zach. She felt rather than saw him leave. Then she was alone with the man who had conceived him.

For a moment she could think of nothing except that Zach had just walked out of her life. She had been preparing for the end, but she had never prepared to have it end like this. The impact of having the love they had shared die in a bitter storm of words and accusations was more painful than she could ever have imagined. But there was no time to mourn.

"It goes on and on and on. Ever widening ripples spreading out forever."

Joelle looked up at Franklin Pennington-Smith's words.

"When I heard about the mine explosion sixteen years ago," he continued, "I felt as though someone had ripped a hole in my gut. I knew who was to blame. I had a dedicated staff who gathered enough facts to make me look like Jesus Christ, but I still knew who was to blame."

"So did my mother." Joelle tried to gather her defenses. All she wanted was a chance to put Zach's departure in perspective, but she was being forced to endure this scene with his father. Her response was filled with venom.

He gave a sad smile. "For the first few weeks after we had to seal the mine, I'd wake up at night feeling as though I was smothering. I quit riding in elevators, I still don't shut the door if I'm in a small room. 'The Voice of Corruption' was about my press conference after the investigation ended. Do you remember seeing me knock down a reporter on my way out of the room?"

"Vividly."

"I looked like an arrogant monster, didn't I? The truth was that I was in a panic. He was between me and the door. The room had begun to close in on me."

Joelle didn't want to believe him. She refused to alter her expression, but she didn't interrupt.

"I took tranquilizers for weeks. Finally the only way I could cope with my distress was to try and put the blame on somebody else. Little by little I let myself believe that I hadn't been at fault. There was some truth to that. I had very little contact with the mining operation, but I was careless in my choice of the men I surrounded myself with. Under my control Pennington Alloy diversified so much that there was no way for me to keep up with everything."

"In other words you were so busy making money that you stopped caring how many people you hurt to do it."

To Joelle's surprise, Franklin agreed. "Yes. That's what happened."

"Is that supposed to make me feel better?" She leaned forward, her eyes blazing with anger.

"No." He rose and began to pace the room. Against her will Joelle noted the older man's resemblance to Zach. The two moved the same way, with the same masculine grace. Franklin's step was slower, more controlled, but it was too similar to Zach's for her to feel comfortable watching him. She looked away.

"I had almost convinced myself that I wasn't to blame, when your song became popular. I was furious. You effectively knocked down all my hard-won defenses. Then when I began to adjust, Zacharias confronted me with his own findings."

"Now you're going to tell me that overnight you became a changed man."

"No, I didn't. Pennington Alloy still has problems. There are men who work for me who shouldn't, practices that should still be abolished. I've been working at altering my business practices for a decade now. Sometimes I do what's right, sometimes I find myself backsliding. Zacharias will still be able to make lists of problems, but the lists won't be as long or as devastating." Franklin stopped pacing and looked directly at Joelle. "Recently I realized that I've gotten too old to keep fighting. Isaac will be a better president than I was."

Joelle didn't want to soften. Sixteen years of her life had been invested in hating this man. Her bitterness was a solid wall that his words could not penetrate. "Why did you want to tell me your story?"

"When I met you in Los Angeles, I told you that I was an admirer of yours. It's true. At first, every time I saw you on television or heard one of your songs it reminded me of my own failures. Later you became a reminder of how far I had come. I could look at you and know that even though Pennington Alloy still had problems, there would never be another disaster like the one that had occurred here."

"And now you're turning it over to your sons."

"They are three fine men."

"It's a happily ever after, isn't it? Except for the men buried in Pennington Alloy #2. Except for my father and my brother who will never see the sunlight again." Joelle stood and faced him.

"Except for those men and for you, my dear." Franklin walked over to stand in front of her. Up close she saw that he had the same warm brown eyes as his son. She wished he didn't. "Don't let the past ruin your life as it's already ruined so many. Zacharias loves you, and I think you love him. Put an end to this bitterness."

Somewhere inside her was a small voice that echoed his words. Put an end to bitterness. Put an end to bitterness. But the words died before they could reach her throat. She was not ready. She might never be ready. This time there was no healing hymn to set her free. "I can't forgive you," she whispered.

"I've forgiven myself." He smiled a little. "That's enough for me. You have only to move on with your own life."

JOELLE FOLDED THE LAST PAIR OF PANTS and packed them in her suitcase. She was ready to leave. Zach's father had left an hour before, and she had taken her time packing. Her head whirled with snatches of dialogue and her body felt as though it was bruised and battered. She was as confused and upset as she had been the day she left Los Angeles.

Finally there was nothing left to do except go. It was apparent that Zach was delaying his return. She wasn't sure why she had waited; she still intended to leave. Saying another goodbye would only cause them both more pain.

So why was it, she asked herself a half hour later, that she was still sitting on Zach's front porch waiting for him to come back? Hadn't they said everything that could be said? Hadn't they severed the bonds they had formed in their weeks together?

Evening was approaching when she finally picked up the heavy suitcase and carried it to her car. She had long since ceased to function rationally. She had spent the afternoon futilely waiting for a man she had no future with. It had not been a time of soul-searching or decision making. She had simply waited for him because the thought of never seeing him again was more painful than another goodbye.

She could not leave without one more look at her farm. She drove the short distance with no realization of having done it. Parking in her driveway for the last time she looked out over her childhood home. The yard surrounding the house was lush and green with neatly trimmed shrubs, some of which were covered with flowers. She could hear the sound of the spring bubbling as it rushed into the springhouse, and in the distance she could see the rich, dark soil of the vegetable garden waiting patiently to receive the plants that would never have a chance to grow there now.

She walked up the path to the house and stood on the front porch. A light breeze rocked the swing. The front door was locked. She realized that Zach must have closed up the house after he had explained her absence to Carol and Jake. She fumbled in her pocket for her keys, unlocked the door and went inside. Always before she had been overwhelmed with bittersweet memories as she had looked around the familiar structure. But this was no longer the house of her childhood. More than the floor plan had changed. Now the house held new memories.

The halls echoed with the sounds of the workmen who had put so much into the renovation. The stove standing proudly in the living room was a reminder of Jake, just as the porch swing was now a reminder of Carol and the wisdom she had tried to share. And everywhere she looked, Joelle saw Zach. He had not been a major part of the renovation itself, but he had visited often, making suggestions and assisting in his quiet way. He had helped her choose colors for the wall, refusing even to let her settle for white in the closets. He had been the one to design the placement of windows and skylights in the kitchen to make use of the sun for additional heat in the winter.

No, Zach had not spent much time in the house, but Joelle knew that didn't matter. He was firmly planted in her memory. For years to come little things would bring him to mind. If not here, then anywhere that she went. She left the house, locking it behind her.

She climbed the hill and discovered that all signs of the abortive picnic had been cleared away. Here, Zach's presence was almost tangible. Lingering where they had spent wonderful, intimate moments together was too painful. The memories were too good, and good memories were harder to live with than bad ones. She walked back down the path, past the house and up the incline to the springhouse. The door was locked, another example of Zach's thoughtfulness, and she unlocked it with trembling hands. It was here, where they had shared their first night of love, that she finally gave way to the tears that had been building all afternoon.

It was dark before she locked the door again and walked to her car. She had spent the last months making the farm and farmhouse a home. Her intention had always been to keep the property as a place of refuge, a retreat that she could use when the world began to close in on her. Now she knew that it could never be that for her. Staring out over the picturesque landscape, she wondered if she would ever come back again.

CHAPTER FOURTEEN

THE GARDENER HAD BEEN THERE that day. Joelle knew it the second her Saab pulled through the front gate. The wild, exotic landscape surrounding the white stucco house looked newly tamed and subdued. She was sorry she had missed Mr. Huckamato. He was one of the few people in Los Angeles with whom she could make intelligent conversation.

"Now that's not true," she admonished herself out loud. She did have friends here. There was no point in being negative. It would be easy to blame her irritability on the sprawling heat-and-smog-enshrouded city that was her home. But her problems had nothing to do with her location. There was a part of her that had always loved the city of angels. It was a vital and alive metropolis that could be invigorating or draining, depending on her state of mind. Now draining was too mild a word.

She didn't care enough to park in the garage. It was designed to blend into the house that looked like a garage itself. Wrenching her key from the ignition, she lay her arms on the steering wheel and rested her head on them.

It was mid-August. In one week she and Tim would do their first and last concert together. Never again would she subject herself to the rigors of dealing with him on a daily basis. On top of the loss of her relationship with Zach, the reentry of Tim into her life was the last straw.

It was not that Tim was behaving badly. On the contrary. Joelle had never seen him behave better. He was still arrogant and manipulative, but he was trying to temper those traits. She had seen him swallow his anger in a new attempt at control, and she had seen him give in on points he would have fought to the death for in the past. She was suspicious of his motivations, but if the changes were real, she had to applaud them.

It was the intimacy with which he treated her that annoyed Joelle. She had no objection to appearing to be friends with Tim in public. It would hardly be advantageous for the world to think that they were bitter enemies. But the speculation about their relationship had spread like wildfire when she had come back from Pennsylvania. She had refused to give interviews about her reasons for disappearing, and to his credit, Tim also had kept silent. But their mutual avoidance of publicity fueled the prevailing theory that Joelle had left town because of a fight with Tim. Now their concert was seen as a reconciliation. What would have been a sellout anyway, sold out that much faster.

And though Tim held strictly to their agreement that he would not pretend to reporters that he and Joelle were a couple, he managed to treat her with a gracious intimacy in public that said more than a thousand interviews could have. She could not fault him for being nice to her. She could only wish that September would come quickly.

Her disappearance had done more than feed the speculation about her relationship with Tim. It had increased her record sales. Her agent had negotiated a new contract for her that was a dream come true. She had only to sign it to insure her success for the next five years. There had been offers of concerts in all the major cities in Europe and feelers from one of the top movie studios. What had begun as an attempt to find herself had ended as a brilliant career move.

Joelle didn't feel brilliant. She felt hot and tired and thoroughly disgusted with her life. And she felt lonely. She had friends, but in the frantic pace of her world in L.A., there was no time to spend with any of them. She was beginning to forget who she was again.

She pried herself off the seat and slammed the car door behind her. She was in no hurry to go into the house, but she knew if she didn't, Maria, her housekeeper, would come looking for her. Maria was relentless about her duties.

Inside, Joelle greeted the older woman. Maria was wearing a starched white uniform and almost immediately she faded into the background. It was more a conscious attempt to appear inconspicuous than a melting into the white walls, although the effect was the same. Joelle was alone again.

Upstairs in her bedroom she stripped off her clothes and filled the Jacuzzi. The pulsating streams of water began to soothe away the tensions in her body, but nothing could set her mind free. She was stuck with her memories and with the hopeless feeling of loss that invaded her every time she let her defenses down.

Where was Zach right now? It was eight o'clock Pennsylvania time. Would he be sitting on his front porch, enjoying the cool summer evening, or would he be lying on the sofa listening to his stereo? Perhaps he was spending the evening with friends, even with a woman. She slapped the bubbling water, sending a fine spray to cover the tile around the Jacuzzi.

She tried to think more positively. Of course it was possible that he was busy in Pittsburgh doing work for

Pennington Alloy. But then there were lots of eligible women in cities. Zach's parents would know many suitable females to match him up with. Franklin Pennington-Smith would not want one of his beloved sons to suffer from the malady of unrequited love. She slapped the water again.

Joelle felt the age-old possessiveness of human beings everywhere. She had refused to make a commitment to Zach, but she could not bear the thought of him making a commitment to someone else. He deserved to be happy—and a part of her wanted that for him. But she didn't want to imagine that he had found someone else so quickly. Eventually she was sure her own pain would fade to a dull ache. Then she could handle the thought of Zach and another woman. By her own calculations that should be due to happen in a century, give or take a decade.

Her melancholy thoughts were disturbed by a discreet knock on the door of the bathroom. "Miss Lynd? Mr. Daniels is downstairs."

Even Tim was not completely unwelcome tonight. Joelle needed someone to help her shake off her depression. She had made her choices. Faced with becoming a real part of Zach's life or single-mindedly going on with her career, she had chosen her career. Faced with accepting all of him, even the parts that were painful to acknowledge, she had chosen to leave. She, who had told herself that she was done with making bad decisions, had made the worst one of her life.

Stepping out of the Jacuzzi, she buried herself for a moment in a thick bath sheet that would have been luxurious enough to be a rug for the springhouse. Then, wearily, she slipped into a green caftan glittering with thousands of gold threads and brushed her hair. Tim was waiting in the living room.

"Have you eaten?" she asked after a perfunctory greeting. Tim was examining her from her bare feet to the top of her head. "No. I thought maybe you'd like to go out to dinner."

"It's too hot to go anywhere tonight. I'm sure Maria left enough to share. She has the evening off, so it's probably something simple."

In the kitchen Joelle pulled a large seafood salad out of the refrigerator and tossed it with the housekeeper's special dressing. There were crusty rye rolls to eat with it.

"It's not like you to drop in," Joelle said after they were seated in the dining room and she was picking at her food.

Tim poured them both a glass of wine. "It seemed to be the most advantageous way of getting you to agree to spend the evening with me."

"I agreed to dinner. Not the evening."

"I consider this progress."

"Progress toward what?" Joelle set her fork down and picked up her wine.

"You know what I want."

"No I don't. Enlighten me."

Tim's lips curled back in an arrogant smile. "You always were such a baby about my intentions."

Joelle blinked and then smiled back. "Now I get it. And I thought we might be discussing something more interesting than whether you were going to get me in your bed again. It's so embarrassing when I overestimate you." She picked up her fork and speared a giant shrimp. "You're not, you know. That part of our lives is finished."

"It doesn't have to be."

"There's where you're wrong."

Tim finished his portion of the salad and helped himself to the remainder in the bowl. "You're still mooning over Pennington-Smith, aren't you? What do you hear from Russell Creek these days?"

"I can tell when you're playing games, Tim. Shall I hem and haw and pretend that Zach and I are in frequent touch with each other so that you can catch me in a lie?" With a great deal of effort, she took another bite. "We did not part on the best of terms. Zach's out of my life now."

To Tim's eternal credit he didn't even smile. "For good?"

"I imagine it's for good." Joelle refilled her glass and toasted the man sitting across the table. "To 'I told you sos.'"

"Your words, not mine." Tim continued eating, pointedly ignoring her gesture. "Where do you go from here?"

"I haven't decided yet."

"That's probably a good idea. I don't think you're in any kind of shape to make decisions right now." His eyes found hers. "Unless they involve me, that is."

"Trying for the rebound, Tim?" The cool, mellow white Burgundy was disconnecting Joelle's tongue from her brain. She realized with a pang that aside from the few bites of seafood, she had eaten nothing that day. She set her glass down.

"A case could be made that Pennington-Smith was the one who got you on the rebound."

"Six years isn't a rebound, it's a whole new serve, a whole new game." She giggled a little, and the sound startled her. Jo Lynd never giggled. Joelle Lindsey laughed, but giggles were foreign to her, too. Someone new had taken over her body. "Somehow, I think I've had too much to drink."

Tim frowned. "A glass and a half of wine? What else have you had to drink today?"

"Nothing. Nor have I eaten. But the room is spinning."

"Are you going to faint?"

"FAINTING IS A VERY ESOTERIC EXPERIENCE," she said later, as she lay on the sofa wondering why she had never seriously considered having her living room walls painted another color. Tim had carried her here, and she had awakened to the impression that she was lost in a blizzard. "Fainting makes you realize the darndest things."

"And you're going to enlighten me about those things, aren't you?" Tim lifted her head. "Here drink this first."

She recognized the bitter taste. It was tomato juice and nutritional yeast, guaranteed to connect her head back to the rest of her body. It almost seemed like a shame to drink it. "I'll bet that's the first time in your life you've ever waited on a woman," she said when the mixture was all gone.

"You and I are destined to celebrate our firsts together, Jo. As they go, this one wasn't too bad. Just don't make a habit of fainting."

"Will you bring me the yellow pages? There's one in the drawer under the kitchen extension."

She ignored his muttering and waited for his return with her eyes closed. "Now, will you look up painters for me?"

"Have you lost your mind?"

"Definitely not." She watched him thumb through the directory. "Is anyone open in the evenings?"

Tim scanned the advertisements. "Here's one." He handed the whole book to Joelle and brought her the telephone.

She dialed carefully, squinting at the ad as she did. She felt better but the room still seemed slightly out of kilter. When a man answered, she gave her name and address and told him what she wanted. He promised to get back to her the following day.

"Now tell me why you had to make that phone call." Tim moved the telephone back to the end table.

"I'm taking charge of my life."

"Again? Is this something you do every four months like clockwork?" Tim lowered himself to the sofa and twisted a lock of Joelle's hair around his index finger.

"No. Last time I ran away. There's a difference." She wrapped her fingers around Tim's wrist to stop him from any further intimacies. "Look, you and I have to talk."

"I thought that's what we were doing before you fainted."

"We were sniping at each other, Tim. It's not the same thing at all." She pushed his hand away and sat up. The room stayed where it was supposed to.

"I feel a lecture coming on." Tim moved to the end of the sofa and made himself comfortable. "You do realize you're the only woman who can lecture me and live to tell about it?"

"You know, for years I wondered how somebody as nasty as you are could be so convincing and warm on stage. Now I think I was wrong all along." Joelle pulled her feet up under the caftan and propped herself against the opposite end of the sofa. "Actually, I had it backwards. The question should have been, how can someone as potentially warm and lovable as you be so nasty when he starts to get close to people."

"Is this an encounter group?"

"You could call it that. You'll get your chance to rip me to shreds in a moment." Joelle examined Tim with a critical eye. "You really are a terrific guy. You need to learn how to fight fair, and you need to stop running from intimacy. If you ever do, you'll be a friend to be proud of."

"I don't want to be your friend, Jo. I've never wanted to be your friend."

"You don't want to be anybody's friend, Tim."

He ran his fingers through his curls, spilling them on to his forehead. "Do you remember the teacher we went to see together, years ago?"

Joelle nodded. "He told me to face my pursuer. I think I'm ready, finally, to do that," she said quietly.

"He told me I was like an onion with a pearl at my center. If I peeled off enough layers, I might get to the treasure inside me." Tim made a face, and Joelle laughed with him.

"Quite an image. I don't think I'd want to use it in a song, but it fits you somehow." Tentatively she stretched out her hand. "I'm still in love with Zach, Tim. Please accept the fact that you and I can't ever be that special to each other. I care about you in a different way. And I want the best for you." She waited patiently, hand still outstretched.

He stared at her hand, and for a moment Joelle thought he would take what she offered. Then he stood and smiled his arrogant smile. "Sweet thing," he said, "if I touch you right now, whatever good intentions still alive in me will go right out the window. I think I'll be heading on my way." He turned when he got to the doorway, and their eyes locked. He understood finally that it was over. For the first time he knew what it was like to lose. "If Zach Smith doesn't know what he's sacrificed, then he's a fool." In a moment, he was gone.

Joelle stared at the frostbitten walls. "Are you a fool, Zach?" she finally asked out loud. She lay back on the sofa, too tired to get up and climb the stairs. "Or am I just fool enough for both of us?"

ON THE NIGHT OF THE CONCERT, Joelle sat stoically in front of the series of three mirrors and waited for the woman doing her makeup to finish. She understood that she would look washed out under the lights without it, but that never made the process more enjoyable. "Are you almost finished, Ruth?"

"Just about. I just saw your costume. It's sensational."

Joelle smiled and then realized she wasn't supposed to move the muscles in her face. The costume *was* sensational. She had refused to do a series of clothing changes, insisting that her fans wanted music, not a fashion parade. Thwarted, her designer had thrown himself into one devastatingly simple outfit. The blouse was bronze satin, draped from one shoulder, leaving part of her midriff bare and trailing down one side to her hip. The matching knickers were whiskey-colored velvet. She would wear gold sandals with straps halfway to her knees as her only adornment.

"Where is she?" There was a commotion outside her dressing-room door, and Ruth jumped, barely missing dusting rouge over Joelle's hair.

Joelle rolled her eyes to the ceiling. "I'm in here, Tim. What on earth is the matter?"

Tim strode in the door. He was already dressed. He looked like a twentieth-century pirate with a flowing cotton shirt tucked into skin-tight pants. The outfit suited him and Joelle knew it would be a hit with the audience.

"Don't pretend you don't know!" He flopped down on the counter in front of Joelle's chair and accused her with his expression.

"I can think of any number of things you might be upset about." Joelle waved Ruth away and pulled off the sheet draping her T-shirt. "The man who was supposed to do the lights went into the hospital for observation, my lead guitarist threatened to break his instrument over your lead guitarist's head..."

"You've changed your last song!"

"Ah..." She stood and stretched. "Yes, you're right. I did. I have total control over my choice of material, remember? It's in the contract we signed."

"What kind of crazy decision was it to make a change like this at the last minute?" He rang his fingers through his curls. Joelle could just see his hairstylist's face when he saw what Tim had done.

"Granted, it wasn't the best-laid plan, but it was something I just had to do. Now, will you get out of here so I can dress, please?"

"Not until you tell me you're going to go back to the way we rehearsed it."

"I have no intention of changing back." And she could tell that Tim had no intention of leaving. With a shrug of her shoulders, Joelle went behind the screen in the corner and began to pull off her shorts and pull on the knickers. "I'm sorry, Tim, but this has nothing to do with you. The song is brand new, and I have to sing it."

"I don't know what the song is, and I don't care. But you can't get up there without your band and sing some song with your own guitar accompaniment."

"That's how I started, and that's how I intend to end."

His silence was more telling than his words had been. Joelle knew he had understood that she meant more than just this concert. She counted the elapsing seconds as she pulled off the T-shirt and pulled on the satin blouse.

"What do you mean, end?"

She had expected a roar, not a quiet question.

"This is my last concert, at least it's my last one for a long time. I'm getting out of the performing business, Tim. I'm going to write songs and make albums, but I'm not performing live or going on tour anymore." She came out to sit on the love seat across the room from Tim and strap on her sandals.

"You'll lose your following."

She was bending over, and she lifted her head to shoot him a smile. "That's possible. But if I do, I can live with it."

"It's suicidal!"

"No, Tim. This is suicidal." Joelle gestured around the room. "I thought all I needed was a vacation, a chance to get away from this life for a while and put everything in perspective. I thought I could come back and control it instead of letting it control me. But I'm not strong enough, Tim. It eats me alive."

"You're one of the strongest women I know." He came to sit next to her.

"Sometimes you have to be strong enough to realize that you can't have it all." She tied the last strap and leaned back to watch Tim's face. "Sometimes you have to make a choice and be satisfied with it. I learned that much in Pennsylvania, but it took me awhile to sort it out. Giving this up is easy. Understanding that I had to was the hard part."

"Would Pennington-Smith give up so much for you?"

"If I asked him to he would, I think. But I'm not giving this up for Zach, I'm giving it up for me. I need more from life than an adrenaline high after a concert. I want quiet nights and intimacy and the kind of environment where I can be whole."

"So you're going back to Pennsylvania."

"At first. I don't know what will happen there. I treated Zach and his father very badly."

"His father!" Tim stood and ran his fingers through his curls again. "His father killed your father, Jo. Are you living in a delusion?"

"Franklin Pennington-Smith was part of a system, and that system killed my father and my brother. I can forgive him for his weaknesses, just as I can now forgive myself for my own. Actually, Franklin and I have a lot in common. We're both struggling to be the kind of people we want to be. I guess we'll both keep struggling until we die."

"Always the little philosopher."

"In your own way, you struggle, too." Joelle stood and put her hands on Tim's shoulders. "My last song is important to me. Listen to it without anger, Tim." She leaned forward and kissed his cheek, then backed away. The kiss was for everything they had shared through the years, the good and the bad. "Now, go back and let someone comb your hair. I've got to finish getting ready."

ZACH GOT TO THE ARENA early enough to find a seat where he could see the stage without straining. The bleachers were filling up fast. The crowd was an interesting mixture of people. All ages and types were represented, but the vast majority were around his own age. Had he believed that the word meant anything, he would have characterized most of them as yuppies. Certainly the same people who would have turned out for a Tim Daniels-Jo Lynd concert a decade before would not have been able to afford the price of the tickets to this one.

Zach killed time imagining what was going on backstage. He was sure it was a madhouse, and he wondered how Joelle was handling the uproar after her quiet months at the farm. Actually, he wondered how she was handling her entire life. The stories he had succumbed to reading in celebrity magazines intimated that Jo Lynd and Tim Daniels were back together and a hotter item than before. This was to be their reconciliation concert.

He doubted that the stories were true. A part of him still believed that despite everything, Joelle had loved him. He knew that she was not the kind of person who bounced from man to man on the rebound. In addition she knew Tim too well to fall for his lines. If anything developed between Tim and Joelle, it would develop slowly. She would be cautious.

Zach's hand went absentmindedly to his chin to stroke his beard. But there was no beard to stroke. No one had suggested that it did not fit the corporate image of a Pennington Alloy executive, he had just decided on his own to get rid of it. Somehow the beard was a symbol of his rebellion, and that part of his life was ended. He was the owner of a thriving business that had just secured a long-term government research grant, and he was a consultant to the research and development department of one of the nation's largest steel companies. He was a successful business man, his idealism intact, his feet on the ground. He had it all. All except for Joelle.

Franklin Pennington-Smith, who had been an insensitive father to the teenage Zacharias, was acutely sensitive to the loss that the adult Zacharias had suffered. Zach had walked into his office that morning to discover a ticket to this concert and a note saying that the company jet was on standby for him. At first he had refused to go, wondering why he should open himself to more pain, but finally, he had called the airport.

Now he waited, wondering again why he had chosen to come.

The crowd was settling down as if they had invisible antennae that signaled the beginning of the concert. A local deejay came on to warm them up, and after a few minutes of nonsensical patter, Tim Daniels and his band appeared. Mass hysteria swept through the arena.

Zach didn't want to be drawn in by Tim's performance. He remembered all too clearly Tim's manipulations and inflated ego. But as a performer, the man was faultless. Joelle had always said that there was more good in Tim than met the eye. Tonight, for the first time, Zach could almost believe that she was right.

Tim's portion of the concert seemed to go on and on. Zach was torn between not wanting it to end and wishing that he could see Joelle immediately. It was this ambivalence that had made him call the airport, this ambivalence that had made him question his decision ever since. He missed her more than he had thought possible, but at the same time he was angry at himself for his feelings. He wanted to forget her and go on with his life. Instead he was sitting in an arena, with thousands of other admirers, waiting for her to appear.

Zach was so lost in his thoughts, that he missed Joelle's introduction. The roar of the crowd alerted him to her arrival on stage. She strode proudly across the wide platform, holding the guitar that he remembered so well. When she reached Tim they kissed, and even across the vast space between them, Zach was certain that the kiss was one of genuine affection as well as showmanship. His hands clenched in his lap.

They launched into a medley that covered most of the songs that Zach had ever connected with either of them. Conspicuously missing were ''The Voice of Corruption,'' and ''When I Come Home To You.'' They sang back and forth, with their eyes on each other, and the combination of their voices had a power and beauty that totally silenced the audience. Zach had eyes only for Joelle. She was stunning on stage, all graceful lines and sensuous angles. The unusual costume managed to accent everything about her, her coloring, her height, her slender body. She was breathtaking.

The medley finally ended, and Tim and Joelle embraced. It was an emotional high for the audience. The cheers went on and on until finally, the stage lights dimmed and Joelle was alone with her own band.

She began with a slow song, a ballad that he hadn't heard before. It was unashamedly a love song. The crowd quieted, and soon she had them really listening. Zach had wondered how she could capture their attention after the medley, but she did, simply by being herself.

On the second song, he began to get suspicious. These were songs he had never heard her sing, although she had sung for him often in the days before she left. They were gentle songs about loving and being loved. They were simple, but not trite. Catchy, but not cute. The crowd was interested.

When had she written them? In the two months since she had returned to L.A.? In the golden days of June when they had shared their lives? Suddenly it seemed imperative to know.

Joelle changed the mood with several livelier songs, including "Simplicity Blues," which he knew she had written in Russell Creek. She chatted in between numbers, telling the crowd a little of what the money from the concert would be spent on or telling funny anecdotes about Tim Daniels. There was a friendly give and take between her and the band and she introduced them all, bragging about their talents and the new record that they were soon to cut without her.

The concert went on and on. Her songs were filled with sentiment without being sentimental. Sometimes they were funny, sometimes they were poignant. She was the voice of a generation and the crowd was sitting forward on its seats, absorbing this new Jo Lynd. She was speaking for them all, and they let her know they were grateful.

Finally the band left the stage and she was alone. Someone brought out a stool for her to sit on and adjusted her microphone.

"Will you bring up the houselights, please?" she asked, and an unseen hand did as she requested.

She was smiling. "That's better. I always hate singing to a blur. I want to see you for this one."

She strummed a few chords as she talked. "I saved this song for last. It's very special to me. Most of you know I disappeared for a while. I stopped growing here, under this artificial light, and I decided to go back to my roots to see what had happened to me. All the songs I've sung tonight were written while I was away. All except for the one I'm about to sing.

"I met a courageous man while I was gone. He taught me things I wasn't quite ready to learn. But I've learned them now. Zacharias, if you're listening, please know that this song is for you."

Zach shut his eyes, unable to look at her as she began the complicated introduction. Her words pierced his heart.

I asked you for a loaf of bread,
A pillow where I could lay my head.
You offered me your soul instead,
But I refused it.
You came to me with moon and stars,
A gilded cage without its bars,
No love more beautiful than ours,
But I refused it.

And now, I wonder where you've gone,
What went wrong, do you hear my song?
And now, I wonder just how long
You'll keep my soul.
Bring it back,
And make me whole.

You'll always have a part of me,
I no longer care if I am free,
Come back and I will make you see,
I won't refuse you.

There is nothing that I can do,
You have my heart, my soul with you,
I lost them both, I wanted to,
I won't refuse you.

And now I wonder if you know,
Where I'll go, what I owe,
And now I wonder if you'll show
Me your soul,
Let me hold it close,
And we'll be whole.

Let me hold it close,
And we'll be whole.

THERE WAS A MOMENT of silence after the last chords of
the guitar died away, and then applause swept through
the arena like a tidal wave, beginning softly and building to a torrential climax. Tim Daniels was back on
stage and they were taking bow after bow. The crowd
was on their feet, Joelle and Tim were singing one last
song together and finally the houselights were brought
all the way up. The concert was finished.

Zach felt the crowd shoving around him. But he
could not move. He could still hear Joelle's voice and
the last song she had sung alone. She had sung it to him.

Now he sat in the rapidly emptying arena, wondering why.

CHAPTER FIFTEEN

TIM STOOD ACROSS THE CROWDED ROOM and watched Joelle field questions from reporters at their celebration party. She was holding an untouched glass of champagne in her hand and there was no smile on her face. She looked as if she had given everything inside her. For the first time since she had told him of her plan to quit performing, he understood her reasons.

"She's something, isn't she?" An attractive young woman from one of the rock fan magazines stood at Tim's elbow.

"She's always been something," he answered, still staring at Joelle.

"Who's the Zacharias she dedicated her last song to?"

Tim took a swallow of his own drink and turned his glance to the reporter. "The man she loves."

The young woman blinked her carefully made-up eyes. "You must know what the world thinks about the two of you. That kiss tonight on stage was pretty impressive."

"The kiss was real, but Jo and I are friends. That's all."

"I have a feeling that's not the way you want it."

Tim swirled his drink. "Are you asking as a reporter or as a woman or just as a person who is trying to give comfort?"

The young woman blinked again and he could tell she was as surprised by the tone of his question as he was. Then she smiled. "You know, you're not anything like what I expected. You're much more human."

"I'm working on it." He looked back across the room and his eyes caught Joelle's. He gave her a half salute with his glass. She smiled and in a moment she was gone. "How would you like to hear the story of my life?" he asked the young woman. "Without your tape recorder."

"I know a little bar with great Mexican food where we can talk until dawn," she said, casually linking her arm through his.

"This isn't the way I usually do this." He pulled her through the crowd to the door. "Gentle conversation is not my usual come-on."

"I've always preferred the unusual," she said with a pixie grin. "Besides, I wouldn't go anywhere with the legendary Tim Daniels. But I think I can hold my own with the real man.

IT WAS CLOSER TO DAWN than to midnight when the limousine pulled in through the front gate of Joelle's house. She thanked the driver, who insisted on checking the downstairs for intruders until Maria, dressed in a white bathrobe that resembled her uniform, chased him away.

Joelle was exhausted and overstimulated, simultaneously. From long years of experience she knew that it would be hours before she would be able to sleep. The party after the performance had gone on forever. Her head still spun with reporters' questions and the answers she had given.

Now she was alone, with her adrenaline still in high gear. Shooing Maria back to bed, she changed into turquoise silk lounging pajamas and wandered through the house examining the work that the painters had done. Two rooms were finished. The kitchen had been painted a creamy salmon, the living room a pale, pale blue. *White on White on White* was sitting in the corner of the blue room waiting to be rehung, and she made a mental note to call a local charity and offer it as a donation.

The house was coming to life. She was trying to make a home for herself again. Joelle had glorious fantasies about what a real home would be like, but she seriously doubted that they would ever come to fruition. She was taking charge of her life, as she had told Tim, and she was going to do what she could with what she had.

Her thoughts were interrupted by the ringing of the telephone. There were very few people who had her number at home. Those who did were off-duty at this time of the morning. She wondered if it was a wrong number. Even superstars with unlisted numbers were subjected to such calls. Answering it was something to do.

"Miss Lynd? This is Sid Fedders."

Her accountant was strictly a nine-to-five man who almost never asked for her opinion on anything. His voice was a surprise. "What can I do for you?" she asked politely, as if it were 4:00 P.M. instead of 3:00 A.M.

"A man called me this evening to get your phone number and address. I told him that the information is confidential, but he keeps calling, insisting that you will want to talk with him. I'd just take my phone off the hook, but I think he's legit. He lives next door to your property in Pennsylvania, and he's been looking out for—"

"Zach? Did he leave a number?" Joelle pressed the phone closer to her ear as if she might miss his answer.

"No. But I'm sure he'll call back. May I give him..."

"Yes!" She took a deep breath and toned down her reply. "Yes, Sid. Give it to him and tell him I'll be waiting. I'm sorry if this has caused you too much trouble."

There was a sleepy mumbled reply and then the line went dead.

Was Zach in Los Angeles? Sid had said that Zach had insisted she would want to talk with him. But he could be calling from Pennsylvania. There was only one way to find out. Zach's number in Russell Creek was firmly fixed in her brain. She had fought against calling him for a week, determined that she must finish up this part of her life first. Now the concert was over. She could call him with no fears.

Joelle dialed the number with a finger that seemed to want to collapse momentarily. The telephone rang and rang, and just as she was about to hang up, a cheerful woman's voice answered.

"Windmill Chargers. Carol Byler speaking."

"Carol? This is Joelle Lindsey."

Carol was delighted to hear her voice, and she seemed thrilled to chat.

Joelle waited for a break. "Carol, is Zach there?"

"No, honey. He's living in Pittsburgh most of the time. Jake and I have moved into his house." There was a short silence. "You haven't been in touch with him, have you?"

"No, but I'm trying to remedy that." Her courage was failing rapidly. "Carol, does he ever mention me?"

"No. But he thinks about you all the time," the older woman said with the wisdom of someone who has spent her life observing people.

"Can you give me his number in Pittsburgh?"

"Sure. He's staying with his parents until he decides where he wants to settle."

Joelle's heart sank. "His parents?" After the way she had reacted to Franklin Pennington-Smith, she couldn't call Zach there.

Carol dictated the number, and Joelle wrote it down.

"Call him, honey. Take that first step."

"Tell Jake I said hi," she said without committing herself. "I'll stay in touch, Carol."

Joelle sat staring at the telephone, willing it to ring. But her need to talk to Zach was more acute than her need to avoid calling the Pennington-Smith residence. She could not be patient. This time when she dialed, her anxiety level had reached a new peak.

What time was it in Pennsylvania? She squinted at the clock and made the correct calculations. She was hours away from being polite. She would wake up a maid or a butler, and they would tell her to call back at a reasonable time. Almost convinced that her failing courage was really common sense, Joelle prepared to drop the receiver in place when a man's voice answered the telephone. It was not a maid or a butler. Joelle knew immediately that it was Zach's father. His voice was unforgettable.

"Mr. Pennington-Smith, this is Joelle Lindsey."

There was a short silence, and she took the opportunity to sink into a chair beside the telephone. "I'm sorry, Miss Lindsey, you startled me. How are you?"

"I'm fine, thank you. I got your number from Carol Byler. I was calling to speak with Zach."

There was another pause, and for a moment Joelle thought that Franklin Pennington-Smith was going to refuse to let her speak with his son. "Would it be more convenient if I called at another time?" she asked.

"He's not here."

She was on a wild-goose chase, and Zach's father was not going to be any help. "I'm sorry I bothered you then," she said carefully.

"Miss Lindsey, Zach flew to Los Angeles late yesterday morning to hear your concert. I don't know where he's staying or I'd tell you."

Then Zach was right there in Los Angeles. "Thank you," she said, her voice filled with real gratitude. "He's been trying to reach me, but I didn't know from where. I'll just have to wait until he calls."

"I'm sure he'll call. It was nice to talk with you, Miss Lindsey."

She owed this man more than polite conversation. In the short silence that followed his words Joelle's past flashed before her in a volatile slide show of memories. The explosion, her mother's anger, the press conference, her song, her rise to fame, all the years when she had made her own concessions to idealism. The last slide was Franklin Pennington-Smith's face when he told her of his sorrow and his own growth. It was time to put an end to bitterness. She understood finally that bitterness was the pursuer she had run from for sixteen years. It was time to start again.

"Mr. Pennington-Smith?"

"Yes."

"I know you don't need my forgiveness, but you have it anyway. And my apology, too."

"I'm glad." His voice seemed a little deeper. "Maybe I did need both of them after all."

"Goodbye."

"Goodbye, and good luck with Zacharias." The line went dead, and Joelle sat holding the receiver in her hands for a long moment until she realized that if Zach was trying to get in touch with her, he wouldn't be able to get through. She replaced it in its cradle and put her head down on the table to wait.

ZACH PACED THE FLOOR of the hotel room. The night had been filled with frustrations. Now he was faced with an endless busy signal on Joelle's telephone. After hounding her accountant for hours and suffering doubts about whether she would give her permission for Sid Fedders to pass along her number, he was unable to get through to her.

His patience was all used up. The concert had been over for hours. It was time to make his move. Pocketing the slip of paper with Joelle's address written on it, he went in search of a taxicab.

THE TELEPHONE WAS SILENT. Joelle toyed with the spiraling cord and waited for it to ring. If she hadn't been certain that Sid Fedders would resign immediately if she interrupted his sleep, she would have called him to see if Zach had gotten her number yet.

Solemnly repeating her mother's homey wisdom about a watched pot, Joelle finally went into the kitchen to make coffee. She needed caffeine in her system like a weight watcher needs a candy bar, but making and drinking coffee was something to do. The possibilities of sleeping that night were remote anyway.

She tried to put herself in Zach's position. What would he think after hearing her songs at the concert, especially the last solo? Would he understand that she had written them because she was desperately in love with him and wanted a reconciliation? Or would he think that she had used their relationship as a spur to her creative powers, and that the songs really meant nothing at all?''

And even if he understood the songs, would he still be interested in sharing his life with her. She had repeatedly rejected him, at first because of his parentage, next because of her own fears about combining career and marriage and finally because she could not totally accept him. She had given him so little in return for the acceptance and love that she had received.

It was difficult, under the circumstances, to believe that Zach would want her back. He was the kind of man who would not like the idea of ending a relationship in bitterness. With a rising sense of panic, she began to imagine that Zach had tried to call just to let her know that he had enjoyed the concert and still considered her a friend.

She was sinking into self-pity. It was the last of a wide array of emotions, and she recognized it just as she was going under. She forced herself to reclaim some of her famous serenity, and drank her second cup of coffee.

When the buzzer sounded she jumped a full foot into the air. So much for serenity, she told herself with her heart still embedded in her throat. Picking up the kitchen telephone, she tried to sound casual. The attempt went unnoticed; the dial tone was not impressed with her dramatic ability. Fifteen seconds later she realized that a buzzer and a ringing telephone were not the same thing. Someone was at the front gate.

She pushed the correct buttons on the intercom in the living room. "Yes?"

"It's Zach."

She didn't want to talk to him through an electrified box. She pushed the appropriate button and went outside to wait for him.

The man walking up the long tiled sidewalk leading to her house was not familiar. The Zach Smith she had known and loved was a casual man with a beard and hair that was neat but too long to be stylish. This man had no beard, and he was wearing a lightweight brown suit of impeccable design. His hair had not been cut in Taylerton.

There was a wariness about this man that hadn't been present in the Zach Smith she had known. He was walking slowly toward her as if he wasn't certain what he would do when he arrived at his destination. She stood in the shadows, aware that he did not know that she watched him, and she tried to quell her panic. Finally she could not hide any longer.

Zach stopped, yards away, and examined Joelle. She was wearing something that looked like pajamas and he wondered if he had gotten her out of bed. The material was just sheer enough to hint at the subtle curves beneath, and he could feel his body react accordingly. She looked composed, as if she were viewing a stranger. He wished he hadn't come.

Joelle was the first to break the silence. "Come inside," she said, "I've made us some coffee." She turned, and Zach had no choice but to follow her. He had already paid the cab driver. It was a long walk back to his hotel.

"I don't want coffee," he said as they walked through the house. He noticed signs that painters had been working inside. The freshly done walls seemed to point out Joelle's decision to stay in Los Angeles permanently and make a real home for herself there. He should not have expected anything different.

Joelle faltered. Serving coffee was an excuse to keep busy while they talked. She felt suddenly vulnerable. Hesitating in the hallway, she finally guided him into the living room. She sat on the couch and Zach sat on a chair nearby. They stared at each other. Neither one could break the silence.

Finally Joelle could stand it no longer. "We used to brag about how nice it was to be quiet together, but this is ridiculous!" She stood and busied herself rearranging the flowers that Mr. Huckamoto had cut for her that morning. "Sid Fedders said that you'd been trying to reach me."

"When you left Pennsylvania, you didn't even leave me a phone number." Zach wondered why bitterness would surface at a time like this. He suspected that it was a defense against the loss he was feeling again. Obviously he had misunderstood Joelle's final song tonight. The woman standing coolly in front of him destroying a perfect flower arrangement was not interested in a reunion. She didn't even seem interested in a conversation.

"I didn't have a chance to leave you anything. I had no warning that our goodbye was going to be so abrupt." Why were they discussing the past like two well-mannered but hostile strangers? Joelle examined Zach under her eyelashes. He seemed so remote, so elegantly untouchable.

"I didn't plan it that way."

"I'm glad to hear that. But it doesn't matter anymore."

He was surprised how much pain he could still feel. He thought he had reached his threshold two months earlier. She had said it didn't matter anymore. Obviously it only mattered to him. "I was at your concert tonight," he said, wanting to get straight to the point. He would get the final parting out of the way, and then he would leave to suffer in privacy.

"Were you?" Now was the opportunity to find out what he had thought of her final song. Now was the chance to find out if there was still any hope for their relationship. All she had to do was walk across the space separating them and ask him what he had thought of the song. His song. But her feet and her mouth had entered a conspiracy to keep her silently rooted to the spot. She was desperately afraid of what Zach might tell her.

Zach waited for a sign that Joelle wanted his reaction to her song. There was nothing. "The concert was quite a success. I'm sure you're pleased."

Joelle's control began to slip. He had ignored the song she had written for him. It was a slap in the face. "Why are you here?" The question, fueled by anxiety and fear, sounded like an accusation.

"I was just asking myself the same thing." Zach stood. "If you'll show me where the telephone is, I'll call another taxi."

"Don't go!" Suddenly Joelle didn't care if she made a fool out of herself or not. She hurled her body at his, wrapping her arms around his waist. "Please don't go."

"Why not?" His words were punctuated by a crushing hug as his arms wrapped around the body that was more slender than he remembered.

"Because when you go, I'm going with you. And I'm not packed yet." Joelle lifted her face to his. "Kiss me, Zach."

Without his beard the kiss was different, but it was no less wonderful. It went on and on, tongue seeking tongue, mind seeking mind, soul seeking soul. Their hands explored every inch of the other that they could reach as if determined to assure themselves that this was really happening.

"Two months. Two whole months!" Joelle threaded her long fingers through Zach's beautifully cut hair as he kissed her neck.

"It felt like forever. I thought I'd never see you again," he murmured.

"I'm sorry. So very sorry."

"Can you feel it?" Zach asked finally.

"Everything."

"There aren't any obstacles between us anymore."

"No. There aren't."

"We have to talk about it."

"Later." Joelle moved back just far enough to take his hand. "Right now I just need to be with you."

She led him quickly through the living room to the kitchen, where she flipped off the security lights that illuminated the deck at the rear of the house. They stepped out on to the spacious cedar platform, and Joelle pulled Zach toward the far end where a series of strategically placed posts hid the hot tub from view. Surrounding it, in giant cedar containers, were Mr. Huckamato's vines.

"I haven't been out here since I got back" she said quietly. "I kept remembering the day you were teasing me about my hot tub and your fantasies about it. Everything reminded me of you, Zach. I'd wake up in the morning and I'd wonder what you were eating for breakfast, how you'd slept. I'd read the newspaper and every article I read reminded me of something we'd talked about. I'd go to rehearsals, and I'd sing the songs I had written about us, and I'd feel as though I was dying inside."

"I got up every morning before dawn and went to work. I stopped at night when Jake or Carol convinced me that I had to. I've been putting in more than full-time at both Windmill Chargers and Pennington Alloy, but it didn't help. I couldn't stop thinking about you." Zach dropped Joelle's hand and his thumbs began to trace identical lines down each side of her face.

She closed her eyes and let his hands soothe away the tensions of the last weeks. He had such strong hands, such capable hands. The hands of an artist, not an engineer. "I never stopped loving you," Joelle said softly. "I never will."

"Were you serious about coming with me?"

"Yes." She opened her eyes, needing to read the expression in his. "Do you still want me?"

"I never stopped. I never will."

Perhaps they had needed to talk after all, because the words freed them both. Their clothes fell away to lie in forgotten heaps on the deck. The warm air of the night blended into the liquid warmth of the tub, and they rested in each other's arms, patiently exploring, testing, tasting.

The night seemed endless; their self-control unflagging. Their coming together was slow and sure and unhurried. Both knew that they had a lifetime of love ahead. They could allow themselves the pleasure of moving slowly toward their destiny.

When patience was no longer possible, they merged, the water swirling around them in endless tiny whirlpools with their movements. They moved as one, caught up in the wordless connection that flowed between them. Defenses had been eradicated; barriers had disappeared. Joelle understood, finally, what it meant to give herself completely. Zach understood the same.

Afterward they sat together, letting the water lull them into an even greater contentment. Mr. Huckamato's sinister flowering vines perfumed the air, and the sky revealed an occasional star. "Everything is perfect," Joelle said finally, breaking the long comfortable silence. "Everything."

"Tell me." Zach had not been able to let go of her since they had stepped into the water together. Even now he had his arm around her shoulders, holding her close. He realized that there was still a part of him that was afraid she would disappear.

"Well, first and best, you and I are together. For always."

"First and best." He pulled her a little closer.

Joelle rested her head on Zach's shoulder. "Second, I have my career under control." She told him of her plans to write and record but not to do concert tours.

"You don't have to change for me," Zach said. "You were right when you said that I didn't accept that part of you that was Jo Lynd. But watching you at the concert, I realized that a part of you will always belong to your audience. I can live with that."

"I couldn't change for you, Zach." She wanted him to understand. "If I did, I'd end up resenting the changes. I'm doing this because I want to. I'm giving up concerts and concert tours because they take too much out of me. They drain me and leave nothing except a few pleasant memories. I want my energies focused on writing songs, on us, on our children . . .

"Children?" He turned her to face him. "Because I want them?"

"Because I want your children."

He was silent, and Joelle saw a shadow mar his expression of total contentment. "Our children will be Pennington-Smiths. Can you cope with that?"

"Their father is a Pennington-Smith, and I love him with all my heart." She traced the worry lines around his eyes. "I know what you're thinking. I want to be part of your family, Zach. I spoke with your father an hour ago. I think that we will be able to accept each other."

It was much more than he had expected. Zach pulled her close and let his kiss tell her how happy he was.

"We'll still have some problems," she warned softly. "I don't know how the rest of your family will feel about me, or if my sisters and brother will understand."

"They'll come around when they see how happy we are together. If they love us, they'll understand."

"Where will we live? Pittsburgh? Russell Creek?" Joelle pinched Zach's cheek. "No more working full-time at two jobs for you!"

"Russell Creek with an apartment in Pittsburgh for the times I have to be there longer than a day."

"Do you know," she said, running her fingers over his face, "that I loved your beard, but you have the most wonderful chin." She kissed a line along his jaw. "Would you like to live in my house in Russell Creek? Carol and Jake could stay in yours and watch over your property. You'll have to sell me a wind machine, though."

"That's hardly an advantageous business proposition considering that we'll be married."

"I'll just have to make it up to you in other ways." Their mouths met and they forgot to talk.

"I'll trade you a wind machine for this hot tub," Zach suggested later.

"I think I'm going to keep this house," Joelle said. "Hot tub and all. I'll arrange recording sessions when you can come and stay here with me. This tub can be your reward for coming to California."

"I thought you didn't like this house?"

Joelle clapped her hand over Zach's mouth and pointed to the vines. "Not here," she mouthed. "They're listening."

He nibbled her fingers until she laughed and pulled them away. "There's nothing wrong with this house that a little love won't cure," she said.

"Will you mind all that upheaval? A house in Russell Creek, an apartment in Pittsburgh, a house in Los Angeles?"

"We'll have three homes instead of one. Everyone of them will be special."

"As special as love can make them."

"And we have lots of love to work with."

"Enough love to last our whole lives," Zach promised as his mouth covered Joelle's to seal their commitment. "You've seduced my soul. I'm totally yours. Does that scare you?"

"It terrifies me. You terrify me because you hold my soul, too. May it always be so."

The warm water lapped around them as they kissed, content in each other's arms. Their separate, necessary journeys were over. The rest of their lives would be spent learning to travel together.

Harlequin Superromance

COMING NEXT MONTH

#206 SOUTHERN NIGHTS • Barbara Kaye
The past is waiting when Shannon Parelli, newly
widowed, returns to the family farm in North
Carolina. Blake Carmichael, who'd silently
worshiped her as an adolescent, is now a prosperous
contractor, determined to fulfill his dream of
homesteading her parents' old place—with Shannon
by his side.

#207 DREAMS GATHER • Kathryn Collins
When gallery owner Amanda Sherwood signs
Grant Wellington for an exclusive showing, she
quickly learns that he isn't just another
temperamental artist. The terms he sets for their
contract prove that he is a man's man who always
gets what he wants. And what he wants is
Amanda . . . with a hunger he's never known.

#208 FOR RICHER OR POORER • Ruth Alana Smith
Despite appearances, Britt Hutton is *not* a Boston
socialite and Clay Cole is *not* a wealthy Texas
oilman. They're both fortune hunters, determined to
triumph over life's hardships. And, moving in the
same elite circles, it is inevitable they will discover
the truth: the powerful attraction they feel is no
illusion. . . .

#209 LOTUS MOON • Janice Kaiser
While searching the back streets of Bangkok for the
daughter he may have fathered during the Vietnam
War, Buck Michaels and social worker Amanda Parr
find themselves locked in a passion as sultry as the
Oriental nights. Everything is perfect, until Buck's
quest becomes an obsession. . . .

Harlequin Intrigue

WHAT READERS SAY ABOUT
HARLEQUIN INTRIGUE . . .

Fantastic! I am looking forward to reading other
Intrigue books.

This is the first Harlequin Intrigue I have read . . .
I'm hooked.

I really like the suspense . . . the twists and turns
of the plot.

I'm really enjoying your Harlequin Intrigue
line . . . mystery and suspense mixed with a good
love story.

*Names available on request.

Take 4 books
& a surprise gift
FREE

SPECIAL LIMITED-TIME OFFER

Mail to   **Harlequin Reader Service®**

In the U.S.   In Canada
901 Fuhrmann Blvd.   P.O. Box 2800, Station "A"
P.O. Box 1394   5170 Yonge Street
Buffalo, N.Y. 14240-1394   Willowdale, Ontario M2N 6J3

YES! Please send me 4 free Harlequin Superromance® novels and my free surprise gift. Then send me 4 brand-new novels every month as they come off the presses. Bill me at the low price of $2.50 each—a 10% saving off the retail price. There are no shipping, handling or other hidden costs. There is no minimum number of books I must purchase. I can always return a shipment and cancel at any time. Even if I never buy another book from Harlequin, the 4 free novels and the surprise gift are mine to keep forever.

134-BPS-BP6S

Name _____ (PLEASE PRINT)

Address _____ Apt. No.

City _____ State/Prov. _____ Zip/Postal Code

This offer is limited to one order per household and not valid to present subscribers. Price is subject to change.

DOSR-SUB-1R